# IN PRAISE OF ANGELS

# *In Praise of Angels*

## A NOVEL OF THE
## RECONSTRUCTION ERA

## RICHARD SMOLEV

ACADEMY CHICAGO PUBLISHERS

Published in 2013 by
Academy Chicago Publishers
363 West Erie Street
Chicago, Illinois 60654

First edition.

Printed and bound in the U.S.A.

Library of Congress Cataloging-in-Publication Data

Smolev, Richard G., 1948–
In praise of angels : a novel of the Reconstruction Era / Richard Smolev.
pages cm
ISBN 978-0-89733-709-0 — ISBN 978-0-89733-725-0
1. Presidents—United States—Election—1872—Fiction.
2. Scandals—Fiction. 3. Political fiction. I. Title.
PS3619.M648I57 2013
813'.6—dc23
2013015970

*For Alan Wolf*

"EVERY PUBLIC QUESTION WITH AN EYE
ONLY TO THE PUBLIC GOOD"

"Well, the wickedness of all of it is, not that these men were bribed or
corruptly influenced, but that they betrayed the trust of the people,
deceived their constituents, and by their evasions and falsehoods con-
fessed the transaction to be disgraceful."
—*New York Tribune*, February 19, 1873.

*Justice (to the Saints of the Press)*. "Let him that has not betrayed the trust
of the People, and is without stain, cast the first stone.

# 1

"GRAINGER TELLS ME you come from good stock, boy."

Benjamin Wright didn't know what to expect during his first moments at the *Philadelphia Courier*. He certainly hadn't bargained for time alone with the man who gave voice to the anti-slavery cause for every sympathizer from Boston to Wilmington years before the first shot was fired.

"I understand you lost two brothers in the unpleasantness. Damned shame. Lost one myself at Antietam. Gangrene. Ugly way to die. Wife and two young boys. But it was the right thing to do, by God. Saved the Union."

Mercer Carlton finished his sentence by spitting a glop of tobacco juice the size of a hen's egg in the direction of his brass spittoon. Some made it over the rim, but most of his projectile just dribbled lazily down the side or twisted its way through a dent mirroring the front of Carlton's boot. Carlton seemed transfixed by the exercise, as if he were counting both the time it took his projectile to reach the bottom and the number of bubbles that popped along the way.

Benjamin clasped both of his hands behind his back. He thought the pose would make him appear serious, possibly even studious. He'd seen photographs of General Grant with his arms stiffened in that fashion, and he'd practiced the gesture, for just this moment. A small dusting of snow was melting on his left boot. He rubbed it dry on the back of his right calf.

"Saved the Union, I tell you," Carlton said. "That's what Lincoln did and they shot him for it, the bastards. And now that we need a time of healing the only thing those Godforsaken Republicans want to do is to throw the President out of office. Grainger tells me your uncle saved his son's life at Vicksburg, and he wants me to see if you're able to be part of the newspaper business." He extended his hand.

Carlton was an odd-shaped man, heavy on the top but with feet so small they didn't look like they'd support him once he stood. His head rose from his shoulders in a slight shift to the left. Fringes of graying hair ringed the sides of his face like lace dangling off the end of a tablecloth, and his stubby fingers were the color of pitch. Benjamin stood in front of him as thin as a sapling and about as naïve.

The *Courier's* office was one cavernous room on top of what had been a stable running an entire block of Market Street. Benjamin poked his head into the first floor before coming up the stairs. Horse stalls had been replaced by two cast iron presses bigger than some of the boats he'd seen in the harbor and four-foot-wide rolls of paper stacked to the ceiling. In the ten minutes he stood next to the door before Carlton finally waved him to come to where he was sitting, Benjamin counted eight desks, five reporters, twenty-two windows, two copy boys no older than twelve or thirteen who each took the ten steps down the stairs to the pressmen below two at a time, and so many pings of mallets on metal typesetter blocks he'd lost track. It was as though he was inside one of the eight beehives he tended on his family's farm back in Grayton, a day's ride to the west, except the *Courier* had the intoxicating smell of tobacco, ink, sweat, damp wool and more ink.

"I'm grateful to my uncle and particularly to you and Mr. Grainger for the opportunity, sir. Extraordinarily so. If I prove myself worthy to join the *Courier* I won't let any of you down." Benjamin made certain his voice didn't give away the slightest hint of his anxiety, for he knew opportunities to get into the newspaper business didn't present themselves routinely to boys who'd been trained to stand behind a plow, to shear the flock, or to make certain the raccoons and foxes didn't devour all the chickens, but who spent their nights writing stories they longed to share with the world. He'd never ventured more than twelve miles from Grayton. He'd been in Philadelphia less than forty-eight hours.

"Let me tell you something about the *Courier*, boy. First, be here on time or don't come in at all. Second, tell our readers the unvarnished truth. Let the other papers in this town fan the flames with their speculation and trash. If you can't give me the facts, get yourself another line of work. Strive for objectivity above all else."

Carlton chopped at his desk with the side of his right hand. "Cold-hearted, clear-eyed objectivity."

Benjamin nodded, as though Carlton had spoken one of the great truths of humankind. He worked hard to remember every word the man was saying. Details counted for everything.

Carlton's desk was cluttered with papers stacked so high the slightest breeze might put the *Courier* off schedule for weeks. He reached for one with the headline *Impeachment!*

"Let me see if you know your civics, Wright. Where will the trial take place?"

Benjamin didn't hesitate. To emphasize the certainty of his answer, he grabbed the lapels of the blue wool suit his mother bought him. He cleared his throat so that his voice conveyed both his understanding and his conviction. "In the Senate, sir."

There had been talk of little but the prospect of the trial since the Judiciary Committee began debating whether it should recommend impeachment to the full House a few weeks before.

"Tell me something interesting about the Senate. Something for our readers." Carlton leaned forward and rested both of his arms on his desk. Benjamin wished that some of the sweat building on his neck and under his arms could find its way to his throat, which was August dry.

"It's in the Capitol, sir. Washington." In his nervousness, Benjamin spurted out the first thought that came to him.

Carlton's expression was a blend of disappointment and more disappointment. He leaned forward for a moment, as if he were about to get out of his chair and head onto some other project. But he hesitated. "You want to be a newspaperman? Start thinking about what will challenge our readers to ask demanding questions." Carlton's chair creaked when he leaned back. "Avoid the obvious at all costs."

Benjamin dropped his hands to his sides. He stiffened his fingers so Carlton couldn't see they were twitching. "The Capitol is the seat of the federal government. It is the place where our congressmen and senators conduct the people's business. Only the House can vote to bring impeachment charges and the Senate conducts the trial." Benjamin exhaled, hoping against hope he might have regained enough of his footing to keep the interview going.

"More, Wright. I need more than what I learned in elementary school." Carlton's words were a threat. "Ask yourself whether what you just told me is a good thing or a bad thing."

Benjamin knew he had to pick his words carefully, for Carlton plainly was a man who didn't suffer fools. "I believe public service is a higher calling." After Benjamin and his parents buried his two brothers, his father abandoned Benjamin and his mother and took a job with a Congressman in Washington. Benjamin spent the past five years of his life trying to make sense of the dissolution of his family. The only way he could accept it was to find some purpose to it all.

Benjamin raised both his voice and his right hand for emphasis. "I believe men such as Washington, Lincoln, my two brothers and even your own brother accepted and then discharged their responsibilities to our country with dignity. I have to believe that

*Chapter 1*

our elected representatives honor that sacrifice by conducting the people's business with integrity." He stopped. There was nothing more to say.

Carlton looked as though a dentist was pulling at one of his molars. "A higher calling? Conducting the people's business with integrity? What bullshit. Spend two days in that swamp and you'll discover the only creatures drawn to Washington are men who think they can make a dollar or two or ten stealing from the machinery of government and the mosquitoes and lobbyists who feed on their blood." Carlton flicked his right hand as though he were swatting away a gnat. "Didn't I just tell you to give me the facts? No one is going to pay a penny for this paper to read your schoolboy pap."

Carlton fished through one of the drawers of his desk until he found the small guillotine that he used to shave off the tip of his cigar. "Open your eyes to the world. Study Plutarch and Rabelais. Read the Boz and Shakespeare so you'll understand why men act the way they do and how to express yourself. But for the love of Mary, don't preach to me or to my readers about some mythical vision from the Lord Himself. We're in the truth business, Wright. That above all else."

Benjamin twisted his neck in the hope his shoulder blades would stop grinding into each other. His stomach felt as though he'd been kicked by one of his plow horses.

"There are only two facts you need to know about Congress, boy. The rest is interpretation and ferreting out the truth those scalawags try to hide."

"Sir?"

"The first is that the Capitol is located at thirty-eight degrees, fifty-two minutes and twenty seconds north latitude and seventy-seven degrees, zero minutes and fifteen seconds longitude west from Greenwich."

Benjamin asked Carlton what else he needed to know about
the Congress.

Carlton's spittle had reached the bottom of the spittoon. "The
second fact is that it's for sale."

Benjamin nodded. This had gone far worse than he'd hoped.
He turned his body slightly, anticipating that Carlton would
express his regrets and wish him well in whatever other occupation
he chose to pursue. What then? There was no work to be had on
the docks or in the mills; thousands of veterans who deserved what
few jobs existed spent their days playing cards and swilling what
alcohol they could get their hands on. Benjamin would be con-
demned to return to the farm.

But what Carlton said next was a gift from God. Nothing short
of that. "Wait. Grainger said he wanted to read something you
wrote. Three hours. That's what I give all my reporters to come up
with their stories."

"A story about anything in particular, Mr. Carlton?" Both of
Benjamin's hands were in the air.

"Write what's in your heart, boy. Write about why you're standing here today in a brand new wool suit." Carlton pointed to desk
number seven, whose top was as bare as one of the farm's back fields
in winter. A copy boy in a brown sweater and threadbare boots
brought five pieces of paper, an ink well and a quill. The reporters
barely raised their heads as Benjamin walked past them. Each man
was older than Benjamin by at least ten years.

A little before one, Benjamin put four pages on Carlton's desk.
"My story, sir. Not just my story. The story of every family that
paid the price of the war." Benjamin returned to desk number seven
and stared intently at Carlton as the man read what Benjamin
had written.

*Grayton was filled with flags and tearful goodbyes and the sweet
smell of April's promise the morning the men and boys—thirty-seven
strong—marched south toward York where they would join up with*

## Chapter 1

*the Pennsylvania 54th. The young boy pleaded, lied, tried every means he could but he was only fourteen. Even if he had been sixteen, General Grant hardly could ask a mother to give up her third son. He cheered his brothers' good fortune as much as he envied their adventure. He wondered why they both looked so somber on a morning filled with the anticipation of victory.*

Carlton was expressionless as he read what Benjamin wrote of that morning.

*When war is fought at a distance it is a spiritual exercise. When war is an abstraction it is a celebration of good triumphing over evil. But the blood on the ground is the blood of our brothers, our fathers, our husbands, our sons. There would be blood in this war as there is in every conflict. The men were certain it would be Confederate blood, as certain they would be home for the harvest, sweet corn, timothy hay for the animals, jasmine honey, apple cider, and squash the size of your head. The mothers, the sweethearts, only wanted their men to return in one piece.*

Benjamin closed his eyes. The rest of his life could all begin here. Or it could all end.

*It was a warm July morning, less than one hundred days from the time the father and his two sons went off to defend Abe Lincoln's vision for the country. There were no clouds, but the sky to the south was filled with heavy black birds of prey, scavengers, omens, as fate would have it.*

Carlton scratched through some of those lines. They were too maudlin for his taste. But he kept intact the description of the grinding sound of the death wagon carrying Benjamin's two brothers, how Jacob lashed Willie's arm to his body so they could bury him in one piece, the frenzy and the putrid smell of the maggots swarming over the bloody stump, how Matthew's face had been torn in two. He was the handsome brother. Carlton nodded when he read Benjamin's description of their mother's screams, the taste of vomit in Benjamin's throat, the clanking of the shovel against

the thirsty ground, tears and sweat pouring out of him in cathar-
sis, the neighbors' sentiment, their pain for the family, their fear
for their own boys and men. He leaned back in his chair for what
seemed an eternity.

Carlton finally called Benjamin to his desk.

"How old did you say you were, Wright?"

"I didn't say, sir, but I'm a couple of months shy of twenty-one."

Carlton paused. "Your father was your brothers' commander
at Hoke's Run?" And when Benjamin only nodded, Carlton said,
"My God."

Benjamin was afraid the thumping in his chest would drown
out the pounding of mallets on metal. He wondered how he'd
explain his failure to his mother and to Susanna, his sweetheart
whom he'd left in Grayton with promises to fetch her to join him
in Philadelphia once his feet were firmly on the ground. But he
smiled as broadly as he'd ever done before when he realized that
would be a discussion they'd need not have.

Carlton shouted to one of the copy boys. "Derek. Put a supply
of paper and ink on desk seven for Mr. Wright."

# 2

"GRANT'S RUNNING FOR PRESIDENT now, that's for certain."
Benjamin and everyone else in the newsroom froze at the sound of
Carlton's pronouncement.

Mornings were all the same at the *Courier,* all save Sunday,
when the presses were quiet, with Carlton slapping the top of his
desk when he had something to say in case everyone in the room
wasn't paying attention.

Benjamin worked hard to fall into the rhythm of the place:
the afternoon shouts of the typesetters a chorus like a hidden crew
bellowing to their captain from the bowels of a great schooner, the
quiet times just after the paper was out the door, or when Carlton
was off with his mistress, a long-legged, blonde Polish dancer
named Mitzi who was the *Courier's* worst kept secret, and the
morning belch from Carlton that sent reporters scurrying so that
a few hours later the criers could tell everyone within earshot the
*Courier* still had one more scoop.

Benjamin was standing next to Jesse Greene at the other end of
the room. He lowered his voice. No sense letting Carlton know he
was a step or two behind him. "What's that all about?" Greene's job
at the *Courier* was to be certain there was enough money in the till
every Friday to pay all the bills.

"What set this particular fire burning is that President Johnson
tried to fire Ed Stanton as his Secretary of War and replace him
with General Grant. The Senate passed a resolution last night saying that as it approved Stanton's appointment the President can't

fire him without its consent. Let's increase today's run by a thousand. People will love reading about this fight."

It wasn't clear to Benjamin whether Mercer Carlton heard every conversation in the newsroom despite the chaos of the place or whether he simply bayed at the moon once an idea took hold of him. He shouted from the other end of the room. "Jesse, you're full of malarkey. All this talk about removing Stanton is just a smokescreen." Carlton fished through the papers on his desk for a cigar.

"The Radical Republicans aren't doing anything more than trying to keep the Democrats from gaining more seats. I applaud their opposition to slavery but now that the question of how we put this country back together is the question on the table, they want to disenfranchise the Confederates because they know that every white man in the South will support the party that opposed emancipation. That's our focus on this story, men. Forget the words they're using and treat this as an old-fashioned power struggle for the control of the Congress for years to come." He snipped off the end of his cigar and rolled the other end around his tongue as though it was caviar. "Damned fools down there. What a bunch of idiots we have running the country."

Carlton started repeating himself, but the reporters already were pulling on their coats and covering their ears against the frigid weather they were about to encounter. Greene assured Carlton his vision had carried the day. He didn't add it almost always did.

Greene laughed, as though he enjoyed being reproached by his old friend as much as he relished the picture of Stanton barricaded in his office. He leaned on the cane he used to support a wooden stump since a Confederate cannon ball took most of his left leg on its arc of destruction at Shiloh. "Keep your eyes and ears open, boys. This promises to be fun."

And with that, Benjamin bounded down the stairs, determined to be the first to uncover a quote or a bit of gossip that would find its way into the lead column that night. His heart raced at the prospect it might.

February was a dismal month in Philadelphia. A storm blew up the coast on the tenth and buried the city in sixteen inches of snow. That was followed by bitter cold and an ice storm that snapped tree limbs with such a commotion the veterans of Gettysburg swore they were back in battle. The alehouses were a refuge allowing the men of the city the chance not only to get out of the cold but to spread the gossip of a deteriorating government in Washington.

Thomas Jefferson frequented the City Tavern on Market Street when he was writing the Declaration of Independence, but on this miserable morning it was filled with Lincoln's soldiers. The only thing they cursed more than the cold was the need to protect the integrity of the Union they'd fought to preserve. Benjamin figured that would be as good as any place to take the pulse of the city.

Four men stood at the end of the bar with glasses of whiskey in their hands. They were a rough lot, needing a shave, a bath, and a job. Each wore some piece of his uniform, an overcoat or a blue muslin sweater vest, their insignias on display as though their commanding officers were just around the corner. Benjamin approached them with respect, the way he'd been taught in Grayton to treat the men who'd put themselves in harm's way and had the good fortune to return. He ordered a glass of rye, asked if he could do the same for them.

"May I ask you gents a question?" Benjamin hadn't bothered with names or the purpose of his visit. "Have you heard about what's blowing up in Washington over Stanton's removal?" The news hadn't yet spread widely, so Benjamin explained what he knew.

The man standing closest to Benjamin spoke first, in a bit of a Scottish accent. When he turned his head, Benjamin saw his right ear had been blown off the side of his face. Pink scars rippled down his neck like small garter snakes.

"Who in the name of Mary does Stevens think he is, threaten-ing to impeach the President over something as foolish as whether he has the power to remove some mate from office? He's the President, for the mercy of Jesus. Did I just spend three of the most godforsaken years of my life either getting shot at or eaten alive by flies and maggots for this nonsense to take over our government?" He swallowed what was left in his glass, shoved it toward the bar-keep for another. "What unit were you in, brother? Where did you serve?"

Benjamin hesitated. He always was embarrassed by the ques-tion. He could have lied about his age, given a false name, and fought with the same ferocity as his brothers. And he might as well have done so. Rachel and Jacob were as lost to him as if he had met the same fate. He was diminished by the question but could do no more than give the answer he gave every time he was asked.

"I envy your service, gentlemen. And honor it." To his relief, the men accepted Benjamin's explanation and hiked their glasses in honor of his dead brothers. Willie and Matthew gave them kinship, but when they learned of Benjamin's association with the *Courier*, they fell into animated conversation about the challenge to the President's powers.

After another round (or was it a third or a fourth?), the tallest of the bunch, a brutish sort whose shaved head bore a bayonet scar as long as Benjamin's hand, eyed the rest of the men in the tav-ern. "Anybody here from the 17th Regimental Regulars? We should assemble our arms, march on the War Building and throw the black heart Stanton out ourselves. He can't disobey my Commander in Chief and get away with it, by God."

Another one of the men said, "I'm told Washington is on high alert for another attack and soldiers have been ordered to their posts."

There was almost a precise link between the amount of liquor consumed and the heat and volume of the men's ambition. The drunker they got the bolder their threats became. Benjamin took in as much of the liquor and the bravado as he was able and then bundled himself up for the walk back to the *Courier*. He had two hours to write up his story.

Carlton, Greene, and T. P. Grainger were at Grainger's desk. When Grainger saw Benjamin enter the room, he held up his glass and motioned to Benjamin to join them. None of the other reporters had yet returned. Benjamin felt both anointment and dread at the prospect of still one more drink when Grainger poured a whiskey for him and slid it across the top of his desk.

"This will warm you up. It's as cold as Greenland out there." Benjamin wasn't accustomed to drinking hard liquor at any time, let alone the middle of the morning, and certainly had no need for another drink on top of the batch he'd consumed, but he couldn't say no. His throat burned at the first touch and his eyes were stinging, but he worked hard to keep his composure. Carlton nodded with seeming approval, as though another threshold in their relationship had been traversed.

Grainger was as tall as Lincoln, angular and as patrician as if he'd been the President himself, the way he sat upright in his chair. He started the *Courier* as a single tear sheet during the Millard Fillmore years and built it up to the point where it outsold all the other Philadelphia papers. Mercer Carlton was the first man he hired.

Benjamin delighted in the intimacy of the meeting. This is how he imagined life in the newspaper business. Colleagues shaping the public dialogue, framing the debate of both Philadelphia and the nation. There could be no higher calling. He straightened his back on his chair.

"I've been tracking down some of the rumors flying around about the state of affairs in Washington," Benjamin said. "I just got back from the City Tavern, where the men are planning to get to Washington themselves, to retake the War Building for the

President, and to oust Stanton by force. I wanted to write up the story about how the people support the President."

Carlton pulled a piece of tobacco from his tongue and scowled. "There's no story in that, Wright." He looked at Grainger, who seemed cross that Carlton would stanch Benjamin's creativity, and then added, "But I like your initiative. The men needed to get out of the cold. It's the liquor talking. Nobody's going to charge into government buildings with their bayonets flashing."

Carlton turned to Grainger. "The boy is on to something, though, T.P. Washington is in an uproar. Word is Stevens is preparing to bring charges to an impeachment committee within a matter of days. He's got that motherless bastard Stanton and even Grant himself in his pocket. This impeachment talk is a bunch of bull crap, but that's beside the point. We're not doing much good sitting on our asses in a snow storm in the middle of Philadelphia. Is there money in the kitty to pay for a trip to check things out first hand?"

Benjamin's disappointment over Carlton's reaction to his idea of a story lasted only until Grainger spoke. "Why don't you take Benjamin down there and look into what's really going on?"

To Benjamin's delight (and, to his amazement), Carlton neither resisted nor hesitated. All the other reporters' plates were full and Carlton could use another set of eyes and ears. He stretched his arms. "Pack some extra clothes in a satchel and meet me at the train station first thing in the morning. You wanted to learn the newspaper business, Benjamin. You're about to get a million dollar education. Sanctimonious sons of bitches. God, this is going to be delicious."

Benjamin couldn't believe what he was hearing. Washington. History unfolding. An effort to impeach a sitting President. And he—a boy of limited schooling possessing of a gift of words whose source he could not even identify—would have a front row seat. A thought entered his mind. Should he telegraph his father to let him know he'd be visiting? But what if Jacob said nothing in return?

*Chapter 2*

Carlton said first thing in the morning. Benjamin had been too excited at first to ask what that meant and too embarrassed afterwards, so he arrived at six. The train wouldn't leave for three hours, but no matter. Benjamin had never seen one this close. He was determined to learn everything he could about it, to capture every detail that might find its way into one of his stories.

The conductor, a tall, barrel-chested man, asked Benjamin what business he had in the station so early in the morning. When Benjamin explained he was a reporter preparing a story on the railroad business, the man was so happy to learn his name might be in the *Courier* he let Benjamin explore the train inside and out. Benjamin was learning to exploit the *Courier's* name for the calling card it was.

"Ask me whatever you want. I've been in the railroad business since there were railroads, long enough to earn the right to be on the first train that will go the entire way from Philadelphia to the Pacific Ocean." He paused, as if he already were on that train. "Then I'll finally retire to a small place I own in Annapolis."

"The Pacific Ocean? How extraordinary. Are there really tracks running three thousand miles, through Indian territory and over mountains?" Benjamin was surprised at his naiveté.

"There will be, soon enough. Great progress is being made. I can't imagine it will be more than another year or two before I make that trip. I'm too old to see much of the future, but you are coming of age in an exceptional time, my friend, an exceptional time."

For all his creativity, Benjamin had a hard time imagining such a remarkable journey.

He thanked the conductor for the license he'd given him to explore the train and first touched every part of the engine the conductor allowed him near, from the engineer's cabin to the undercarriage. The wheels were nearly as tall as he was, gleaming steel catching the morning light, bolted to monstrous steam-driven shafts so

21

wide it took both of his hands to circle them. When he moved back to the next car, the stokers were more than happy to take a break from loading the coal that would drive the beast to explain with broad, sweeping gestures how the whole contraption worked, their faces and hands and clothes already black as a starless night.

There were two Negro porters in the passenger cabins, another four in the dining car, all getting ready for the trip by making certain their crisp white jackets, black pants, and clean white gloves were spotless. The men smiled and nodded politely as Benjamin ran his fingers across the soft leather chairs and beveled glass windows of the first class cabins, and the brass handles on all of the doors. The men in the dining car were covering the tables with starched white tablecloths, positioning each so that the small openings cut into them fit directly over the four small holes drilled into the table top to give the passengers' glasses a place to nestle. Each man spoke of his responsibility with pride.

Benjamin thanked the men for their time and then walked to the back of the train, where the boxcars were being loaded with everything from two hundred cases of champagne and sixty bales of damask silk that had sailed from Cherbourg to the port of Philadelphia to three thousand mason jars full of dried cranberries that started their journey in Prince Edward Island. They were all, like Benjamin, on their way to Washington.

The conductor was right. It was an extraordinary machine and an extraordinary time to be alive. The adventure of the journey turned his thoughts to Susanna. They promised to wait for each other until the time was right for them to begin a life together. On the day he left, Susanna handed him a handkerchief upon which she had embroidered the words, *Remember Me Always*.

Susanna said she was afraid she'd lose Benjamin to the pull of the big city, to the intensity of the *Courier*, to the fancy restaurants, and fancier women. She feared Benjamin would have little use for a simple farm girl. And yet, for all of Philadelphia's attractions,

## Chapter 2

Benjamin hadn't forgotten Susanna, hadn't changed his mind about her being the one with whom he wanted to spend the rest of his life. He regretted not having the time to visit Grayton, but he hadn't been at the *Courier* long enough to ask for that indulgence.

Benjamin fingered that piece of linen as he vowed to take Susanna on a train to touch the Pacific Ocean once they were married and the transcontinental railroad was completed.

That's what he would do.

That's how they would celebrate the beginning of their lives together.

# 3

"WATCH YOURSELF, BOY. This town is full of horse shit."

Carlton didn't bother turning toward Benjamin as he maneuvered over the planking set above the gravel and mud surrounding the train station in Washington. For all his care, globs of mud oozed through the cracks between the boards onto his boots. He bent over and wiped off as much as he could with yesterday's edition of the *Courier*.

"The locals want the national government to take care of things and the government wants the locals to take care of things, so nothing ever gets done around here." Benjamin had spent enough time around Carlton to know that his vision of a true newspaperman has the ability to turn even the smallest bit of muck into an editorial.

Carlton started barking orders to the cluster of boys scurrying up to carry his luggage in the hope of receiving a new five-cent piece for their trouble. All the while, he was going on about the sorry state of affairs in the Capitol with such commotion Benjamin hardly picked up every third word the man was saying. But he was still too thrilled about the train ride to do much of anything other than to marvel at the experience. The amazement of whizzing past farms and towns as though he were riding a magic carpet, the absurd site of men gauging the wind when they peed off the side of the car so they wouldn't spoil their shoes, the sense he had stepped into tomorrow.

Their carriage strained as it moved through the slop around the station, the wheels lumbering through the ruts as best they could, the horses breathing heavily with each step. It wasn't until it turned onto the paved New York Avenue that the horses were able to fall into rhythm. Carlton continued his rant, but no matter how much he went on, the headiness of being in the center of the nation's government buoyed Benjamin's spirits.

When the massive white dome of the Capitol came into their view, Benjamin nudged Carlton and said, "So that's thirty-eight degrees, fifty-two minutes and twenty seconds north latitude and seventy-seven degrees, zero minutes and fifteen seconds longitude west from Greenwich, Mr. Carlton?" It was a stunning sight to behold.

Carlton spit some of the cigar he'd been rolling around his tongue. "When I'm this close to the place, I can't even say for certain, boy. If there were some way to distort the lines of latitude and longitude and find a way to make money at it, those bastards would do that as sure as I'm sitting next to you. I don't know how your father can stand to work in the place."

Benjamin tensed. He'd opted not to send the telegraph.

The room at Willard's wouldn't be ready for several hours, so they left their bags with one of the porters. After all that time on the train, Carlton said he needed to stretch his legs. "Come with me, Benjamin. I'll show you what all the fuss is all about." Benjamin was grateful for the distraction.

A short walk up Pennsylvania Avenue took them to the President's house. It was an imposing structure, white marble shrouded in haze. Benjamin put his hand on the wrought iron fence surrounding the grounds.

But Carlton was in no mood to linger. He grabbed the right sleeve of Benjamin's jacket. "Andrew Johnson lives there and Thaddeus Stevens wants him out. That pretty much sums up why we're here."

Carlton pointed to his right, to the Capitol dome Benjamin already had sited with geographic precision. "And that's where the lynching will take place." The first major Constitutional crisis in the nation's history was reduced to a couple of jabs.

Benjamin wondered how a man like Carlton becomes a man like Carlton. Was he once new to the world, energized and as optimistic as Benjamin felt himself? Did he gradually evolve into a shrewish critic of everything that came in his direction? Or was he plopped down on this earth ready to stand to the side of anyone and anything and mold some narrative out of his slanted vision of the way things ought to be? Benjamin hoped that twenty years on he wouldn't be the same crusty caricature. He wanted to believe there was more to the newspaper business than barraging the public with cynicism and bias.

"I don't think of Stevens as a bad man. He has been a loud and consistent voice on the question of freedom for the slaves." Benjamin didn't want to lose Carlton's affection by saying something either school boyish or unduly patriotic. He'd learned that much from his short time in the newspaper business. But there were two sides to every story.

Carlton looked pleased. "You've done your homework."

Carlton continued, "Stevens has gotten old, though. He's sickly now." He was composing the *Courier's* story as they walked. There was no need to tell Benjamin this was the theme Carlton wanted him to use in his stories about the impeachment saga.

"If he were ten years' younger and had his health, he would have reined in the radical wing of his party. He's just a figurehead now who probably doesn't even know he's being used. It's a damned shame."

Benjamin made note of the comment not because of its criticism of Stevens, but for Carlton's objectivity and touch of sympathy for the man. In the combustion of the *Courier's* rush to get the paper onto the streets before the *Sun* or the *Mirror*, Carlton was a tsar in both his thinking and in the way he demanded fealty to his ideas. A man was either his ally or his enemy. There was the black of the *Courier's* ink and there was the white of the *Courier's* paper stock, but there was no gray.

Carlton pointed toward a square of elegant houses standing directly across from the President's house. "Staying too long in this city changes people for the worse. Watch for that characteristic in the people that you meet."

Had this place done that to Jacob? Benjamin had no time to think about the answer to that question for Carlton stopped talking long enough only to light his cigar. "Do you see that white stucco house with the green shutters at the corner of the square?" Benjamin nodded. Whatever thoughts he had about his father would have to wait until the end of his boss's ramblings.

Carlton continued to talk as they walked toward Lafayette Square. "You know the name Dan Sickles?"

Anyone who knew anything about the war knew the name. "The general who led an entire regiment into a slaughter at Gettysburg?"

"A year or two before the troubles broke out, Sickles lived there with his wife Teresa. He was in the Congress. New York City. Like everybody else, he came here promising to be a reformer, but soon enough he was firmly in Buchanan's pocket. His wife was gorgeous, though. They were quite the couple around town."

Carlton took Benjamin by the arm and walked him closer to the house. "The trees in the square were much smaller then." He turned and looked across the square. "Despite having the ear of the President and a perfectly charming woman in his bed, Sickles had trouble keeping his pants on around other ladies. His whoring finally drove poor Teresa to take up with Bart Key. You know the family? His father wrote the Star Spangled Banner."

"I know the song. Everyone knows the song. I don't know the family."

Carlton pointed to a building diagonally across from the stucco. "Key used to wait at a window at the club in that building for a signal from Teresa that the coast was clear." Carlton then stopped at a stand of trees just inside a wrought iron fence to which someone had tethered a horse. "Sickles discovered their affair. He had two thugs ambush Key right where we're standing. They shot him twice. Sickles put the third bullet in him even though the poor bastard didn't even have a weapon on him."

"What became of Sickles?"

"Everybody in this town somehow is linked to someone else. We're here because Ed Stanton is making a hoo hah about not leaving his office. Stanton was the lawyer who beat the charges. He told the court Sickles had gone temporarily insane."

Carlton coughed and then spit into the gutter. "Temporary insanity. Can you believe that pile of manure? If courts start letting criminals walk away Scot free because they went crazy for a minute, half the wives in Philadelphia and certainly all the wives in my house would kill their husbands and start over with new ones. What a country." Benjamin made note of what Carlton was saying. There might be a story for the *Courier* lying in the records of the Philadelphia courts.

"Sickles?" How do we close the story on him?" Benjamin was learning that to a good newsman, every question leads to another, every story has a beginning, a middle, an end, and a postscript.

"The war came along and he became the worst general the Union had, God save all of us. Washington has this almost magical ability to elevate incompetent boobs."

"And Theresa, what of her?" Benjamin needed closure on the heroine's role.

"She died of a broken heart. The doctors said it was tuberculosis, but I know better." The comment made Benjamin think of his mother, for she was destined to do the same. He couldn't think of a worse fate. Damn Jacob for that.

Carlton paused. "Schuyler Colfax lives in that white stucco now. Powerful figure around these parts. He's the Speaker of the House, but he's hungry for more. There's talk Grant will ask him to be his running mate once the election season heats up. Schuyler Colfax. Remember his name. He thought he was the man to bring honor and integrity to the government, but he fell under the sway of Washington's seduction. Remember too he lives in a house haunted by its past. I don't know how and I don't know when, but the ghosts of this place will overtake him."

Carlton took a long drag on his cigar. "Grainger wanted me to teach you the newspaper business. Here's today's lesson. Nothing in this town is as it appears on the surface, Benjamin. Nothing. Remember that as you witness what's about to unfold."

# 4

MERCER CARLTON SETTLED HIMSELF into his seat in the public gallery at the House of Representatives. Carlton's gift of a two dollar piece assured a place for Benjamin along the back wall of the gallery despite Stevens' mandate that only one representative from each paper be allowed entry.

Benjamin was wedged next to two women in their forties dressed in their finest clothes for the event and perfumed at ten in the morning as though they were attending the opera. They were not alone. Virtually everyone in the gallery preened for the event. Soldiers in full regalia. A man in white tie and tails, as if he'd just come from a ball, a passel of women even more glamorous than the ones who pressed against him. But there wasn't a black face in the crowd.

Benjamin wriggled his right hand free to make note of that fact on his pad. Carlton would want to remind his readers they'd we'd just given up tens of thousands of young and promising lives to liberate the slaves, but the slaves themselves hadn't been freed enough to find even one place to stand in the halls of Congress.

Still, Benjamin would never forget his first vision of the place. Marble columns soaring toward a vaulted rotunda that seemed to touch heaven itself. Statues surrounding the great hall, exquisitely sculpted busts of the men who had shaped America, the House chamber itself, even packed to the gills, as rich in mahogany and marble as it was in tradition. But as awed as he was, he stayed focused. He belonged here, pencil in hand. He had a job to do. He was a newspaperman.

The room became quiet in an instant when Schuyler Colfax entered from the door at the rear of the chamber. All eyes turned to him as if commoners were watching a Roman senator enter the Forum. A tall man, with graying hair and a full and deep white beard, his back was ramrod straight. He moved slowly, as if to allow everyone the time to absorb the unfolding history. Benjamin thought of what Carlton said when they were standing in front of the man's house the night before and wondered what he'd been like in his youth, or even a few years ago.

The parade of representatives followed, men all dressed in black, as if to a funeral, dark ties, darker expressions. Not one man looked to the crowd, not one sought the glance of a friend. They were here to make history, either to bring down a President or to do what they could to stop the exercise. This was solemn and serious business on both sides of the aisle. Benjamin leaned forward on the balls of his feet. He didn't want to miss a word.

Colfax recognized Aaron Baker, a Democrat from Maryland. Baker was wide as a barn, with a voice belonging in a taller man's body. His words rang through the hall. "Mr. Speaker, we meet today on the birthday of our first and perhaps finest President, George Washington. In his honor, and to honor the brave men who gave so much to their country of late, I most respectfully move that we read into the record Mr. Washington's Farewell Address and that the House then adjourn to show this day the honor it so rightly deserves."

The chamber exploded with laughter and the echo of men in the aisles slapping each other's back and repeating the humor. More boos than applause filtered down from the gallery. His fellow Democrats walked to Baker's desk and shook his hand or patted his back. Baker's face was the color of a tomato that spent too much time on the windowsill. The Democrats knew the Republicans had all the votes they needed to do whatever they wanted to Johnson; they were powerless to stop the coming stampede. Baker's gallows humor at least was a blessed respite from the inevitable.

Colfax, though, would have none of it. He slammed his gavel with a force Benjamin thought would splinter it. In a voice the texture of shattered glass, he threatened to empty the chamber if there were any more outbursts. No public hanging was going to be put off by such frivolity.

The door to the chamber opened. Thaddeus Stevens led the Committee on Reconstruction onto the floor of the House. He was so bent over and moving so slowly from whatever disease was killing him that Benjamin had difficulty imagining what a striking figure he'd posed in Washington when he was as powerful a man as could be found there. Stevens had cheekbones so high on his face and so chiseled that Benjamin wrote on his pad the man might have Cherokee blood. Stevens' eyes were lost in shadow. He leaned against an aide for support.

The other members of the Committee followed Stevens into the room as acolytes follow their priest. Carlton would report to the men in his newsroom he had never seen a more pompous lot, or men more full of their own ambition.

With the solemnity of a man knowing he would be remembered for the ages, Stevens read the resolution of impeachment. Benjamin strained to capture every nuance, not so much of the words themselves (for the text of the resolution would be available by handbill within a matter of hours), but for the reaction of the men on the floor of the chamber and of the people in the balcony. He owed Grainger the best possible story he could muster and he owed the possibility of his own career nothing less.

Stevens paused between the words high crimes and misdemeanors, as though he wanted each vowel and consonant to become part of the masonry holding the Capitol together. He concluded his remarks with a dare to the opposition. "Gentlemen of the Committee, you have heard the charges. I am prepared to rebut any response the other side might wish to make."

And how the Democrats seized the opportunity. It didn't matter what they had to say as long as it lasted long enough the impeachment vote might be delayed.

Carlton twice left the room for a cigar and the privy and once for a light dinner at Oscar Reed's restaurant.

Crowds milled around the Capitol for blocks on every side.

The entire police force of Washington and some army regulars had been called out to maintain the peace. The image of armed men patrolling the steps of the Capitol left Benjamin cold. They were carrying the same Winchester rifles Willie and Matthew had strapped to their backs the last time Benjamin saw them alive. They were unable to hide their fears, unable to join the boisterous celebration of the men and boys at their side who had convinced themselves of the rightness of their cause. It was a hideous way to remember them.

The noise from the crowd was deafening, but the work of the Committee dragged on. Finally, well past ten in the evening, a frail and dark Thaddeus Stevens began an attack on the President that left him so limp that a clerk had to finish his oration.

The vote was almost an afterthought. The Republicans held together. Their one hundred twenty-six votes was nearly three times that of the Democrats.

Carlton was so revolted by the whole charade he stormed off to John Welcher's pub and gave Benjamin his proxy to write the story he'd been sent here to cover. Benjamin didn't need a coach to write the telegram he would send back to the *Courier* with instructions it be printed in its entirety. He scribbled the message as he waited for the audience to thin. *We have lost the battle for decency and level-headedness to a group of Republicans so bent on bringing down this President they will stop at nothing. God help and save this Blessed Republic from what they are about to do.*

Benjamin looked at what he'd written. He was surprised at how the words flowed. It wasn't that he doubted his ability to shape the sentences. He'd proven how adept he was at that when he became Grayton's voice of homage to its fallen. But those words were paeans to a noble cause and to a hero's death. The spectacle that had played out before him today and into the night, however, was nothing but partisan bickering, gamesmanship to create the appearance of civility, and the crushing brutality of a wide majority of votes. There was nothing to honor about this side of Washington. Stevens and his crowd deserved nothing but scorn.

The crowd in the visitors' gallery rushed out to get one of the better tables at Willard's or at the Executive Grill. Benjamin held back. He wanted to be able to describe for the *Courier's* readers the expressions on the faces of the major players in the impeachment process as they left the well of the House.

A guard allowed Benjamin to stand in the lobby but far enough away from the representatives that he was able to hear only a smattering of the words the men shared as they moved out of the chamber. His eyes focused on Colfax as another member lightly took his arm. A younger man, a full head shorter than the Speaker, he might have been his uncle.

"Mr. Colfax, may I have a word?" Schuyler Colfax turned at the sound of a voice he recognized as that of Oakes Ames, the Gentleman from Massachusetts, as Colfax called his fellow members of Congress even outside the chamber. He leaned against his aide for support.

"Mr. Ames, this is a sad day for the country."

"It is, indeed, Mr. Colfax, but there will be better times ahead. The railroad line to California is nearing completion. The nation soon will be united as never before. One only can imagine how the lives of our people will be transformed by this magical invention. You can be proud of the job you have done on behalf of the American people by making such important legislation possible."

"Our job, Mr. Ames, is to deliver the future to America."

"The Credit Mobilier is performing better than we had expected when we last spoke. Our contracts have turned out to be quite profitable. Our friends will not be forgotten."

Carlton's words came back to him. Nothing in Washington is at it appears on the surface. There might be a story here. There could be a story anywhere in these halls. Benjamin wrote down the words *Credit* and *contracts* and *railroad* and the letters *M* and *O*.

Colfax turned to his colleague. "We must talk, Mr. Ames, but now is not the time. Perhaps lunch tomorrow would be convenient?"

# 5

"LOOK AT THIS BUNDLE of jack straw. Eleven separate charges. Ten of them are all about Johnson trying to throw Stanton out of office and Stevens throwing this Tenure of Office Act business back in his face. One charge seems to complain about Johnson giving public speeches that made people laugh at the Congress."

Carlton had been parading around the newsroom with one of the handbills detailing the charges spouting his version of today's story, and the story for the next day and the day after that, from the moment the copyboy he'd sent to meet the train from Washington rushed one into his hand. He'd known what the *Courier* was going to say about the allegations for days, but he needed to see what words Stevens actually used before publicly labeling him a scoundrel.

It wasn't as though Johnson had been caught giving military secrets to the French or had helped himself to public funds. The charges Stevens drummed up were a crazy quilt of complaints about Johnson trying to throw Stanton out of office and of not respecting Congress.

Carlton fished into his coat for a cigar. He bit off the end and then spit out a piece of tobacco. "I suppose not respecting them is better than shooting the fools."

He put the handbill on Benjamin's desk. "Run me up five hundred words for tonight's paper. Give the boys each page as you write it. I want the type set as fast as we can to beat the rest of the rags in this town to this story."

Carlton headed toward his desk and then turned back. "It's all a bunch of bullshit, Wright, so don't get hung up on the words they used. Let the people know what's really going on. The *Courier* has championed the anti-slavery movement since we opened our doors. We spilled a ton of ink praising the man's work with the underground railroad. But God damn it, Stevens has gone too far this time. You don't reunite a country that's just been through the bloodiest war in its history by putting your boot on the throat of the enemy you just defeated. That's the *Courier's* message, Wright. Tell it straight and tell it fast."

"And the facts, Mr. Carlton?" Benjamin asked. One of the copy boys stopped as though Benjamin had accused Carlton of heresy. Benjamin surprised everyone within earshot with the audacity of his comment. However much he accepted Carlton's view of what had transpired in Washington, he even surprised himself that he might find the courage to question whether the job of the *Courier* was to report or to shape the news. He shared its newsroom with Mercer Carlton long enough to come to understand the man stood squarely for the unvarnished truth so long as it fit within his definition of what that truth should be. But however much he might have been intimidated by the man at the beginning, pushing back on the point felt just right.

Carlton squinted. He walked close enough to Benjamin's desk that only Benjamin could hear what he was about to say. "Those *are* the facts, Wright. Those are *all* the facts that our readers need to know." He then stood straight and made certain everyone within earshot heard what he was about to say. "Greene. Hold the first two columns open. Wright is going to feed you the lead article in exactly the terms I just described it. You'll have the first hundred words in half an hour." He looked again at Benjamin. "Exactly the terms I mentioned."

Carlton's booming voice brought the room to life. Two copy boys raced to Benjamin's desk before he'd finished reading even the first portion of the handbill. Their quick, gulping breaths only ramped up his sense of urgency.

Benjamin had no training in the law, but Carlton's assessment seemed accurate enough. The articles of impeachment were swaddled in haughty legalese, but they all boiled down to Johnson's desire to fire a man Lincoln had put into office.

As anyone who has spent more than five minutes paying attention to the recent brouhaha in Washington can attest, Thad. Stevens and the Radical Republicans want to crush the defeated states of the South. They want to impose military rule. They want to take away the very power to govern those states. Long-time readers know the *Courier* has championed the anti-slave cause since the paper opened its doors. We applaud Stevens' motives. There can be no doubt he stands with the freed Negroes. But as much as the *Courier* supports that cause, we give our greater support to the need to preserve the institution of the presidency, particularly at this fragile moment in the nation's history.

Benjamin felt as though he were channeling the muses of a history who needed to be memorialized so future generations would understand both the venom and the hypocrisy behind the Republican's rhetoric. He rarely paused over a word, never reread or doubted what he'd written.

Andrew Johnson sees the reconstruction process differently from the Radical Republicans. He wants to bring the Confederate states back into the Union gradually. He wants a healing to take place so the freed slaves can grow into the freedom the blood of our brothers achieved for them. We may disagree with those views, but the fact he possesses them does not present grounds to run the man out of office.

The Radical Republicans know the Constitution doesn't allow them to bring Johnson up on impeachment charges because of his views on the future of the secessionist states, so they have trumped up charges they hope fit within the meaning of high crimes and misdemeanors the Founding Fathers set as the standard for removing the President.

"Wright," barked Carlton. "This is good. Give me more of the same. Hurry." Benjamin's hand was aching from pushing his pen so hard and so fast across the page. It would take days to wash away the splotches of ink stained onto his skin.

The Committee on Impeachment filed eleven separate charges against the President. Ten of them relate to his effort to remove Edwin M. Stanton as his Secretary of War and to replace him with General Grant. Who better than the Union's finest commander to put in that post? Johnson inherited Stanton in his cabinet when Mr. Booth dispatched Mr. Lincoln to God's grace. He should have the right to begin his time in office with a fresh slate. But the Radicals aren't interested in anything other than imposing their vision of reconstruction on the defeated states. That's why they seized on the trumped-up argument that the Tenure of Office Act requires Congress to approve the removal of cabinet officers who were placed into that position in the first place with the consent of Congress. They argue that as Johnson won't support that law, he is violating his oath to support the laws of the United States and thus can be removed from his office.

The Founding Fathers never intended the impeachment process to be used for such purposes. Never. We rue the Radical Republicans' lack of proportion as much as we regret their effort to use the impeachment process for such blatantly political purposes. The President who can call our fathers and brothers to spill their blood for their country should and must be above such backbiting.

"This is just what I wanted, Wright. Greene." Carlton handed Benjamin's page to Jesse Greene. "Remove the line praising Grant. The last thing we need to do is to encourage that drunken old bastard to get himself messed up in Washington. If we're not careful he could end up as President and we'd all be in a deeper pile of dung than we're in now."

The eleventh charge of impeachment, which is called the Omnibus Bill, strikes us as particularly troubling. It is a kitchen sink of charges that Johnson ridiculed and brought the Congress into disrepute. Perhaps we at the *Courier* are biased in favor of the Bill of Rights because it was written here in Philadelphia, but as we understand it, words spoken in Washington also enjoy its protection.

Benjamin felt as though he'd ridden through a hurricane. He had almost no strength left to say another word. But there was no need. T. P. Grainger nodded with approval as he read what had been typed. He then broke into a smile and read aloud what every Democratic sympathizer in Philadelphia (and even a few in New York and Washington) would be quoting for days. "If any level-headed man has any doubts about what the Radical Republicans are up to, he need only read the Omnibus Bill. The charges are a boiling kettle so filled with obfuscation the Senate could find justification for either impeaching or canonizing the President and still get it right."

Jesse Greene started first and then the others in the room broke into applause. Benjamin reddened and then smiled.

## Chapter 5

Grainger put his hand on Benjamin's shoulder, leaned over and said for only Benjamin's ears, "Carlton and I have been talking, son. The impeachment trial likely will last a month or more. Events will be playing out in the Senate and in the salons of Washington where decisions really are made. That's a lot of ground for one man to cover. You did a good job at the committee hearings. Your eye is keen and your writing strong. We'd like you to share some of the burden. All of the rooms in the city are spoken for and you may have to take your bedroll, but we'd like you to accompany Carlton to Washington for the trial."

He paused, held up the last page Benjamin had written. Benjamin could hear the newsies in the street hawking the *Courier's* version of the impeachment charges, their voices becoming fainter as they ran away from the building to their designated corner. By the time Grainger extended his invitation, dozens of men, perhaps hundreds, were already taking a side in the debate Benjamin had defined for them. He was certain that by darkness, every tavern in Philadelphia would be filled with men shouting his quotes as though they had taken a life's oath to defend them.

If anyone had told him, when his mother talked about his leaving Grayton to pursue his dream in the newspaper business, that within a few months he'd be giving voice to the opposition to the political railroading of a sitting president from office, or now, better still, that he'd be an eyewitness, Benjamin Wright would have dismissed the notion to a young boy's dreams.

But it was real, as real as the badge of black ink on the meat of his hand marking him as a man devoted to putting words on paper, to moving men to spirited debate, to defining the public dialogue, as real as the affirmation he received from his colleagues.

Benjamin thanked Grainger for putting his trust in him, assured him he'd be diligent. And then he started writing silently with only the tip of his finger, *So this is what history feels like.*

# 6

THE TRIAL WOULDN'T START for another two weeks. The *Courier's* readers needed something to feed on beyond anticipation. Grainger came up with the idea of looking at the war three years on. On April 9 it would be that long since Lee took Grant's hand in surrender in Wilbur McLean's sitting room at Appomattox Courthouse.

Each of the *Courier's* reporters were to spend two or three days back at his home asking whether the sacrifice had produced anything beyond broken bodies and splintered futures. It would be an interesting exercise for Benjamin, for he would need to discipline himself to look at Grayton as an outsider visiting the place for the first time. Benjamin hadn't been schooled in objectivity, but he was determined to heed Grainger's advice and to stand outside himself and pretend he was taking one of Matthew Brady's photographs.

It was a soaking March afternoon. The roads near the farm were badly rutted and washed out in spots, mud halfway up his horse's legs. Benjamin would write about how the government needed to stop merely talking about fixing the mess the savagery left behind and begin fulfilling its promise to repair what the war destroyed.

The rain kept Rachel inside. She wasn't even aware Benjamin had ridden up until she heard the commotion in the barn while he was unsaddling and washing the mud off both himself and his Haflinger. They embraced on the porch without saying a word. She felt thin. Fragile. Distant. Benjamin could write an entire piece for Grainger out of nothing but the woman's silence.

The house was cold. Rachel never fussed for herself. Benjamin put two logs on the fire. He stood with his hands as close to the flame as he could bear. It would take some time for the chill to lose its grip.

Rachel seemed even more hollow than when he'd left to join the *Courier*. Her cheeks sunk further into her face. Her eyes were more hidden. She'd cut her hair short so as not to have to deal with it. It only accentuated how veined and sore her neck looked. She was wearing one of Jacob's old work shirts over a pair of well-worn britches. And her breathing was shallow.

"It's been a remarkable two months, Mother. Not just Philadelphia, but the Capitol itself. I've been so fortunate to be exposed to a world I knew of only from pictures. I never knew so much marble and gold existed." Benjamin prattled on almost end-lessly about the hearing, the glitter of the restaurants, the elegance of the people and their houses, the stories that Carlton told as though the whole world wanted still one more. The house hadn't seen such an animated conversation since Willie and Matthew were wrested from it.

Rachel took his hands in hers, rubbed them, the way she did when he'd lost one of the mittens she knitted for him. "I don't want to lose another of my men to Washington, Benjamin. Don't do to Susanna what your father did to me." Her voice was stone. She felt herself a widow from the moment Jacob and the boys marched off, for he'd never really come back any more than they did. The war pressed against him the way that hot iron is pressed against an anvil. Washington consumed what little was left.

Benjamin tried to twist his hands free but his mother tightened her grip. "Love Susanna, Benjamin. Not Washington. I'm not ask-ing you to come back here. I knew once your Uncle Curtis started talking about that job in Philadelphia this old place didn't stand a chance. I didn't try to hold you back then and I'm not trying to do so now. I'm just asking you not to lose sight of the difference between what's real and what's a stage play."

She smoothed his hair. The gesture took Benjamin back. When the boys were little and Rachel needed to get them presentable she'd put a bit of saliva on her hand and then run her fingers over their heads. It was the last thing she did to Willie and then to Matthew before Benjamin nailed one of their coffins shut and Jacob struggled with the other. They were connected for that instant.

"You're all I have left now, Benjamin. Make me proud."

He felt both chastised and angered that fifteen minutes into their time together Rachel could greet him only with criticism. "I'm learning my trade, Mother, learning the craft of writing. You can be proud of that. I had my own byline on the story we wrote about the impeachment charges. It's in my satchel for you to read. There hasn't been a story as important as that since Mr. Lincoln's assassination."

"Proud that I have a son who doesn't abandon his family, Benjamin. Proud that he's man enough to accept his responsibilities to his wife and children." Her words were more than a rebuke. They bound him like shackles.

Benjamin moved away from the fire. He was unwilling to stand idly for any more of his mother's complaints. "I'm not Jacob. Please. No more of that."

"And I don't want you to be." They looked at each other but said nothing, as if each was afraid to raise the volume of the conversation to the flash point. Finally, Rachel waved her arms. "Enough of this talk. Run along and fetch Susanna. I want to see the two of you together again. I want to be reminded what a handsome couple you are. Bring some joy back into this house."

Benjamin was only too glad to be released from the emotional prison of his mother's hearth. His return to Grayton was not enough of a gift for Rachel, but he had nothing else. His coat was still soaked from the ride. He grabbed a horse blanket in the barn on his way toward the Madigans'.

He was relieved to be away from the woman. He felt compassion for her. She'd been scarred by the war as badly as any soldier, but what right did she have to scold him for his father's failings? She'd shut him out of her life for the past several years. Burying her two older boys gave her that right, but how could she now claim to know the content of his heart? He wondered whether Grainger's story would be about how the war turned allies into enemies.

He moved slowly at first, picking his way as best he could through the slop. He stopped at Willie and Matthew's headstones, picked the fallen branches off their graves, swept away the leaves that had piled up, told them where he'd been, where he was heading, wished they could be a part of it all. There was no point complaining to them about Rachel's pain. They'd suffered enough. They'd earned their rest.

When he moved again, his steps were slow and measured, but his pace and spirits lightened when, within a few hundred yards of the Madigans' door, he heard the pianoforte. Susanna was giving a lesson to one of the children who paid fifty cents for an hour of her time.

Benjamin looked through the window, taking care not to be seen. He recognized the student, a young redheaded girl, from her father's funeral. His name had been Kelsey Phillips. He was one of Hunter's men at 1st Bull Run, only twenty-seven when he was shot in the back of his head near the train station in Manassas, Virginia during the retreat after the First Zouaves lost their gunnery.

Benjamin knew all their names, all their stories, for as a boy who could mold words into eulogies, it was his job during the war to turn slaughter and fear into gallantry so widows and children and mothers would remember as heroes even those who at the end ran like the frightened children they were.

The young girl was perhaps nine now, the oldest of three children he left behind. Benjamin would write of the void of Kelsey's loss, and of how the neighbors rallied to fill the emptiness, always falling short, however brave their efforts.

Benjamin sat quietly on the porch until the lesson stopped. He picked the mud off the bottom of his boots with a stick and let Susanna's sweet voice surround him with memories of the dozens of funerals when the entire congregation dropped its voice to a whisper so that Susanna's could carry both *Amazing Grace* and the souls of the newly dead beyond the rafters.

"Benjamin?" Susanna scooted her student along. Benjamin slipped his notebook and pencil back into his pocket.

They kissed. For the moment their lips were together there was no Carlton, no bustle of the newsroom, no grandeur of the Capitol. There only was a girl ready to become a woman who tasted of the licorice drops she kept on the edge of her piano as a reward for her better students. "I was afraid you'd forget about me, Benjamin. I can't compete with the fashionable women of Philadelphia."

There had been one. A friend of Mitzi's, a gift from Carlton, a liquored wrestling match. Benjamin had been left dirty. He would not speak of her in front of Susanna.

He rubbed the small of her neck with the index finger of his right hand. It hadn't been that long since they saw each other, but the softness of Susanna's skin startled Benjamin. He was filled with a desire that if Susanna had allowed to flame would have turned them to ash.

"I'm so glad to see you. I hadn't expected you back from Philadelphia so soon." Susanna held both of Benjamin's hands. Her eyes were flecked with hazel. It was as though he hadn't left. Contentment welled up in her.

Benjamin studied Susanna's face in the late afternoon light. He traced the line of her cheeks and the well of her eye with the index finger of his right hand. She was even lovelier than the photograph of her he took with him to Philadelphia. He would write of how the war had been unable to strip Susanna of her simple beauty. He leaned in and kissed her a second time.

She pulled back. She needed distance, needed air, but then she pressed both her lips and her whole self against him in a way that shattered boundaries. Their bodies nestled together as if they had been made for no other purpose.

"I missed you," said Benjamin. There would be time to tell Susanna the real reason for the visit, if Benjamin ever chose to share it. But the words were an oath of truth, a pledge. He didn't want Susanna to pull him back to Grayton. He wanted them to move forward together. "I can't wait until you can join me there."

Susanna smiled, but tensed. "It's such a big city, Benjamin." He knew that a future with him in a place outside the only home she ever knew frightened her. But he wanted to believe that the idea of a future without him, frightened her even more.

Benjamin understood and respected Susanna's fears, for they were his own. "I'll always take care of you, Susanna." He reached into his pocket and touched her tears with the handkerchief she made for him. The gesture evoked more. Their ambivalence united them as almost nothing else could.

"Nothing and no one will harm you. I promise."

They kissed. They could not will themselves to stop.

Benjamin would not write of this moment, of their longing, of their fear of being either together or apart, of the sweet taste of Susanna's lips.

This was their story, not Grainger's.

# 7

BENJAMIN RODE to John Henderson's place in the morning, three miles down the Grayton Pike from Rachel's farm. The spring snowmelt in the Grayton River joined the seemingly endless rain to wash out a line of fencing around John's sheep meadow. His ewes would be lambing in a couple of weeks. John was patching the holes in the fence so the little ones wouldn't scamper off and get themselves eaten by the wolves who roamed in the pine and sycamore trees surrounding his farm. Benjamin threw himself into the job. John's boys were way too little to be hammering fence posts back into the ground, so he was both grateful for the help and in a talkative mood. He was interested to learn about Benjamin's time at the *Courier* and happy to help with Grainger's story.

"Has it really been three years already since the end of the war? I've lost track of the time." He paused, leaned on the cane that supported his right leg. "I suppose that's right. The boys are two. Casey and I were married as soon as I got back. Three years. All that time passed in a wink."

John's reaction to returning to Grayton mirrored the other stories Benjamin heard over the years, a mixture of relief and guilt at having survived when so many comrades fell along the way, the sense that they never would be called on again in their lives to reach for such a noble calling, that they were living a second life they weren't certain they deserved.

Benjamin wanted to take John back to the crucible of bullets and cannonballs flying, bayonets slashing, the ground awash in blood the morning Willie and Matthew were killed. "What do you remember when you think about the battles?" Grainger's assignment wasn't about the war itself, but the aftermath of the war, but Benjamin so needed to know about his brothers' final hours he turned every opportunity to have a conversation with one of the survivors from the Pennsylvania 54th into a search for answers. To a man, they were stoic, unwilling to talk about what happened at Hoke's Run. It was as though they had taken the same oath as monks or prelates. Benjamin always carried with him the question of what they were protecting. Or whom.

He'd asked John before, not long after he returned in the quiet of night, so unlike the heraldry and high expectations of his leaving. They sat in a pew in the back of the church, long after the other worshipers left. Benjamin hoped he might draw John out in a confessional place. But it was too close to the endless privation, to the hollowness of the fear that was his constant companion, to the memories of the boys he'd sent to their deaths, to press him to speak when he plainly couldn't. Benjamin hoped that time, a new wife, two small boys, and the renewal of still another spring healed over some of his wounds.

"Is that question about all battles or about Hoke's Run in particular?" asked John. He understood Benjamin's inability to stop seeking answers about his brothers, for his thirst was no different from the boys under his command in their tents the night before a planned battle, boys who wanted to know not only whether they might be able to summon the courage to die as heroes but why they had to die at all. The war was becoming a distant enough memory and Benjamin was far enough along into his own life that John seemed more open to Benjamin's question than he'd been in the past.

"I'm happy to hear whatever you have to say," Benjamin said. He removed his work gloves and reached for his note pad, as if the gesture were becoming reflexive. He inhaled deeply, hoping he finally might see a glimmer of reality and summoning every ounce of energy he could muster to capture all of John's words.

"It was a difficult morning. Hot as all get-out. Our troops were under Abercrombie's command. Your father and I each led a battalion." John wasn't a large man, but he commanded respect because of the quiet dignity with which he carried himself. His hair was cropped short. His hands were calloused and cut from stringing barbed wire. "Neither of us had any idea what was expected of us. We'd been soldiers for all of eighty-two days."

"That was the first real test for the 54th. Everyone must have been so afraid," Benjamin said. He couldn't imagine what was going through his brothers' minds the first time they were summoned into battle. "And one thing I've never understood is why Abercrombie would put a father and his sons in the same battalion. Wasn't there concern he might put their safety before that of others under his command?"

"Your question, Benjamin, assumes Abercrombie thought about such things. Like everyone else involved in the mess, he was making things up as he went along."

"Was the opposition in as much disarray?"

"The Confederates were as frightened as we were, but they were a tenacious lot, by God. They were led by Stonewall Jackson, although he hadn't gotten that name yet. He was one tough son of a bitch. I saw him shoot one of his own men who tried to flee. After that, his troops didn't dare do anything but advance."

John spoke more softly as he shared his memory of the boy no older than seventeen or eighteen who came charging at him with his bayonet spiraling wildly about his head as though he were some sort of a spinning toy. The boy was so close that John could see his freckles, could smell the damp stink of his clothes as his blade sliced though both the flank of John's horse and his right boot, almost severing his leg just below the knee. The blade was covered in dirt, shit, and the insides of the horses and men the boy had to scramble over to get close enough to John to thrust his bayonet. His shot hit the boy in his right eye. It had been the color of a robin's egg before the bullet jammed it into its socket. The boy crumpled like one of the twins' rag dolls, the contents of his head spurting out of him as though he had become a fountain of blood and brain. That was John's introduction to the art of war.

"One thing I'll never understand about that morning is why so many of our men were exposed in an open meadow." Benjamin paused before continuing, as if he were remembering what he'd studied about the battle. "They were led into a massacre they could have avoided if they'd marched two hundred yards to their right, through the trees." Benjamin pored over every map, every eyewitness account, every newspaper and magazine article he could get his hands on. He knew Abercrombie sent two battalions up the hillside toward the Confederate stronghold at the top. Both could have used the trees for cover. One chose the open field. "Whose decision was that?"

At some point in every war the battles blend into one continuous fog of cannon smoke, thundering horses, shells exploding and bullets thumping into skin with the sound of rocks thrown against a wall, followed by the mournful wails of men too wounded and weak to do anything other than to hope death will come quickly. But not Hoke's Run. John had the expression of a man who couldn't forget his first all-out battle any more than he could forget the first time he touched Casey after he returned from the war.

"Could you describe the attack on Baker's Ridge?"

John let the silence gather, as if he were hoping Benjamin would move onto another topic. When he finally spoke it was with some hesitation. "A small band of Confederates were spreading cannon fire from a bunker they'd built on the top. Abercrombie ordered us to take them out." John was talking so quietly Benjamin had to take a step toward him. "Your father and I each took twenty men."

And then he described the chaos of it all. The woods were full of horseflies the size of bats and of baffles and traps the Confederates had planted. John worked his way slowly, painstakingly, through the maze, always dropping to the ground when snipers caught his men in a vulnerable spot. The 54th had never been fired on before that moment, but John was able to maintain his composure. But whether driven by frustration, or fear or both, Jacob veered into the open meadow in the hope that he could escape the hell of it all. His men followed their commander as if he'd discovered a preferred strategy. Jacob lost seventeen men and two sons in less than one minute of cannon and rifle fire, fear, apoplexy, and madness.

John fell silent. It was as if he couldn't find a way to describe to Benjamin what a horrible mistake his father had made in that moment of panic; as if he knew there were no words of comfort that Benjamin would accept no matter what he said. He picked up a fence post. He handed the sledge to Benjamin. Benjamin put his notebook in his rear pocket and put his gloves back on.

In a way, Benjamin was grateful for John's discretion. That he was opaque, that he hadn't criticized Jacob was a gift of sorts, better than a half truth, better than a lie. John's silence allowed Benjamin to believe what he chose to believe: that it was Abercrombie, or perhaps John himself, and not his own father's lack of will, that led Willie and Matthew into slaughter.

# 8

THE RIDE BACK TO PHILADELPHIA was a jumble of disappointment and anger toward Rachel, of Susanna's lips, the hint of licorice, the fear she truly might be afraid to leave Grayton when he so wanted only to look forward. Leaving Grayton the first time felt like an adventure beginning. This time it felt as though everyone and everything there was holding him back.

Benjamin leaned toward his horse's mane, struggling against both the wind and the need to put all those thoughts aside and to begin focusing on the job at hand. He'd be in Washington in only two days, witnessing the impeachment of a sitting President. It was time to put on his reporter's hat and to ignore everything else.

And when he finally got there, the town was a carnival. Crowds far larger than those that came for Lincoln's second inaugural. Bookmakers taking bets on the outcome of the trial at tables on street corners and in the lobbies of every hotel, with the odds favoring the ouster of Johnson on at least one count holding steady at three to one. Pleasure houses at all hours overflowing with customers. Mansions on Connecticut Avenue brimming with sweet brandy, candied fruits, braised beef, and oysters on the half shell at the endless stream of parties.

Carlton threw himself into the celebrations with the gusto of a sailor on shore leave. He told Benjamin to report on the mood of the common man by wandering through the city with his eyes open and notebook always at hand. On the evening of the first day of the trial Benjamin found himself standing in front of the President's house. A light mist chilled the already cool night air.

It had been a day of little more than procedural skirmishing. The talk of the city wasn't of what had happened in the Senate, but that Johnson would be so magnanimous as to respect the tradition of the annual White House reception for Congress by inviting into his home the very men who were forcing his removal.

Benjamin stood outside for hours, both to watch the carriages unload their cargo of glittering ladies and round men in their brushed silk top hats, and then to catch a glimpse of the President graciously bidding safe passage even to those who would do him the most harm. Standing behind the barricades the armed guards had thrown up around the perimeter of the President's property, Benjamin was impressed by Johnson's dignity as he bowed his head to guests who had spent their afternoon attacking him.

Two men disembarked from a covered carriage. Benjamin went rigid at the sight of them, turned his head away at first so he wouldn't be recognized, but then, as if someone or something else was controlling his neck, locked his eyes on them. Both were dressed in their evening clothes. They had to walk past Benjamin to enter the building, so they were coming directly toward him. One of the men stopped.

"Benjamin? My Lord. I had no idea you were in Washington."

The man was slightly taller than Benjamin, thin, almost reedy. His voice was soft. "Mr. Kelley." The man turned to his companion. "I'd like you to meet Benjamin Wright." He nodded in Benjamin's direction. "My son." His voice quivered.

Benjamin gulped for air the way a drowning man might try to salvage a few last breaths. Three years. It had been three years since he'd spoken to the man, over two years since he'd received even the smallest of notes. And now, as if out of nowhere, his father stood four feet away from him acting as though they'd last seen each other only a few hours before. Should he hug the man or spit on him? Kelley extended his hand. Benjamin somehow composed himself in time to acknowledge his greeting before Kelley pulled his hand back.

Jacob leaned in and whispered. "Seeing you gave me quite the start. But at the same time, I am pleased we met this way. I'm surprised to see you in Washington, but as you are, we should find time to talk." He pulled back a bit to glimpse his son. "You've grown. You've filled out quite a bit." Benjamin could find no words for his father.

"I have given a great deal of thought to what I would say to you when we met after such a long absence on my part. I do not have the right to ask your forgiveness, Benjamin, but I do want to see if we have the ability to find some common ground. Please, let's find time to talk."

Kelley pulled Jacob toward the building before Benjamin could respond to the invitation or to tell his father where he might find him if he cared to accept the invitation. In a way, he was grateful he didn't have an opportunity to respond to his father, for his brain was so addled he might have spoken in Sanskrit if he had been able to find his voice.

The first words Jacob spoke had been conciliatory. They could not have been planned, for he had no way of knowing he would see Benjamin in the crowd, or anywhere in Washington, for that matter.

Benjamin moved toward the President's house until he was stopped by a soldier with a rifle across his shoulder. He whispered his father's name, uncertain why he was doing so, but driven by a need to speak to the man.

And then Jacob was gone, swallowed into the sea of men and women entering the President's house. Its windows were aglow with candles. A row of torches lit the drive. Beads of rain sparkled on the bare tree limbs like small crystals. The strains of the military band wrapped the onlookers like a blanket against the chill and the damp of the evening. Benjamin stood where the soldier had stopped his progress. It took him some time to remember he'd been sent here by Grainger for a purpose. He was a newspaperman, here to report on the moment, not to wallow in his own pity. He turned back to the crowd milling around on the main lawn, listened to their conversations, shared their uncertainty about what damage to the good of the country might come out of the trial. As the minutes wore on, Jacob's image began to fade.

Several in the crowd danced and passed around flasks of bourbon as though they were part of the invited political and social elite. Stories and rumors flowed as freely. One that spoke most certainly to the outcome everyone expected was that Ben Wade, the president pro tem of the Senate, and the man who would succeed Johnson, already had selected the members of his cabinet.

# 9

THE TRIAL ITSELF it couldn't have been a more boring spectacle.

What should have been high political drama was little more than a series of endless days of low-level clerks testifying about how laws were enacted and then enforced.

Mercer Carlton and the others lucky enough to hold tickets held court each evening in the bar at Willard's for the reporters representing the hundreds of papers from around the world who had sent men to cover the action before venturing off to Chamberlin's or to one of the town's soirees, gaming rooms, or brothels. For the price of a drink or a bowl of stew, these reporters bought all the details they needed to send a wire back to their own papers that would be the next day's headline and byline.

*If they're going to drive the man out of office, they at least should come up with a witness more compelling than some clerk.*

*The man is disgracing the office with his drunken attacks on elected officials of good moral standing.*

A small man with a large waist held up his stein and shouted, "Show me one." to laughter from both sides of the lobby.

It saddened Benjamin that well over half the stories in the country's newspapers were the second-hand accounts of what journalists too lazy or too uninterested to learn for themselves picked up by loitering around the lobby with a glass of beer in their hand. The press owed its readers more. Grainger said as much, but Benjamin didn't need to be told.

*He had no right trying to remove Stanton. It was an act of an anarchist.*

*Oh, come on, man. Be reasonable. Lincoln appointed Stanton before the damned foolish law he's hiding behind even went into effect. Lincoln died before he could appoint the man to a second term. The whole argument is pretense and you damned well know that.* The chorus of voices was growing by the moment.

*And why does that scoundrel Ben Wade even get a vote? He'd be voting to throw Johnson out so he can crawl into the job himself. Someone should check the rules of the Senate on that.*

One side of Willard's lobby was set aside for Johnson's supporters. The Radical Republican papers filled the other side. By five on trial days, the lobby was filled with the dissection of the day's events from both perspectives. Like clockwork, Friedrich Bols, the Willard chief doorman, who weighed three hundred pounds if he weighed an ounce, and who always dressed as though he might be called to serve the Kaiser on a moment's notice, would shout *Ozapft ist!* and the festivities would begin.

*They actually put someone on the stand today to testify he saw Johnson take a drink at a dinner at the President's house. They want to impeach the man for having a drink, for the sake of God.*

Carlton shouted, "That's a good idea. If I'm going to keep educating you bastards about this country's history, someone should bring me a bourbon. For the love of Jesus, that's the one thing the Southerners got right."

*Today, some boy who couldn't get a job shoeing horses spent three hours explaining that some asinine piece of legislation had been enacted into law. Is this what Jefferson meant when he wrote about high crimes and misdemeanors?* The cries of support from the Radical Republicans nearly drowned out the derisions from Carlton's side of the room.

*If the President won't enforce the laws of the United States, what's he doing in office?*

## Chapter 9

To shouts that he had no answer and was running from the question, Carlton announced he had to pee.

At the beginning of the trial, these sessions provided Benjamin a bit of amusement. He even wrote a short piece about the ritual Grainger put on one of the inner pages under Benjamin's byline. At Carlton's insistence, he was spending every minute of every trial day outside the Senate door in the hope of catching a glimpse of the President's arrival, to see if he wore an expression of confidence, perhaps one of fear, or at the very least, some gossip that might find its way into the *Courier*. The sessions at Willard's at least gave him a sense of being part of the bigger scene playing itself out all over Washington.

Johnson never obliged the Radical Republicans the pleasure of the indignity of sitting at his trial. As the trial moved into its second week of little more than a parade of low-level clerks and gossipmongers, the crowd around Benjamin thinned.

It took several days for Benjamin to shed his embarrassment and to ask Friedrich what in the world he was shouting.

Bols threw his head back and bellowed, "The barrel has been tapped, boy. Remember those words and you'll never be without friends."

Just as the absurdity of the Republicans turning a petty dispute into a Constitutional test was sapping Benjamin's belief in the goodness of his government, the way that the people learned of those events was stripping him of his respect for his fellow journalists.

Depending upon how far they had to travel, it took the outlying papers somewhere around three days to arrive in Washington. Benjamin compared the stories to his own notes and his own recollection. To a man, he could remember the exact moment when someone who had the good fortune of a seat for the day shared whatever came to mind. The fact that some of the things that they remembered after too much alcohol and that others reported after even more alcohol might never have happened didn't stand in the way of their becoming the historical record of the most important Constitutional event in the country's history.

Benjamin came to wish he could have more respect for either the politicians who made the news or the reporters who covered it. The spectacle playing itself out in front of him wasn't the lofty principle that Washington, Madison or Jefferson had envisioned when they established three branches of the government and a free press to keep them honest. It certainly didn't speak to the high moral justification of the taking of thirty-seven of his brothers and kin and friends from Grayton, but by the end of a war it always is impossible to discern the purpose for which it started.

Benjamin's time in Washington convinced him that while the Republicans spoke in the soaring constitutional rhetoric their lawyers had crafted, there was nothing in their partisan bickering except a hunger to win at all costs.

Benjamin felt himself surrounded by the Holy Trinity of opportunistic politicians, sharp lawyers, and newsmen whose papers thrived on falsehoods and controversy.

Divining the truth from that triumvirate seemed to Benjamin an exercise in trying to understand why oats tasted the way they did by sifting through what came out the back end of a horse.

# 10

THE PUBLIC FACE OF THE TRIAL was in the Senate. The gathering of the votes necessary to support impeachment, however, took place in quieter venues such as the sitting rooms of the boarding houses where several of the members of the Senate lived while Congress was in session. Still, Catherine Ream was sent into a tizzy when she received a note from one of Ben Wade's aides that Wade intended to call on her daughter Vinnie later than afternoon.

"It's that wretched Mary Todd Lincoln. I shouldn't say that out loud, Vinnie, but I'm tired of everyone treating her like a saint. Of course, what they did to her husband was awful, but it scarred all of us, not just her. She's been playing the wounded little bird for three years now and her act is getting tiresome." Catherine stopped only to bark orders at the three Negro girls she'd asked to help get the place spotless.

"She's been complaining about your commission to do her husband's bust since you received the honors. And now they're talking about raising funds to send you to Europe to finish the piece. I'll wager she's trying to interfere. She's probably sending the man as her emissary to deliver the bad news. Oh, Vinnie, it would mean so much for you to complete the project and I don't have to tell you how badly we need the money. This place is falling apart around us and with your father's illness he hardly can keep things up."

Her mother touched Vinnie's hair. It cascaded down her back in rich brown curls. "You're so pretty, so young. It's just vicious jealousy talking when people say you've gotten all of your work only because you play the coquette around men you're trying to impress. I hate that kind of talk. They don't have your talent so they make things up. Oh, my precious baby. I don't want Mr. Wade to tell you that you can't complete the Lincoln bust. That would be so awful. You know how to talk to men of his stature. I'm sure you'll find the right things to say."

Vinnie may have been only twenty-one, but she had seen enough of men like Ben Wade to know she shouldn't display any fear, whatever the purpose of his visit. Her youth masked both her sophistication in the ways of Washington and a spine as firm as the marble she molded into poetry. If Wade were delivering Mary Todd Lincoln's message, Vinnie would absorb the news with grace and thank the man for his time, nothing more. She had her own cadre of supporters, so the battle would be far from over on the strength of one visit. Vinnie dabbed a bit of rouge on her cheeks and pronounced herself ready for whatever the president pro tem of the Senate might have to offer.

Three men stood as Vinnie entered the room. Wade seemed flustered, but Vinnie thought it might be the heat. Although only a few days into May, the temperature rose well into the nineties early into the day. The onset of summer's humidity and the stench from the Potomac made the city almost intolerable at this time of year. The press of outsiders who came for the impeachment and stayed through the weeks of trial only made it more crowded and oppressive.

Vinnie's mother was busying herself with instructions to her young help on where to place the lemonade and sugar cookies they had brought into the room. Vinnie declined anything for herself.

After the introductions were made, Wade spoke first. "Miss Ream, I have but a moment, so let me be brief. I must return to the Senate chambers for the afternoon session of this most difficult trial. I feel our country's pain that we must endure this ordeal, but the President has given us no choice and the Constitution compels that we proceed."

Her mother was surprised, but Vinnie was unfazed either by the topic the man discussed or the fact that he'd jumped to his point so quickly and with no reference to Vinnie's work as Washington's leading sculptress.

"I appreciate what you are going through, Mr. Wade. But surely you didn't come to my home to unburden yourself about the nation's difficulties." Vinnie's mother put her fingers to her lips, in a signal that Vinnie should let the men state their business before she said anything.

"My colleagues will speak in greater detail, Miss Ream. The purpose of my coming is to stress the importance to the well-being of our country of our concern." Wade was flustered by Vinnie's composure and self-assurance. He seemed to be hurrying out of the room as he spoke. "With that, I truly must take my leave."

The men who accompanied Wade stood rigidly and then sat somewhat awkwardly. Catherine chatted amiably while pouring more lemonade and passing around the plate of cookies. Both men needed something in their hands and accepted her offer with gratitude.

Their names meant nothing to Vinnie. Washington was a small enough town that even though the administrations changed with some frequency, it was possible to know who was running the important government offices, particularly for a woman who spent so much time walking through the Capitol on her way to her studio. Not recognizing their names, Vinnie asked the men's responsibilities in the government. They told her they were attached to the Senate leader's office.

The taller one spoke first. Vinnie thought better of telling him some of the glaze from her mother's cookie was glistening off his mustache, but the sparkles were the only thing she could see when she looked at the man. He had the voice of a church baritone. "Miss

Ream, your mother has told us you are quite conversant about the details of the impeachment. It's not surprising it has been the dinner table topic of the boarders here. That's no different from what is taking place across the city. Likely, the country."

Vinnie shook her curls. She played with the end of one that had fallen across her shoulder. The taller of the two men continued. "As you know it will take the vote of two-thirds of the fifty-four senators to convict on any of the impeachment counts. There are nine Democrats whose votes are lost to us. Adding those to the three Republicans who already have sided with the President leaves only six more Senators who can defect from the cause."

"Where does our Senator Ross fall in your calculation?" The men seemed surprised at Vinnie's directness. "We've spoken periodically about the trial at dinner, as have the other boarders here, but I don't know much about the Senator other than he appears to be a good man who will vote his conscience."

The trial had drifted mindlessly into a sea of nothing. Talk around the city was that Johnson would be driven from office only by the weight of the Republican control of the Senate and not by any of the evidence mustered against him.

The shorter of the two men spoke. He seemed animated by Vinnie's reference. He leaned forward on the sofa. "Senator Ross is an important vote. We were hoping you might talk to him on our behalf, encourage him to consider all aspects of the case. There are those who would be extremely grateful."

Vinnie understood why Wade made such a hasty retreat. It hardly would be seemly for the man who already was outlining his inauguration speech to be a witness to an attempt to influence the vote of a sitting Senator through any means, but particularly difficult to explain away his involvement in bribery.

Vinnie wasn't surprised. As the trial limped toward its conclusion, it was hard to go anywhere in the city without hearing men and women talk about the unrelenting pressure being brought to bear on the uncommitted senators.

The Radical-dominated legislature in Tennessee passed a resolution directing Joe Fowler to vote for impeachment or to find another job. The Methodist General Conference prayed that every senator—meaning especially Waitman Willey, a Methodist from West Virginia—be saved from error.

Sprague of Rhode Island was told his re-election depended upon a vote with the Republicans. Only Lyman Trumbull of Illinois, who was viewed as too honest to bother trying to bribe, was left alone.

Vinnie looked to her mother. She saw the fear in the eyes of a woman whose husband's rheumatism forced the family to rely heavily on Vinnie's work and who herself had spent the last five years working eighteen hour days to hold the boarding house and her family together.

That Edmund Ross might hold out against impeachment was a surprise to the Republicans. He wasn't a man of means. If he were, he wouldn't be boarding at Mrs. Ream's house. He wasn't known for his independence on the floor of the Senate. In fact, he'd voted consistently with his party. What did he hope to gain by hinting he might vote against impeachment?

The taller man seemed to have regained his composure. At least, to Vinnie's disappointment, he had taken a napkin to his mustache and no longer sparkled like a Christmas ball. "We ask nothing more than you use the occasion of the dinner table to speak to the Senator, to draw out some of his views. Spend some time with him on your lovely porch in the evening. If there are things we might learn from those discussions, we will continue to be most appreciative."

Whatever others said about the reasons such a young girl should receive both recognition and high profile commissions, Vinnie never thought of herself as a temptress. She found the whole notion that a Constitutional crisis should turn on a sexual innuendo to be as ridiculous as it was offensive. She looked to her mother. She nodded and lowered her hand to the top of her bodice. "I believe I understand."

The smaller man looked as though he would explode. "Your country will be most grateful." The men were so certain of the rightness of their position the absurdity of the statement meant nothing to them.

Vinnie was careful not to let her true emotions show. She hadn't been asked to prostitute herself, merely to engage the Senator's attention. She was being asked to create a diversion from the stress of always trying to follow the right and righteous path. She would be alluring and subtle, playful and democratic. If she could draw those emotions out of the marble and bronze with which she shaped her sculptures, couldn't she bring the same qualities out in herself?

"I appreciate your concerns, gentlemen. I believe we share a desire to see justice done." She held out her hand, half expecting a fight between the two men over who would be first to bow and kiss it. "If you'll excuse me, I must bathe now. It's been dreadfully hot. I'm certain you'd like me to be as soft as a tea cake when the Senator arrives home."

Vinnie Ream told the men everything they had come to hear.

Her belief that Andrew Johnson should remain in office was a matter she decided to keep to herself.

# 11

THE TO-DO ABOUT THE IMPEACHMENT was the best thing that happened to Willard's since the end of the war. Every room was booked for weeks at a time. The pub and restaurant overflowed from noon until well past midnight. Newspapermen from all over commandeered the corner of the bar under the portrait of Lincoln standing next to a marble pedestal with a law book in his right hand and took turns shouting down Carlton and his counterparts at the *Herald* in New York, the *Tribune* in Chicago, and the *Star* in Kansas City.

It was here on Thursday at around four-thirty that a tiny black child who couldn't have been more than eight limped quietly to Benjamin's side and put a crisp white envelope into his hand. The boy smelled of the caramel whomever had penned the note had given him as a treat. Benjamin gave him a nickel to thank him and to scoot him on his way but the boy said he was told to wait until he received a response to the message inside the envelope. It was written on a piece of stationary from the Congress. The curiosity in the back of Benjamin's throat had the texture and taste of sour milk

*Benjamin—I must confess both my surprise and pleasure at seeing you the other night. You've grown into quite the young man. Is there any chance you would consider having dinner with me? If so, I'd be honored to see you at Bleecher's on Saturday at 7:00. Father.*

The reporter in Benjamin counted the errors; places where Jacob had started one word only to replace it with another, or struck a letter that was out of place. Jacob was obviously on edge when he wrote the note.

But that curiosity was almost instantly overtaken by a sense he could open himself to his father only by betraying his mother. He looked at the young lad; standing silently, rubbing his finger along the edge of the nickel. Benjamin was prepared to send the boy on his way with the message declining the invitation, but when he saw Carlton taking a break from one of his seemingly endless diatribes about the fool-headedness of the Republicans, the need to talk to someone older, more experienced in the ways of the world, brought Benjamin to his side. He asked if Carlton had a free moment to discuss something other than the trial.

"Pee first, then talk, Wright. A man's got to respect his priorities."

Carlton was fidgeting with the buttons on his pants when he walked to the wicker chair next to Benjamin on the veranda. He motioned for a waiter to bring them two pints of ale. When Benjamin pointed to the small messenger who'd followed them outside, Carlton ordered a glass of lemonade for the child. He then squinted the sun out of his eyes while he read the note.

"That's right. I'd forgotten your father worked for Pig-Iron Kelley. He's one corrupt son of a bitch, but the voters in your district love him." Carlton pointed to the name on the top of the letterhead. "Have you ever spoken to your father about what it's like to be a bagman for a Congressman?"

"We haven't communicated in years." Benjamin explained their chance meeting the other night.

The bluntness of the fact seemed to catch Carlton short. He looked at Benjamin with some surprise. He didn't say anything until the waiter had set the two pints on the table between their two chairs and was out of earshot.

"Years? He's your father, Benjamin." Carlton stopped, but offered his judgment before Benjamin said anything in response. "That's quite odd."

Jacob stayed on the farm for about two weeks after they buried Willie and Matthew. He wasn't the same man who left in April, head high, chest out, and heart full of expectation. He didn't move from his chair on the porch for hours at a time, all day and well into the night. If he slept at all it was on some hay strewn on the floor of the barn. He didn't eat. He didn't try to comfort Rachel or even look at Benjamin. It was though he was afraid Benjamin might ask if his brothers died as heroes or Rachel might seek some detail about what happened to her boys. And then his orders came to return to his regiment and he was gone. After the war he sent Rachel some money and a message that he was taking the position in Washington. He never asked her to join him there.

"May I ask you something personal, Mr. Carlton?"

"Mercer." They'd never spoken with such intimacy.

"Mercer. Do you have children?"

Carlton's voice softened. Saddened. "We had one. A girl. She'd be sixteen now but she died when she was only three. Tuberculosis. She was my princess. We couldn't have any more after that."

"Forgive me. I didn't mean to bring up painful memories."

"You needn't worry about that. I don't have a moment when Valerie isn't in my thoughts."

Carlton sipped from his glass. He waved to the small boy, who was nursing his lemonade with an expression of wonder. "But if I'm now allowed to ask a personal question of you, Benjamin, how is it that you and your father haven't spoken for such a long time?"

"Neither spoken nor written. Not a word, until this note."

"How so?"

"I've been asking myself that same question for years. I lived through so much of my mother's grief I only see him through her eyes. I don't think it would be fair to my mother if I accepted the invitation." Benjamin called for the child to come to his side.

Carlton put his hand on Benjamin's arm. His touch was light, but firm, more to guide than to comfort. "He's your father, Benjamin. I can't imagine what he's gone through or what he's thinking now that he knows his son is in the same city, but when a man loses his family he has almost nothing left. You're likely to have a family some day. Think about that before you turn down the invitation."

And so two days later, Jacob stood the moment Benjamin entered the restaurant, held out both of his arms, as if they might embrace, but then dropped them to his side when Benjamin came no closer than five feet and nodded silently. They shook hands, somewhat rigidly. Jacob's shirt was missing the third button from the top.

A thin, young woman in a brown tunic came to their table. She wore a garland of white flowers in her hair, as if someone had anointed her the May Queen. Benjamin exhaled a bit of relief at the distraction, for he hadn't yet come to terms with where this evening might lead. Her voice was gentle. He ordered lamb.

The woman had to lean toward Jacob to hear his request. Benjamin and his father both watched the woman move toward the kitchen. It was so much easier than turning to each other and beginning their conversation in earnest.

Jacob fingered his spoon. "It's unusually warm for this time of year." He paused. "You look good. Strong. Healthy." He took a swig from his tankard.

Benjamin said nothing.

"Don't repeat what I'm about to say, but my personal view is that this impeachment trial is a lot of malarkey. It's like a fever that needs to run its course." Jacob was talking quickly. Benjamin assumed he was as disoriented as was his son.

"Did you want to discuss anything in particular when you invited me to dinner?" Jacob pulled back in his chair at the abruptness of the question.

"I hardly know where to begin." Jacob looked around the restaurant. "What an extraordinary coincidence we met the other night. I'm so pleased we did. I couldn't stop thinking about that moment the entire time I was with the President."

Benjamin broke off a small end of bread while Jacob continued to talk somewhat nervously. "I wasn't certain whether you'd accept my invitation. I'm flattered you did. Honored."

The man across the table from Benjamin was not the same man he knew before the war. The Jacob that Benjamin remembered had dawn to dusk energy, calloused hands from straining against the plow, cuts from the barbed wire always needing tending, and a booming voice that could fill their eighty acres.

Now, Jacob's skin had the pasty look of someone no longer in the sun. His eyes, once capable of sighting a rabbit at a hundred yards or of bringing down a buck in full charge through the woods with a single shot, now searched Benjamin's features as if he were going blind and wanted a memory to sustain him once his world went dark.

Jacob spoke slowly. "I don't have the right to ask for your forgiveness, Benjamin. The best I can do is to ask for the opportunity to start over. I don't know if you're planning to marry or to have a family of your own, Benjamin, but once you do, you'll understand why I'm asking for another chance. There is nothing worse than a parent failing his children as I've failed your brothers and you." Jacob folded his hands together, as if in prayer.

Benjamin said nothing. Jacob spoke after a moment in which he searched for some way to shift the conversation to another topic. "I read several of the articles you've written for Grainger's paper. You can be quite proud of the name you've developed for yourself in such a short time. I know I am, although I must confess your facility with words is not a gift you inherited from me." Jacob tried to smile. Benjamin nodded, but suppressed any other reaction.

"Your writing has a hunger, Benjamin, a yearning I must confess I don't understand. It frightens me somewhat."

Plates were set in front of them. Mugs of beer were refilled. The strong odor of the lamb and the dark brown color of the sauce spooned over it startled Benjamin, as though he'd forgotten they were sitting at a dining table. They both hesitated, as if they were wondering whether actually touching the food in front of them would break the spell of their conversation. After a moment, though, Jacob speared one of the scallops with his fork.

"Sometimes when I write I don't know where the words come from myself." Benjamin wasn't certain whether to append the word "Father" or the word "Sir" or "Jacob" at the end of his words. "Please pass the mint jelly, if you would be so kind."

Benjamin leaned into the table. "If I exhibit a hunger, perhaps it's a desire to fill the void left by Willie's and Matthew's death. And by your leaving. Especially that."

Jacob looked at his son for some time. Benjamin had crossed an invisible divide. The father no longer was talking to a young boy. Benjamin would stand fast for an explanation.

Jacob coughed once and then a second time. When he finally found his voice, it trembled. "I don't know if I can explain what I did any more than to say it was the only way I felt I could go on. I couldn't live every day of my life with your mother's judgment condemning me. You were an innocent victim of the demons possessing of my mind. For that I am truly sorry. But I can do no more than to apologize."

Benjamin felt a stinging taste of disappointment at the idea his father could so casually cast off years of abandonment. He shifted uncomfortably in his chair.

"I understand the pain I caused, Benjamin, but I lack your command of words, your sensibilities, so I can say no more than I already have. I've honored my financial obligations to your mother. Credit me that much. We can't remake the past, my son. Tell me about your life now. I am curious. Genuinely so."

The question seemed honestly asked, but Benjamin hesitated. "Before we probe into my life, I believe I've earned the right to ask a few more questions about yours." Benjamin was unable to shake the image John Henderson described of the butchery at Hoke's Run, the idea of Willie and Matthew bounding through an open field at their father's order, as rabbits scurry in frenzy to avoid being devoured by a coyote.

Jacob was silent. He rubbed at his temples.

Benjamin put his hands together. "Was it you who led my brothers into enemy crossfire in an open meadow with no trees or rocks or even tall underbrush where they could hide or did you act on someone else's direction?"

Jacob had the look of a man who had seen a phantom. He hesitated, but Benjamin demanded an answer. "It is so terribly hard for me to speak of that morning. Please don't ask me to relive that moment. Not now. There is no limit on the number of questions you may ask, Benjamin, but please, do me the courtesy of changing the subject." He had the expression of a man praying for mercy.

The tone of Benjamin's voice left no doubt who was in command of their conversation. "If you won't answer that, tell me this." He leaned into the table. The force of his body pushed Jacob back into his chair.

"You left me alone with a woman who had nothing left for herself, certainly nothing left for me. Even if you felt you had to distance yourself from Mother, why did you never once so much as inquire about my well-being? Why didn't you get word through Uncle Curtis or some other means you were curious about the plans I had for my life after school, whether I was healthy, whether I was able to take care of everything that needed to be done at the farm?

If you will answer only one question it should be why you abandoned your only remaining son."

"I feel as though I'm one of the witnesses at Mr. Johnson's trial being cross-examined by Mr. Stanberry." There was far more hurt than humor in Jacob's comment.

"I'm not a lawyer but I am beginning to define myself both to myself and to the world as a writer." Benjamin paused, thought again about all of those days and nights alone on the farm. "Or perhaps I became a reporter because I've been asking those questions and a thousand more since the morning you left."

Benjamin leaned back in his chair, folding his arms across his chest. "You asked for new beginnings. If we have any chance of that we need to start with those questions. So I repeat myself." His voice left no doubt that Jacob needed to respond if their conversation were to move beyond this threshold.

Jacob's shoulders sank. "I have failed you, Benjamin. I am not a weak man, just a broken one. I once had your idealism, your thirst for what is righteous and good."

He paused, sipped from his beer and then grabbed the edge of the table to steady himself. His voice was more forceful than it had been a moment earlier. "Let me change the subject slightly. Do you remember when your Mother and I bundled you boys off to Washington to see Mr. Lincoln's inaugural?"

"Until you brought my brothers home, it was the one thing I remembered about my youth above all else. How could I not recall that experience?" The pleasantness of the memory surprised Benjamin. It was as if Jacob's reaching back to a time in their lives before all of the pain entered had inched them closer for that instant.

"*The mystic chords of memory, stretching from every battlefield and patriot grave, to every living heart and hearth-stone, all over this broad land.* I always will remember those words. Every schoolchild in the Union states memorized them."

"*Yet will swell the chorus of the Union, when again touched, as surely they will be, by the better angels of our nature.*" Jacob smiled. "Every soldier memorized them as well, Benjamin."

Jacob lowered his voice. "From the moment Lincoln was elected the Southern states started voting for secession. Talk of the war was everywhere. Your mother and I knew I'd be called into service within a month or two after Lincoln took office. We presumed I'd be killed in one of the battles. I never could explain why I felt compelled to join the Union forces, or why I was willing to die for such an intangible belief as the idea of a unified country. In retrospect, we would have been better off letting those fools go off on their own."

Jacob paused. "Your mother and I wanted you boys to hear from Mr. Lincoln himself why your father might be leaving your lives. I never imagined your brothers would be lost and I'd still be standing at the end of the war. Never in a million years."

As though he were assembling a jigsaw puzzle, Jacob moved the scallops around on his plate with his fork before he went on. "I had your ideals once, Benjamin. I left mine on the fields at Hoke's Run when I spent the entire day picking through piles of bloodied bodies so I could find your brothers and bring them home to be buried. And then I couldn't find Willie's arm and had to start all over again. It's been almost five years and I can neither cleanse my eyes of the image of turning over hundreds of bloody corpses and looking into the tortured faces of the dead in the hope of finding my sons nor get the wretched smell of their rotting flesh out of my nostrils."

Benjamin rubbed the side of his right arm with his left hand.

"And as you know the details of that horrible morning, you know the answer to your question as well as I do. I am responsible for Willie and Matthew's slaughter."

Jacob put his head in his hands and then used his napkin to wipe his eyes. "There. I've said it."

Jacob held out his hands, but Benjamin refused to take them in his. "I have no answer to your second question, my son. If I can wish you only one thing it is that you never have to bury either your child or your wife, Benjamin. I pray you never have someone who belongs to you in that way ripped from your hands."

Jacob's hands fell to the table as though he lacked the strength to keep them suspended in the air. He then looked as though he had forgotten something.

His head titled back slightly. "Ah yes. You asked for the mint jelly."

He slid the small emerald bowl toward his son.

# 12

EVERY LIMB ON MERCER CARLTON'S BODY was on fire.

Convinced he was suffering from malaria, typhoid and cholera at the same time, Carlton fought the assurances of the doctor Willard had summoned in the middle of the night that it was nothing more than overindulgence, that quinine and an ice bath would bring down the fever and that bed rest and a colonic wash was all he needed.

Carlton refused to accept the fact he would miss the most important moment of the most important trial in the nation's history for anything less than a plague on his body of Biblical proportions. No self-respecting journalist would be absent from the gallery the day the Senators were to vote on the articles for something as base as a virus in his bowel. Benjamin assured him repeatedly the true extent of his illness would remain their secret.

Benjamin stood at the door to the Senate of the United States with Carlton's ticket pressed in his hand. He marveled at the prospect of a young farm boy from central Pennsylvania being gifted with the almost mythical opportunity to witness this event. He was immune to the crush of people around him.

Men pressed wads of bills in Benjamin's direction in the hope of buying his ticket. One hundred dollars. One hundred-fifty dollars. Sums that would take Benjamin years to gather (and that would establish his life with Susanna in a way he only could dream) would be his for the taking. But he thought of the disdain he had for the journalists he'd taken to calling the Willard witnesses. He owed his chosen profession more than that. Benjamin handed his ticket to a black-coated usher without a moment's regret.

The floor of the Senate was so dense with both Senators and Representatives it was hard to see anything other than the tops of men's heads. Chairs to the right of the chamber had been roped off for the members of Johnson's cabinet.

The gallery was packed, with men and women not only in every seat, but at every open space in every aisle. The women dressed once again in their very best clothes, as if something of this magnitude required every jewel and piece of finery in their closet.

It was as though the Grim Reaper were being introduced when Thad Stevens was carried up the Senate steps and into the chamber in a chair. Every Republican vote so mattered that the weak were carried in from their hospital beds. The crowd around Benjamin whispered the name of Senator Howard when he was brought onto the floor of the Senate on a stretcher.

Salmon Chase gaveled the session to order. He warned that if anyone in the gallery spoke, the entire gallery would be removed. Benjamin held his notepad firmly in his hand. It seemed everyone else in the gallery—those from the press and those lucky enough to have gotten a ticket from whomever they knew in power—brought along paper and pencil to track the votes. The only sound coming from the gallery was the scratching of lead against paper, as though a swarm of crickets entered the chamber through an open window.

The Radicals moved first. A motion was made by someone whose voice Benjamin couldn't identify to call for the first vote on the eleventh article, the omnibus bill that had been the subject of Benjamin's article in the *Courier*. The Republicans rammed the vote through to the howls of the protesting Democrats.

The Senate Clerk called for the roll call. The core of the Radicals quickly fell into line. The Democrats held their positions. Eleven votes for conviction and six for acquittal. That much had been expected. The air in the chamber was heavy with anticipation for what was coming next. The clerk called the names of those Senators who hadn't yet voted, asked each to step forward and be heard. It was time for those Senators whose votes couldn't be assured by either side to speak.

When William Pitt Fessenden stood at his chair, he towered above those around him. A Republican with the independent streak of his native Maine, he wrote a friend he would rather spend the rest of his days planting cabbages than violate his conscience. "Not guilty."

Someone in the gallery whispered, "That's one that got away from the Radicals." Pencils scattered feverishly. Fessenden's vote seemed to startle the chamber into the reality the outcome might not be preordained.

When Joe Fowler of Tennessee spoke, his voice was almost a whisper. The entire gallery leaned forward as though a wave had tilted their schooner to the port side. The clerk asked him to repeat his vote for the record. "Not guilty."

James Grimes of Iowa, recovering slowly from a stroke, had to be helped to his feet. There was no hesitancy in his voice. "Not guilty." That was the vote of John Henderson of Missouri as well.

*He's going to make it.* The gallery seemed to inhale at once. A man two seats away from Benjamin holding a $50 betting slip—four months' pay—looked at the slender paper as though it were a poisonous snake about to lunge at his throat.

*The uncommitted are holding together.* The whispers from the gallery caused a number of the men on the chamber floor to turn their heads to see who was talking.

*There are still votes of other Radicals. They only need one to hold firm.*

Three names were unaccounted for.

Thad Stevens motioned for Ben Wade. Wade approached him. He leaned his ear toward the old man, the way a priest leans into the near dead to capture their final words. Wade walked toward one of the Senators who had yet to be called. He began gesturing toward Stevens as he spoke.

Chase pounded his gavel. "One more outburst and I will empty not only the gallery but the entire chamber of all but the Senators." As if the air had been released from a bellows, the chamber fell eerily silent. Wade walked to his chair as though he had been caned by his teacher in front of a class of nine-year olds.

Edmund Ross rose to his feet. The gossip around Washington had been that Ross was the man most likely to bow to the Radical pressure. Any other vote was hemlock to a man of political ambition. Benjamin looked to his left. A small young woman no older than him, with dark, thick curls and fine white skin, sat upright in her chair. She brought her hands to her lips, clenched her fingers together as if in prayer. Her eyes were closed.

Benjamin moved to the side of his chair so he could get a better look at Senator Ross. He seemed vaguely familiar, but Benjamin couldn't be certain whether or where he had seen the man. His time in Washington had been a blur of new circumstances and new faces.

Ross cleared his throat. "I am aware that friends, position, fortune and everything else that makes life desirable is about to be swept away by the breath of my mouth."

There was nothing of the pompous oratory so customary on the Senate floor, no grand gestures or flowing rhetoric. Benjamin heard the soft but determined voice of a man who was profoundly touched by the responsibility he'd been given.

Ross turned to the gallery, as if he were searching for an ally. "Perhaps forever." Benjamin knew at that instant Ross would side with Johnson. He felt his heart pounding so hard he feared Chase would complain about the noise and threaten to empty the gallery. His fingers were numb, as though he'd been caught in a snowdrift.

## Chapter 12

Ben Wade slumped in his chair when he heard Ross speak the words, "Not guilty." Thad Stevens turned his head away from the proceedings and lay stiffly on his stretcher.

The small woman a few seats away from Benjamin whispered, "Thank you, Edmund." Benjamin saw she was crying.

The gallery exploded like a pricked balloon when Trumbull of Illinois and then Van Winkle of West Virginia voted for acquittal. Men were screaming at the top of their lungs. Women were hugging and crying, some in glee and some in despair.

What you seven have done is sinful. We should call you the Sinful Seven.

You've made a mockery of the proceedings.

God bless you all. You have saved the nation.

*If this is what you call salvation, God help this country now. We will need His intervention from the likes of you.*

Chase pounded his gavel so fiercely Benjamin thought the desk beneath it might collapse. Guards moved toward the gallery. One of the Republicans jumped to his feet and asked for a recess. There was no point voting on the other articles if the Radicals couldn't win a conviction on a charge as broad and vague as the omnibus bill. Over the shouts of the Democrats that justice was being perverted, the motion was called and the delay was granted. The whole affair hadn't taken half an hour.

Benjamin was swept along with the crowd onto the stairs of the Senate and into a blistering hot morning. He squinted against a blinding sun. He was overwhelmed by the roars of thousands of Johnson supporters and the shouts of even more Radicals. Rows of armed guards stood between them with their bayonets poised.

Guns were being fired into the air. A bell rang at the church two blocks from the Capitol. Then another, from what seemed a bit farther away. As the news swept to every part of the city, a new clarion was heard, until the whole of the city to Benjamin was an echo of joyful noise.

Benjamin found a spot along a column where he was safe from the crush. He inhaled deeply to catch his breath. He resolved to do more than to be a passive witness to this moment in the nation's history. He had seen a man rise above the pressures of party and of peers. Benjamin could shape what history recalled of the man just as he had framed the dialogue over the impeachment charges. It was as though Carlton's illness had given Benjamin the opportunity to realize his destiny. He had to seize the moment.

Benjamin knew his purpose at that instant was to let the world know how it should remember Edmond Ross before those whose impeachment hopes he dashed shredded him like so much confetti.

# 13

ON THE MORNING OF THEIR WEDDING, Susanna and her younger sister Millie braided the manes of their quarter horses with white ribbons. The colts stood majestically, as if they understood the solemnity of the moment. Susanna pricked her middle finger with a needle to draw a small drop of blood to color Rachel's cheeks. The sun was vibrant, the congregation filled with joyous anticipation as Carson Madigan took his daughter's hand and walked her toward the door of the First Methodist Church of Grayton.

Carlton fussed like an old woman, straightening his tie and picking dirt out of his fingernails as he stood next to Benjamin near the altar. He must have touched the pocket in which he carried both rings a dozen times as Susanna floated toward them. Benjamin had never felt luckier or more ready to begin a new adventure.

Rachel couldn't and didn't even try to control her tears. Grainger put his arm around her shoulder. Jacob hadn't been invited, of course, and Benjamin hadn't told Rachel of their meeting or of his thoughts about whether reconciliation was possible. All that talk, if it ever were to come, was for another day. And she looked weak. She needed to hold onto Benjamin's arm with one hand and the back of each pew with the other as she made her way down the aisle to her seat. And everyone said a prayer for Susanna's mother, who died before she was able to marry off either of her daughters.

Benjamin scanned the rows of friends and guests. He sent a letter of invitation along with his story about Ross to the Senator at his Washington office, although it was hardly necessary. The story the *Courier* printed about the day that one man's integrity triumphed over raw political power grabbing was reprinted in almost every sympathetic paper in the country.

Benjamin was determined that his version of the impeachment vote would be the one history remembered. He worked throughout the night of the vote to capture the mood of the Senate chamber when Ross put the public good over his own.

The world spun dizzyingly since the vote. The *Washington Herald,* a Radical paper that supported Wade and Stevens down the line, picked up the gallery cry against the Sinful Seven who ignored the pressure of the Republicans. The phrase stuck. Forces gathered around the men of conscience to assure none ever would hold elective office again.

The Republicans nominated Grant in Chicago. He picked Schuyler Colfax as his Vice President. The Democrats conceded the election to the war hero by offering the nomination to Horatio Seymour of New York. The prize was Johnson's for the taking, but he demurred. Loyalists saw to the rebuilding of his Tennessee home that was burned by the Federals. He was ready to return where he belonged. By the dignity alone of his opening the President's house to the members of Congress on the night that his trial began, Benjamin was certain Johnson had earned his rest.

Grant campaigned by staying home at his farm in Galena, near the Mississippi River in Illinois. Seymour rarely left New York. The Southern states that refused to give the freed slaves the vote weren't allowed to participate in the election and those Blacks who could vote were strongly in Grant's corner, so Seymour never really had a chance. There wasn't much fodder for a newspaper in that, so Carlton told Benjamin if he was going to get married, he might as well pick a slow news day.

Susanna was perhaps three steps away from him when Benjamin saw Senator Ross enter the church. Their eyes met for an instant. They both nodded, and then Benjamin turned to the preacher so he and Susanna could become one.

It wasn't common around Grayton to have a member of the United States Senate go to the trouble of attending a local wedding. That Edmund Ross would do so caused quite a stir once it became known who he was. After the toasts were made to the bride and groom, Grainger and Carlton raised their glasses to a man of uncommon principle and political courage.

Ross spoke softly when he addressed the couple. "At the moment, I must confess I have more time on my hands than friends. My party has abandoned me both in Washington and in Kansas. The fact I was sent there to vote my conscience seems beside the point. Benjamin, you honored me with your kind words. A footnote in the history books may be my only reward for that vote. If that is my lot, I hope the men who write about the episode use your words. Grainger, my thanks to you as well."

"I hate what the Republicans are doing to you, Senator. You're being ostracized for doing nothing more than demonstrating you are a man of unflinching integrity. You're paying an unduly harsh penalty. The Republicans are a terribly unforgiving party."

Susanna tugged on Benjamin's arm, as if to say, *not today, Benjamin.* She accepted the idea, however grudgingly, of following Benjamin to Philadelphia. But on the day of her wedding, Susanna would not compete with Benjamin's other life. She was entitled to be selfish, to demand his time, his attention, his devotion. That was a small enough price to ask if he wanted her to overcome her doubts about the steps he was asking her to take. Sacrifices should be met with sacrifices, but a brand new husband's attention is hardly a sacrifice.

Grainger raised his glass toward the Senator. "I'll share a secret with you, sir. Those of us in the newspaper business like to have our readers think of us as professional cynics. And the Good Lord knows we've witnessed enough foolishness out of our elected officials to justify that attitude. But in our hearts, we root for men like you, Mr. Ross. We really do want to believe Washington can summon men who stand for something outside their own parochial interests. Your vote made me proud to know you, Senator."

Benjamin moved closer to the group. He looked back at Susanna, who had moved toward Rachel. Rachel's stare passed judgment on Benjamin as if he were no better than Jacob, abandoning his wife to the seduction of Washington's power, its flattery of the ego and its bottomless need for adulation. Benjamin turned away from her anger.

"But the *Courier* is a Democratic paper, is it not?" Ross seemed to have forgotten he was attending a wedding and began speaking in a serious tone. "You hardly undertook the endeavor to heap praise upon the Radical cause. Until last May, I believed myself part of the Republican army."

In the background, Benjamin's Uncle Curtis began scratching on his fiddle. He was accompanied by Carson Madigan's brother, a freakishly tall man with broad whiskers that bordered an infectious smile, who had finished tuning his banjo. They were trying to find themselves on the same place in a Virginia reel.

Grainger nodded with respect. "I like to think the *Courier* stands for what is good and right and purposeful in our government. You proved yourself worthy of being included in that category, sir."

Susanna tugged on Benjamin's arm forcefully enough this time to pull him from the cluster of men. "And I like to think I can dance with my new husband before the evening grows too old. Your politics will still be there in the morning, gentlemen. Tonight belongs to the two of us."

The men laughed. Grainger relit his cigar. He patted Benjamin on the back. "She's a fiery one, son, watch yourself."

## Chapter 13

Ross bent and kissed Susanna's hand. "Mrs. Wright, you are correct. I apologize for the distraction. More than that, I encourage you to pull your husband away every time you see him fall too deeply into the cesspit of politics." He raised his glass. "To the bride and groom. Long life. Much happiness. Bring out each other's smiles."

Susanna already had pulled Benjamin into the center of the ring of guests. Carson Madigan began clapping to the music. Someone else began whistling the tune Curtis was playing, and another man in the crowd started playing the spoons. Susanna took both of Benjamin's hands in hers and curtsied. He bowed stiffly (he never had reason to learn how to dance), and looked toward Rachel. She put both hands to her lips and threw him a kiss.

Susanna threw her arms around Benjamin's neck and deeply kissed him. The crowd cheered and Benjamin was swept away in a whirling sea of pearl organza and the loveliest woman he had ever seen.

# 14

"ARE YOU HUNGRY?" Susanna pulled back the curtain. A mass of Canada geese blackened a corn field and over their heads, two eagles let the morning air carry them off to their day's adventure. They'd boarded the train in Philadelphia yesterday morning and by nine tonight they'd be in Chicago. It was as though the entire railroad had been built for their honeymoon.

"For you." They'd begun their exploration of each other as soon as the porters announced to the passengers it was time to turn in. Their bed was tiny; but neither complained—space for one was all they needed. "Don't be surprised as we grow old if I ask you from time to time to join me on an overnight train ride." They both smiled at the idea, and then kissed yet again. "Imagine, Susanna, one day we'll be able to take a train all the way to the Pacific Ocean. Can you believe that? I can't wait for that opportunity."

"I smell coffee. And bacon. Let's get dressed, Benjamin. I'm starved."

"Ask and it shall be yours, my love. Ask and it shall be yours."

The dining car was almost full. A thin dark porter with long, bony fingers, in a bright white coat and spit-shined shoes escorted Susanna and Benjamin to a table with two open seats. A large man, broad across the chest and so dark from the sun Benjamin presumed he spent his days in the fields, put his coffee cup carefully onto its saucer, stood with his napkin still in his left hand, and extended his right. "Peter Dey. I'm delighted to have the company." A humble man, Dey stopped short of identifying himself as the railroad's Chief Engineer.

They smiled, exchanged greetings, sat and ordered large breakfasts for them both.

"This is extraordinary. To think we're moving past all this wonderful countryside so quickly and yet sitting at a table with fine china and linen." Susanna tapped on the window. "And look at this, they think of everything." She ran her finger around the space where the table cloth had been seamed to make a hole for glasses.

"Your first time?" Susanna, who still was warm with the evening she'd spent with her new husband, blushed as though Dey were asking about that time of discovery.

"Is this the first time you've ridden on a train?" asked Dey. "If so, I welcome you both with pleasure."

"You say that as though you own the train. Is this really yours to welcome?" Benjamin asked.

Dey smiled. "In a way. I do have some responsibilities here. Each of us working to build the railroad feels the same sense of pride in what we're doing."

Benjamin extended his hand a second time. "With good cause, my friend. You have every right to be proud of what you're accomplishing."

The porter poured them both orange juice and coffee. He put a small bowl of sliced fruit in front of each of them."

"Bon appétit." Dey nodded. "And you, sir?"

"I am with the *Courier.* A reporter."

Susanna leaned her shoulder lovingly into Benjamin. "He's being unduly modest, sir. My husband is the *Courier's* leading political reporter. I'm sure you've read his stories about the impeachment trial. Senator Ross was so impressed by what Benjamin wrote that he came to our wedding. Can you believe that? A United States senator in Grayton."

"Impressive, indeed."

"And all because of my Benjamin." Benjamin squeezed Susanna's hand. Not to quiet her, but to thank her. He really was her Benjamin.

"You work for the railroad? Susannah asked what position Dey held. When he told her what he did, she continued with some excitement in her voice. "Fascinating. Would you mind if I asked you a couple of questions, Mr. Dey?" Susanna put her spoon on the side of her plate, folded her arms on the table and leaned in. It wouldn't have done the man any good to resist because Susanna started peppering him before he had a chance to say anything.

"How many men does it take to lay a mile of track? How do you feed them? Shelter them? How do you move supplies? Have you encountered problems with the Indians?"

Dey smiled. He looked at Benjamin. "I thought you were the reporter, Benjamin. It sounds as though she will keep you on your toes. But those are all outstanding questions. Let me explain."

Benjamin sat back in his chair and watched as the two of them went back and forth as though they'd known each other for ages and were reconnecting after a long absence. At one point he asked whether Dey would mind if he took notes, and when the man agreed, Benjamin placed his reporter's pad by his right hand. Susanna paused from her questions only long enough for the porter to place a plate of scrambled eggs and bacon in front of her, some wheat cakes in front of Benjamin and a plate of toast and a dish of jam and butter between them.

"What does it cost to put down a mile of track?"

It was the next question in a logical series of Susanna's questions, but it seemed to catch Peter Dey short. Where he had been fielding Susanna's questions with agility, almost with romantic vigor, he looked away, as though he wanted to be somewhere else. Where his movements had been fluid, leaning into Susanna's questions, they became rigid, almost unyielding. He was silent for a full minute. Without saying as much as a word, Dey seemed to be hinting there was a story behind the answer to Susanna's question.

"Peter, let me ask something slightly different, if I may." Benjamin had questioned enough people in the pursuit of the *Courier's* stories to know when their body language was telling him to pull back. "I'm interested in the organization itself. What business entity is actually responsible for building the rail line? Who pays and feeds the workers, hires supplies and handles the hundreds of other tasks that go into a project of this magnitude?"

Dey exhaled, as if he was grateful for the reprieve from Susanna's last question. He answered quickly. "A corporation known as the Credit Mobilier. It was set up some time ago." The name sounded vaguely familiar to Benjamin. He was having trouble placing it into context.

"And who owns the Credit Mobilier?"

"Largely, the same men who own shares in the Union Pacific. I don't know all their names, but one of the largest shareholders is Oakes Ames, a Congressman from Massachusetts." Benjamin recognized the name. An image came to him from the day that he saw Ames talking to Schuyler Colfax outside the House chambers. He flipped to the page in his notebook where he had written the word *Credit* and the letters *M* and *O*, tried to remember any snippet of their conversation.

Dey paused, as though he were debating whether to say more. "You said you're from Philadelphia. I'm told that a lawyer from your city just sued Mr. Ames claiming an interest in some shares."

Susanna leaned forward in her chair. Benjamin understood the implications of what Peter Dey had just told them, but in her eagerness, Susanna spoke first. "I presume that means the shares have considerable value." It was the same question Benjamin had been poised to ask.

Dey smiled in an awkward way. "Men rarely bother filing lawsuits over trivial matters." He hesitated. "Let's leave it at that."

Benjamin respected Dey's need to set boundaries to their conversation, but there was one more piece of information he needed so that he could set about the work he had to do to pursue this story. "And the lawyer's name?"

Dey looked at his watch. "I must be going. We will be arriving in South Bend momentarily. I have a meeting with some suppliers that will keep me there for at least two days." He took Susanna's hand, kissed it and wished them happiness on their honeymoon and beyond. He began rising from his chair, turned and headed toward the exit.

"And the name, sir?" The strength in Susanna's voice seemed to surprise Dey as much as it surprised Benjamin. Diners within earshot put down their forks or cups and watched the scene unfolding at this end of the dining car. Dey turned back toward the table. After a moment's hesitation, he leaned toward her and whispered, "Henry McComb."

Susanna leaned into Benjamin. He'd already written the words *Credit Mobilier* and *cost of construction* and *lawsuit* and the names *Henry McComb* and *Oakes Ames* in his notebook.

Susanna ran her finger across the words on the page. "We should find out how all these tie together once we get home."

# 15

"HENRY MCCOMB? That mousey little bastard?" The mention of the man's name brought Carlton out of his chair as though he'd been bitten by a spider.

"What did the good gentleman do to deserve the back of your hand?" Benjamin asked the question as he walked toward Carlton's desk and then poised himself for one of Carlton's broadsides.

"Good gentleman? I could fire you for calling him that. The lowlife sued the *Courier* three years ago claiming we tarnished the reputation of one of his clients by saying he ran slaves in his early days. What we printed was true, of course, but it cost us a small fortune to get the matter thrown out of court."

Carlton scanned the story Benjamin wrote after copying McComb's complaint line by line in the clerk's office. "There hasn't been much to write about since the brouhaha over the impeachment died down and the election is behind us. I can't think of anything I'd enjoy more at the moment than seeing old Henry's name on the front page of the paper and watching him weasel around for some explanation of what he's up to." He leaned back in his chair, put his left foot on an open drawer in his desk, and began rolling his tongue around the end of one of his cigars.

Benjamin couldn't wait to tell Susanna their efforts had been so well received. Susanna helped write the story the night before in a drafting session that resulted in them being half naked in front of the last embers of their fire.

"This Credit Mobilier outfit must be robbing the government blind on what it's charging to lay down the track. These shares must be worth a king's ransom. That's the angle we'll play on this." Carlton had the anticipation on his face of a man with a large trout on the end of a line. "By God, Wright. This is why I got into the newspaper business in the first place."

Carlton scratched his pen over a few lines in Benjamin's story. "I don't want to get sued again over this, so let's print one copy. You can walk it over to that worthless dog's office and tell him he's got until noon tomorrow to point out any inaccuracies. Greene. Greene, where are you, by God?" Jesse Greene looked up from his desk. "Increase tomorrow's run by five hundred copies. Wright's on to something big."

Carlton's pleasure with what Benjamin found improved his aim. His spit arched directly into the middle of the spittoon.

McComb's offices were on the second floor of a three-story brick building kitty-corner from the new city hall and around the block from the courthouse. There was nothing particularly elegant about the building or about the sign Henry McComb, Counselor at Law stenciled across the window closest to the doorway. The letters seemed slightly off-kilter, as though the sign painter hadn't bothered to use a straight edge.

Benjamin examined the soles of his boots before stepping on the strip of carpet laid on the marble flooring. He climbed the stairs deliberately, taking each step slowly so as not to display his nervousness, and knocked on the door to the law office. After a polite period, he moved the door open.

Four men were hunched over papers strewn over two desks. They sat opposite each other, each man engrossed in the pile in front of him. Two men were clean-shaven, one had an impressive handlebar mustache, and one a full beard. Each of the men was dressed in the same frock coat that had become popular among Philadelphia's business class since the war, open at the top and drawn to a tighter fit around the waist. One of the men was drinking tea.

"I'm sorry, sir. I didn't hear you knock. May I be of service to you? My name is Kimberly, David Kimberly. I am Mr. McComb's chief clerk." Although the man's accent suggested he was raised not far from Grayton, he pronounced the word clerk with a hard *a*, as though he either had studied at Oxford or emulated and imitated those who had.

Benjamin extended his hand. "Thank you. I am Benjamin Wright. My employer is the *Philadelphia Courier*. I'm certain you're familiar with the paper. I came across Mr. McComb's name in a court filing and would like a moment of his time to answer some questions about the matter. We intend to publish a story about the litigation in tomorrow's edition and want to give Mr. McComb the opportunity to point out any inaccuracies in the story."

"A newspaper?" Kimberly's voice suggested he held the whole newspaper business in disdain. "The *Courier* is a bit Democratic for my taste, but I know of it." Kimberly turned to the other clerks sitting at the two desks, each of whom was trying to make it appear he wasn't eavesdropping on the conversation. "As Mr. McComb's staff, we are responsible for all court proceedings. I'm certain if directed to do so by Mr. McComb one of us could answer your questions. Do you have a card of introduction I might show Mr. McComb?"

In the months since he'd presented himself to Grainger, the topic of printed business cards never entered either their conversation or Benjamin's consciousness.

"At the *Courier* we identify ourselves by our bylines." Benjamin made no effort to hide his feelings for this dandy. "Is Mr. McComb available? My questions are not for his *clark*."

The bearded clerk started to laugh, but then buried his head in the pile of papers on his portion of the desk the moment Kimberly turned in his direction. Finally, a door opened and an owlish man with his eyeglasses pulled low on his nose poked his head out of the opening. He spoke with a shrill voice. "Kimberly, what business does this man have here?"

Benjamin didn't wait for Kimberly to set the agenda. "Mr. McComb, my name is Benjamin Wright. I am with the *Philadelphia Courier*, T.P. Grainger's paper. I discovered your lawsuit regarding the shares in the Credit Mobilier and would like a moment of your time."

"It is a private matter. It is not for the newspapers." He squinted at Benjamin. "Grainger? It is especially not for the *Courier*.

"But sir, the complaint that you filed suggested that high government officials were involved in some sort of. . ."

McComb cut him off. "I will prove each of the allegations of the complaint in an appropriate forum at an appropriate time. I have nothing to say to the press about the matter."

"This Oakes Ames. What is his involvement?"

"How did the Credit Mobilier manage to win the contract to construct the rail lines for the Union Pacific?"

"What government officials other than Ames are involved?"

McComb would have no more of Benjamin's questioning. "All of your questions will be answered, young man, but not in your newspaper. There are reasons for my silence and they do not involve you. If you have no other business here, my staff and I are quite busy."

Benjamin took the story out of his pocket. He handed it to McComb. "As you please, Mr. McComb. We will run this story in tomorrow's edition. You have until noon to give us written notice of any alleged inaccuracies. Good day, sir." He looked toward the clerks at their desks. "Good day, Gentlemen." His heart was racing with exhilaration at having gone toe to toe with the whole lot of them.

It took Mercer Carlton less than a minute to announce his conclusion of the reasons behind McComb's stonewalling to the newsroom. He stood in order to erase any doubt that everyone should pay attention to what he was about to say. "I asked the conductor on my trip to St. Louis last month how they paid for the whole affair. Do you know what he told me?" He paused for emphasis. "The government is giving away land and money to the railroads to build the damned thing. Thousands of acres and millions of dollars. And then the same men controlling the Union Pacific who were getting all these grants set up this company to lay down the track, so they're entering into contracts with themselves. Some of the shareholders were and still are in the government. That's got to explain the references to high offices. McComb's suit has to be about the money the government is pouring into the railroad."

Carlton reached into his pocket and put a five-dollar gold piece on his desk. "Find out everything you can about this Credit Mobilier. Who owns it. What it does. What it's worth. What it costs them to build the line and what they're charging the government. It's got to be thousands, tens of thousands of dollars. I'll bet you five dollars, Benjamin, these government contractors have stolen more than five hundred thousand dollars."

"Mr. Carlton, you know I just got married. I can't be a betting man like you."

Carlton put his hand on top of the coin. "Fifty dollars if you find out McComb and his people cheated the government out of more than five million dollars. No bet. That's what you get for that feisty bride of yours if you find enough to prove I'm right."

Carlton shouted the length of the *Courier's* newsroom. "Grainger. You've got no reason to be particularly gracious to the railroads, do you? I just wagered fifty dollars of the paper's money we've found ourselves the story I've been hungering for."

# 16

It was Grainger's idea to send a telegram to Oakes Ames asking if he'd spend an hour or so with Benjamin. Ames' response was both breezy and, as Carlton said, pure crap. *Happy to talk. Always glad to let the American people know how we're handling their business. Call at my office at 10:00.*

The space was cavernous. Two sofas, four cushioned chairs, a desk the size of a church pew, an even larger and more luxuriant carpet, three massive oils of Washington, Jefferson, and Paul Revere, and a view across the great lawn all the way to the White House. Benjamin felt as though he was about to meet with the King of England. A pitcher of lemonade sweated on a table between the sofas. Two aides busied themselves with paperwork, pretending not to hear every word between them once the pleasantries had been exchanged.

"Mr. Ames, my paper is planning a major feature on the building of the transcontinental railroad. I was wondering if I could ask you. . ." Benjamin was relieved to get the words out without showing his anxiety.

Carlton warned Benjamin it might be difficult to get a straight answer out of Ames, his exact words being, *The man is a politician. He wouldn't know the truth if it bit him on the ass and he won't give it to you anyway. Just keep coming after him. Watch his eyes. Watch his hands. I'd tell you to look for signs he's lying, but he'll be lying all the time, so look for signs he's nervous.*

Ames cut him off. Short and tightly coiled, with a salt and pepper beard but, as had become the style of the day in Washington, no mustache, Ames had a thick Massachusetts accent. He spoke with a slight lisp. "Phenomenal undertaking, Mr. Wright. We've already built eleven hundred miles. The first few hundred were relatively easy, of course. We had reasonably flat land." Ames leaned into the table. "But whoever said the Appalachians are gentle hills never built a rail line through them."

Ames leaned back in his chair, roared at the joke he'd told a thousand times and moved ahead with the power of the railroad he was building before Benjamin could ask another question. "Of course, in the East we had a rather short hop to cities for supplies and such. Now that we're in the territories, we have to haul everything hundreds of miles. Steel, lumber, food, lodging, hookers." Ames slapped the table. "I wish I'd thought of that name. If the whores followed Grant's divisions instead of Hooker's I suppose we'd be calling them Grants, but whatever name you give them we actually had to transport the ladies."

Benjamin feared their time moving away from him, wondered whether and how he might retake control of the board in the chess match into which Ames so cleverly had turned their interview. But Ames was far too nimble to cede as much.

"And Indians. By God, they don't want us coming through their land. And the flies. Biggest goddamned things you've ever seen. The size of birds. I don't know for the life of me why the Indians want the damned territory so much. Have you ever seen buffalo shit, Mr. Wright? Are you from the city or did you grow up on a farm? Buffalo shit is nothing like horse or cow dung. For one thing, it's the size of my head. For another it's so hard we could build a trestle out of the stuff and drive two trains over it at the same time. I don't relish the idea of going over the mountains, but by God we will. The American people want this railroad. It will transform this country in ways we can't imagine."

Ames had set aside thirty minutes for the interview. He'd used twelve telling stories that were irrelevant to anyone other than someone trying to hide the truth behind the Credit Mobilier and the reason Benjamin called on the man in the first place.

Benjamin needed to regain his bearings. He leaned forward in his chair. "Mr. Ames, could you tell me why the Credit Mobilier stock is so valuable that Henry McComb would sue you to get it back? What assets does this company have? What are its prospects for the future that its stock would be so valuable?" The two aides seemed to hesitate for a moment in their movement of paper from one pile to the next. Benjamin wrote out the questions he wanted to ask Ames. Those were fairly down on the list, but he realized he'd get nothing out of Ames unless he hit him in what might be his soft underbelly. Benjamin ignored his script.

If Ames had any adverse reaction to the question or to the topic of Henry McComb or the Credit Mobilier he didn't betray any emotion. But he looked surprised at the seriousness of Benjamin's questions. He was direct in his response. "The Credit Mobilier is the construction company that's building the lines. It got paid forty-two thousand dollars a mile for the first hundred miles or so. The price goes up as we move west because we have to haul materials a lot farther and to cross much more difficult terrain. I don't have those numbers in my head. I'm sure my staff can pull them out. If not, the Treasury Department has payment vouchers. I'm sure you can get access. I've heard about Mr. McComb's papers, but I haven't seen them so I can't comment."

And then, with the nimbleness of a dancer, Ames turned back to the visionary's story of the building of the railroad that would link east and west. Benjamin tuned out on the man's words, for he knew them to be as evanescent as smoke.

"We're anticipating that two million people will settle in California within five years of completion. Two million. Can you imagine that?" The man was an artist, gesturing smoothly with his hands, no hair out of place. No worry lines across his brow.

"Land that only a handful of white men have seen soon enough will bustle with schools and churches and shops."

Ames was a mesmerizing story teller, a master magician, ignoring every question Benjamin could conjure up and parrying every thrust at the Credit Mobilier or the possible hint of a scandal. When his scheduled time was up and Ames reached out his hand to shake Benjamin's, Benjamin realized he'd failed to discover anything beyond his own limitations as a reporter.

As they said their goodbyes, Benjamin was tempted to look inside the Congressman's sleeve to see what he'd hidden there.

# 17

WASHINGTON FELT LIKE a different city, more hackneys on the streets and more paved streets, women in brighter colors and more elaborate hats. But the mood wasn't all festive. Where Willard's had been filled during the impeachment with curiosity seekers and partisans insanely passionate in their positions, this time the public rooms were littered with lobbyists, favor-seekers, and a rag-tag bunch of charlatans who spent their days and nights crafting ways to strip the government coffers of whatever money they could.

Benjamin had convinced Grainger to let Susanna accompany him on the trip by arguing that having a wife on his arm might win an invitation to one or more of the soirees where business and gossip both thrived. Grainger smiled at Benjamin's creativity, but he was prepared to give them this wedding present without much of a fight.

And sure enough, as soon as he learned they were in town, Edmond Ross invited Benjamin and Susanna to be his guests at Jim and Polly Fisk's. Benjamin had never been in a tuxedo. Standing next to Susanna in a floor length lilac velvet gown he thought they were the handsomest couple in the world. This was the life he deserved.

The walk from the carriage stand was lit with hundreds of tiny candles suspended from every tree. Footmen scurried around dressed in red brocade as though they'd just come from Louis XIV's court.

Ross leaned into Benjamin and whispered, "Parties like these are thrown as often by the lobbyists for the railroads, coal and steel companies as by the matrons of Washington's society who restored its mood after the war." He nodded silently at a lobbyist for the cotton shippers from whom he rejected an offer of a new carriage. "Everything is for sale at these parties. Tariffs, votes, cadetships to West Point. It's sad that only a few years ago Lincoln was rallying us to a higher cause. I can't imagine this is what he had in mind."

Benjamin held back. He didn't want to reach back to the part of him that still wanted to believe Willie and Matthew had died for something larger than themselves. Not tonight. Not with Susanna looking so stunning in her lilac gown and the air filled with the smell of honeysuckle and rosemary. Instead, he asked how Ross had managed an invitation after his impeachment vote made him a pariah to so many.

"I still have my seat in the Senate. The Republicans couldn't come up with a plausible way to remove me from office before the next election. Jim Fisk needs my vote for more of his railroad subsidies. He couldn't care less that I'm marked for execution by my own party."

Ross handed his invitation to one of the doormen. "He's aware that I'm of an independent mind and I'll do what I damn well please when the vote comes up, but the only way he knows how to deal with elected officials is to ply them with cash or good liquor and fine cigars."

"He also knows that even in my sorry state I won't take his cash. So he invites me to drink his champagne. I see no harm in that. It's better than sitting alone in my room, even though half the people here won't talk to me and the other half want to run me through with a bayonet."

Benjamin smiled. "As pleased as we are to have received your invitation, Senator, forgive us if we keep a few feet between us."

The woman accompanying Ross for the evening seemed familiar to Benjamin, but he couldn't place her with any precision. He
was reluctant to appear forward in front of Susanna. She was feeling weak since they'd arrived in Washington. The doctor who came
to the hotel (the same man who kept Carlton from the votes on the
impeachment) thought she might be experiencing the early signs of
pregnancy. The idea both elated and frightened Benjamin.

Polly Fisk placed a string quartet in the corner of her ballroom
and ostrich feathers in her hair. White-gloved waiters circled the
room with flutes filled with champagne and trays bulging with caviar and small bits of pointed toast. When Ben Wade walked within
earshot, Ross called out his name and asked if he'd like to reacquaint himself with the daughter of the woman who ran the boarding house the Republicans had financed. Wade stopped and turned
in her direction. 'Judas' was the only word Wade spoke before continuing through the crowd.

Susanna spoke first. "I would have presumed Mr. Wade's comment was meant for you, Mr. Ross. But he seemed to be looking at
Miss Ream." Vinnie only smiled.

There was a mystery about the exchange that piqued Benjamin's
curiosity. "Reacquaint? Do you know Mr. Wade, Miss Ream?"

"We met only once." Her answer was simple. The smile she
gave to Ross suggested she was holding back the meat of the story
behind her comment.

"I am a newspaperman. You know I am duty bound to investigate whatever story might exist behind your charming smile," said
Benjamin. He paused, wrinkled his brow. "Excuse me for sounding
forward, but have we met before?"

Vinnie shook her head. "I don't think so, sir. But as to your
questions, you are not working this evening, are you, Mr. Wright?"
Vinnie's hair was auburn. Her eyes were hazel. Her skin was pale,
almost ashen, delicate as porcelain.

## Chapter 17

Ross put his hand on Benjamin's arm before he had the chance to say he always was on duty when a story might be looming. "Let me give you and Susanna an education in the ways of our government." They moved slowly toward a table groaning with ham and turkey and all manner of delicacies. Pointing to a tall man supporting himself with a cane, Ross said, "Governor Bullock. He's buying Georgia for himself and his cronies."

He directed them to a group by the south windows. "They'll be legislation introduced within a week by that crowd protecting the cotton growers. If you walk down New York Avenue you'll see the house the good senator from Virginia is building with the lobbyists' money." Susanna rubbed the inside of Benjamin's arm, as if to remind him she was there for him.

All the while, Vinnie carried herself with the poise of someone fully accustomed to the small flatteries and large favors upon which Washington thrived. As the two couples moved through the room, there wasn't a name Vinnie didn't know. She chatted as fluently about Polly Fisk's children as she did about the price of cotton or when the next tobacco ship would be leaving Charleston for England.

Susanna and Vinnie drifted off to look at the other rooms in the house. A waiter brought Ross another glass of champagne. He motioned toward Thad Stevens. Benjamin recognized him from the Johnson impeachment. "You're familiar with Jay Cooke, I presume. Everyone knows the man."

Benjamin said that Carlton often spoke about Philadelphia's premier banker with some disdain. "He financed the war for Lincoln, as I understand it."

Ross was quick to agree with what Benjamin had just said about Cooke. "That's right. But it wasn't because he believed in the cause or even cared a whit about the elimination of slavery. He made millions. He has some powerful men like Mr. Stevens in his deep pocket."

Ross sighed. "I don't mean to sound entirely bitter. There are some good men here. Fessenden and a few others are men of conscience. Certainly, Trumbull can't be bought. It's just that those of us who want to accomplish something other than the bidding of all those men who shower us with favors seem to be swimming upstream against ever-strengthening currents. The money is getting in the way of what's best for all the people."

Benjamin had spent enough time on the edge of the scene to have the same concern, but he wanted to use the time he had alone with Ross to get an answer to something that had been gnawing at him. "As long as we have a moment alone, Mr. Ross, can you tell me the meaning of the exchange between Mr. Wade and Miss Ream? I must admit my curiosity."

Two women began walking toward them from the door to the parlor. One was dressed in red. She was tall and thin, with white feathers in her hair. The other had chosen ivory. She was shorter and more solidly built. Benjamin presumed them to be younger than his mother, but not by much.

"Some other time, Benjamin. The walls in this town have ears. That's especially true for walls covered in brocade and silk."

"I will change the subject, sir, only temporarily. I suspect the worst, though. I must assure you of that. You are suggesting this whole city is so rife with people using each other for favors I'm certain there is an entire month of stories in that one reference from Mr. Wade. Mr. Carlton will not let the matter rest." What Benjamin didn't say was that there were days he felt that in his own way, Carlton was as much a tyrant as the men with their hands on Washington's reins of power.

"You are becoming quite the cynic, Benjamin. I sensed a bit more of the patriot in the very kind words you said about me."

Benjamin smiled. "Part of me certainly still believes in the idea our government can be a force for good, Mr. Senator." He paused. "But sadly, some of the schoolboy enthusiasm with which I held that belief as a young man feels as though it's slipping away. Still, I don't want to let go entirely of the portion of my soul that needs to believe in that ideal."

"I wish I could find the words to buoy your spirit, Benjamin. I really do. But having been thrown in the ditch by my fellow Republicans for the crime of having voted my conscience, I am at a loss."

Susanna and Vinnie approached the two men. Susanna slipped her arm in Benjamin's. "What have you two been discussing while we were exploring this magnificent house?"

Benjamin looked at Ross and then laughed. "Small talk. Possible stories the *Courier* might explore. The state of the democracy."

"Small talk about the state of the democracy? We were gone less than ten minutes. What were you able to discern about that lofty subject in such a short time?"

Benjamin nodded in the direction of two women who had entered the room just after Susanna and Vinnie. "To understand what we were discussing, I'd like you to watch as those two women cross the room. They're quite pretty, wouldn't you agree?"

Susanna nodded. Benjamin continued. "As they draw closer, though, you notice the dark circles under their eyes, the wattle on the smaller woman's chin, the liver spots marking their hands."

"That's a cruel thing to say about the women, but now that you've directed my attention to their flaws, not an incorrect statement."

Ross laughed. "Let me assure you there was no malice intended, my dear Susanna. Your husband is quite the observant newspaperman. He was just making the point that there are times when democracy is better viewed from a distance." Ross sipped the last of his champagne. "Sadly, we are living through one of those times."

# 18

ALTHOUGH ROSS TRIED TO GATHER whatever information he could about the cost of building the railroad, he had no more friends in Washington. That meant Benjamin had no choice but to sit through the tediousness of the meetings of those House committees whose job it was to pass out appropriations in the hope someone might make a stray comment worth pursuing.

Today, it was an afternoon session of the agriculture committee during an oppressive early June afternoon. The room smelled like a barn full of wet sheep.

Benjamin was fishing for his kerchief when the committee chairman recognized Pig-Iron Kelley. Kelley fidgeted with his glasses and then began reading from a prepared text. Benjamin leaned forward a bit to hear. He was, after all, both the man who represented Grayton in the Congress and his father's employer.

"Mr. Chairman, there is no question our cotton growers deserve our support." Kelley stopped when two members leaned into each other and began a conversation. He looked at them angrily and waited until they finished whatever they were saying.

"But so do our grain farmers and dairymen. Shouldn't we be thinking of their well-being at the same time? I say nothing against our cotton growers when I suggest we should look at the broader question of aid to all of our farmers as part of a larger package rather than exhaust what little revenue we have on only one group."

He waited for some adulation, or at least a positive response to what he'd just said.

"But Mr. Kelley, the question on the table is about cotton, not whatever is grown in Pennsylvania." The speaker had a frustrated Southern twang. The word *grown* seemed to have three syllables.

Benjamin moved closer to the podium. Carlton might be interested in how one of the local congressmen stood for the defense of the farmers he represented against the interests supporting the cotton trade. Benjamin began forming the story in his mind. He would write about how the grain and dairy farmers in Pennsylvania were being served in the debate over how to allocate limited national resources in a country still figuring out how to pay off the debt it took on to finance the war.

Benjamin stopped short when his father approached Kelley. Jacob whispered in Kelley's ear. He opened his coat to show Kelley an envelope in his breast pocket. They spoke for a moment. Jacob nodded and then left the room through a door behind the table where the representatives were sitting. He hadn't seen his son. The whole exchange lasted thirty seconds.

Kelley looked up from his text. "Mr. Chairman, I'm certain we all recognize we must look at each issue individually as well as in the context of the whole. I trust we'll do right by all farmers in due time. I vote to approve the pending legislation."

Benjamin's breathing was labored. He wanted to follow Jacob through the halls, wanted to shout the question of whether his brothers had died so Pig-Iron Kelley could be fifty dollars richer and the cotton growers even more so, whether the poignant story his father told him at their one meeting was some gauzy-eyed vision of the way things might be because that's what Jacob believed Benjamin wanted to hear and not how he'd chosen to live his own life. Benjamin hated himself for believing for an instant that someday there might be a place for Jacob in his life again.

The committee members began gathering their papers. Benjamin approached Kelley. "Mr. Kelley, my name is Benjamin Wright from the *Philadelphia Courier*. You might remember we met casually some time ago outside the Executive Mansion when President Johnson opened it to House members during his impeachment trial. Do you care to tell me what was in the envelope my father handed you that caused you to switch your vote so quickly on the cotton subsidy question? I'd like to pass that information on to our readers."

Benjamin thought he detected a glance of fear in Kelley's eyes, but his response betrayed no emotion. "Your father? My chief aide. He reminded me of another meeting for which I was late. Beyond that, I have no idea what you're talking about. Give my regards to Grainger when you see him next. He's a decent enough reporter and a solid editor." He turned toward the door.

"Mr. Kelley, if you won't tell me what was in that envelope, I'll have to ask my father. After all, the envelope in question was in his coat pocket." There was nothing rash or impetuous about the question. He no longer feared the man.

Benjamin felt Susanna's hand on his arm. "I know what you're feeling, Benjamin. Let it go." He wriggled free from her grasp. This wasn't their wedding, where she could demand his time and attention. This was his business. This is why he'd come to Washington.

Benjamin inched his body closer to Kelley's, as if he were ready to challenge him physically.

Kelley turned for a moment and then looked at Benjamin as though he meant to bore a hole through his skull with his eyes alone. "Yes, we met the night of Johnson's reception. I know that. You're the famous journalist who wrote so harshly about the impeachment and with such pathos about Senator Ross. You have an eye for detail. But if you're so goddamned good at gathering facts, young man, you should know your mother lives on the money your father sends her. She has no other source of income.

## Chapter 18

And neither does he. She'd lose your farm in an instant without that help. If I were you, I'd neither try to put your family or your father's position in such jeopardy nor look for things that don't exist." Kelley spoke with such disdain he might as well have spat the words in Benjamin's face.

"We're talking about the envelope, Mr. Kelley. I presume it contained an amount of cash bartered for your vote. The people who elect you to Congress time and again will be interested in learning how you conduct their business." Susanna pulled even more forcibly at Benjamin's arm.

Kelley leaned into Benjamin. He spoke in a whisper with a voice sounding as though it had been filtered through sand. "You are young and naïve about the ways of the world, but you are the son of a trusted aide and friend, so let me give you some much-needed advice before you do yourself harm. Don't sacrifice your mother in the process either of trying to concoct stories about the workings of the government or of making a name for yourself."

"I am a newspaper man, Mr. Kelley. My job is to expose the truth to our readers."

"You call yourself a newspaperman, Wright, so here's a bit of news. You're incapable of understanding this town and you'll be devoured by it if you try to do so."

# 19

CARLTON FISHED FOR HIS PEN, shook it to get the ink moving, and crossed out Benjamin's description of McComb in the story he'd just handed him.

"We can't call McComb prominent. The best way to annoy the little pecker is to say he's just a fee-for-hire lawyer." Carlton laughed at his own characterization.

"McComb will be as angry over the fact we didn't blow smoke up his ass about what a big deal he is as he will be we're plastering this story over the front page. By dinner tonight, every free man in Philadelphia and Wilmington will be wondering what McComb and his pal Ames are up to." A copy boy grabbed the pages Carlton was holding in the air and bounded down the stair to the pressmen as Carlton shouted that Greene should run five hundred extra copies.

Carlton put out his hand. "You've done well, Wright. This story is going to get some wind at its back. Everyone will be talking about the railroad to California and all the people's money the government is throwing at the men building it. Your friend Ames seems to have put himself smack in the position of being the prime contractor to the government for the single purpose of robbing it blind."

Carlton slapped his palm on his desk, as if to say that observation ended all debate on the question. "The men who are building the damned transcontinental railroad are a bunch of thieves,

Grainger. That's the God honest truth, and the *Courier* is breaking the story. We'll smoke that bastard McComb out of his hole by printing a front page devoted to nothing except how he's trying to help himself to more of the government money than his partners in crime are willing to give him. He'll jump to a denial and we'll be off to the hounds."

Grainger patted Benjamin on the back, but he gave him no time to celebrate his scoop. "Let's not lose sight of the fact you went down to Washington to look critically at the operation of the government under our new President. Write up something about the Congress in broad terms. The atmosphere. What it's like to walk around the halls of the building. Give me about a thousand words by the end of the week."

Benjamin's notoriety (and twelve dollar salary increase) hadn't come without the price of raised expectations. T.P. Grainger greeted Benjamin with the respect of an assignment he fully expected to be within Benjamin's grasp. "Grant has hung a 'for sale' sign on Washington. People want to know about the grease keeping the wheels of their government turning." Grainger made his expectations for the story even clearer. "Let's start by telling them what Congress is up to and then slowly feed them names and details. We can work this angle for the entire summer if we play our cards right."

"Our story is about the men with the government contracts cheating the taxpayers out of their money, damn it." Carlton could barely get the words out before he was looking around for a place to unload his mouthful of brown sludge.

"Stay focused, T.P. Grant's turning the Capitol into a French whorehouse isn't anything new. Greeley's been all over that for months." Carlton stood, so he could press his point with some urgency. "We need something new to tell our readers, and the McComb story is right under our noses for the taking. The news is in the railroad money. That's a Philadelphia story and God damn it, T.P., we're a Philadelphia newspaper."

Benjamin was rooting for Carlton to prevail in this battle of egos and visions for the *Courier*, but he knew he was betting on the losing side. He would be saddled with both tasks and with that, the inevitability of confronting the reality his own father was little more than Pig-Iron Kelley's enabler.

As much as Benjamin wanted to stare Kelley down and to prove even the most powerful members of Congress can't spit in a newspaper's face, he couldn't dismiss the possibility of retaliation. If Rachel lost their farm because Jacob lost his job, her only remaining son would have brought her as much grief as her other two. Maybe more, as it would be by his hand.

"A thousand words by the end of the week, Benjamin. There will be plenty of time to look into this Mr. McComb, but first things first."

His new home was the only refuge Benjamin wanted or needed.

Susanna had done what Benjamin thought was the impossible. She made Rachel laugh. Not just laugh, but go positively giddy over the prospect of being a grandmother. When Rachel visited their two spare rooms in Philadelphia, the two of them were like sisters. And their landlady, Gwendolyn Nicholson, could have been the third. They were inseparable. They visited the finest fabric shops so that Rachel could make clothes for the baby (she'd already made a scrap quilt, but insisted that the clothes be brand new.) Gwendolyn Nicholson acted as though she were the pregnant one, following after Susanna, urging her to slow down as she continued her daily walks, her arms full of gingham and lace for the room that was to become the nursery. When Curtis drove his sister into the city, his wagon was stuffed with the crib and rocking horse that his youngest had outgrown and a new mattress Rachel herself had stuffed with eider down. Curtis also carved a small wooden swallow for the baby and oiled it until its skin was brown as toast.

Benjamin watched from a distance, sitting at their table, his notes spread around him like fabric remnants, trying to respect

Grainger's direction. But there were too many voices around him. Women's voices. Deliciously happy women's voices at that.

Rachel called him. She was in a small room no bigger than a closet. It was, in fact, the place where Reverend Nicholson stored his extra chairs the church needed for Easter and Christmas services and the pot luck suppers Gwendolyn ran to raise money for the building fund. Rachel was standing on a chair, her arms stretched high, but not high enough, toward the ceiling, to tack a piece of fabric to the wall.

"Stretch this across for me, Benji. We need to let it hang down to keep the flies off the baby. I can't quite reach and we can't have Susanna standing on chairs now, can we?" Rachel ran her finger across the fabric, imagined what the space would look like with the new fabric and a hooked rug she was making.

For a moment, Benjamin didn't react. He was too stunned at being called Benji. That's what he'd been called when he was the youngest of the three boys, tearing around the farm behind his brothers, always several yards behind them. Rachel hadn't called him that since they buried Willie and Matthew.

There was a color in Rachel's cheeks and a gaiety in her voice Benjamin thought had been lost forever. She seemed a bit stronger than she had on the day of their wedding, but still weaker than he'd known her to be. Perhaps the baby growing inside of Susanna was breathing life into Rachel as well. Benjamin chose not to ask Rachel about her health, about whether she should use some of her time in Philadelphia to call on a doctor. And how could he ruin Rachel's mood by telling her what he had learned about her husband at Hoke's Run or had seen in the committee room at the Capitol? How could he write about any of that now, of all times?

If Rachel was finding joy in the next generation, what was the point in making her confront the failings of this one?

Who was Benjamin to stand in the way of his mother's happiness?

# 20

THE SECOND TIME Benjamin met David Kimberly was even more unpleasant than the first.

Kimberly wore his pompous and demeaning nature as though it were a second skin bedecked in a great sweeping gray cape with a hint of lavender in the fur around the collar, matching the stone at the tip of his walking stick. The effect—likely the purpose and effect—was to make him look like some dandy who'd just stepped out of a store window.

That they were meeting at all wasn't the surprise. The deeper he dug into the story of the lawsuit McComb brought against Ames, the more Benjamin was convinced they'd meet again. What he was finding was too combustible for McComb to ignore. That Kimberly came to the offices of the *Courier* at eight, the morning after the second story about the suit hit the streets, told Benjamin his reporting had touched a nerve.

Mercer Carlton was positively giddy when a small copy boy announced in a squeaky voice that the man who stood at the entrance to the *Courier's* editorial room was McComb's chief clerk and that he'd asked to be directed to T.P. Grainger. Carlton got out of his chair and did a little two step, part Irish jig and part just plain silly.

"Right between the eyes, my boy." Carlton spoke in a voice that didn't care whether the clerk took the message back to McComb. "Our suspicion that McComb and Ames and whoever else they're in bed with are stealing from the public coffers is dead on target. Why else would the little weasel send his errand boy first thing in the morning to complain to the owner of the paper? I told you so, Benjamin. It's the railroads, for the love of God. It's not the money being made building the transcontinental. It's the money being stolen."

Carlton had walked to the door of Grainger's office, hoping to be invited into whatever theater was about to unfold. Benjamin went back to his desk, by design. Men like Henry McComb don't send their chief clerk lightly on errands. He'd sued this Oakes Ames. Benjamin was certain he'd sue the *Courier* and throw in a claim against Benjamin for good measure. That was one lawsuit he didn't relish describing to Susanna. He winced when the copy boy tapped him on the shoulder and whispered he was wanted in Mr. Grainger's office.

T.P. Grainger sat behind a large roll top desk that once belonged to Zachary Taylor. As a rule, he loved to tell the story about how Taylor lost the desk in a poker game in a Richmond saloon. David Kimberly's visit, however, was no occasion for stories of that sort. Grainger shut the top of his desk, in case this clerk had mastered the art of reading papers upside down.

Kimberly remained seated. He didn't extend his hand to Benjamin. Carlton took the third chair. Benjamin leaned against the wall behind Carlton after acknowledging Kimberly's presence with a simple nod.

"Carlton, Wright, Mr. Kimberly has a proposition from his employer. Would you be good enough to repeat what you told me, Mr. Kimberly, exactly as you said it to me?" It was obvious Grainger disdained the clerk, his message, and the man who'd sent him on this mission.

David Kimberly didn't bother looking at either man. He seemed insulted Grainger had asked him to repeat what had been a simple, if direct message. "Mr. McComb has offered to purchase the *Courier* lock, stock, and barrel. Mr. Grainger has been offered five thousand dollars for his interest in the paper. He has twenty-four hours in which to respond."

"Five thousand dollars. It's your life's work, T. P." Carlton blurted that out without thinking or, probably without caring. McComb would learn of every word of their conversation. "Even if you wanted to sell the paper, which I can't see you doing, that's an insulting number."

Carlton pointed at Kimberly. "T.P., did you call us in here to witness the man's thrashing or to escort him out to the street?"

If Grainger was amused by Carlton's defense, it didn't show. "Mr. Kimberly has more to say."

Kimberly moved slowly in his chair. "I informed Mr. Grainger in the event the offer was turned down, Mr. McComb and Mr. Jay Cooke, whom I presume you know by reputation, are deep into negotiations focused on their starting a paper here in Philadelphia that will make short order of the *Courier*. It's a cruel world, gentlemen. Mr. McComb only is trying to soften the blow."

"Cooke?" Carlton nearly burst out of his jacket. "Jay Cooke? Grainger, I told you the story we should be following is the way in which the men who are building the transcontinental are robbing the treasury blind. Tomorrow's headline is sitting right in this room." Benjamin recognized the name from Polly Fisk's party. The man's money covered a wide patch of geography.

Carlton left his seat and moved toward the door, as if he needed to make some grand exit. "I trust you'll tell Mr. Kimberly what he can do with this offer, Grainger. I'll be working on tomorrow's paper if you need me." Benjamin didn't move.

Benjamin could see Grainger was straining for the right words. He had the responsibility of twenty years of work, thirty employees, and a reputation for honesty on the street outside the *Courier* to think about. He lacked Carlton's freedom of grand and empty gestures. If there were some way Benjamin could have thrown

Grainger a lifeline he would have. But he was powerless to do anything other than to watch the strain of Kimberly's threat sink into Grainger's marrow.

"Benjamin, be good enough to show Mr. Kimberly out. Mr. Kimberly, you may tell Mr. McComb I'll have a response to his proposition some time tomorrow."

Grainger ran his finger gently over one of the ridges of his desk, as if he were saying goodbye to an old and dying friend.

# 21

"MERCIFUL JESUS, T.P. You can't seriously be thinking about McComb's offer. I've never known you as a man to bow to pressure." Benjamin faded into the corner of Grainger's office. He wanted to hear every word these two old friends, colleagues and comrades in arms were about to say to each other, but didn't want to get in the way of their twenty-year friendship.

"Cooke is a powerful man, Mercer. Much more powerful than the President himself." Grainger spoke so softly Carlton had to lean toward him to hear what he said.

"That's because this President has proven himself to be a petty criminal and a cipher. He can't take a breath without inhaling the vapors of the special interests crawling all over his skin like leeches. The man is a whore." Carlton was surprised by the disdain in Grainger's voice.

"He should have stayed in the military." Carlton was trying to find some way to move his colleague in a different direction. "He was a damned fine general."

"He wasn't Lee's caliber of general or man, but what's the point debating that now?" Grainger spoke with resignation. "It was Lee who laid down his sword. History only cares about those who come out on top."

"And on this particular battle, T.P., we're destined to come out on top. For the love of God, man, look at McComb's threat for what it is. We scratched the surface of a story that our instincts tell us has fraud and government looting and the railroads all over it, and the first man McComb runs to is the man who made millions on those same railroads. What does that tell you other than we're onto something big and have a duty to pursue it?"

Grainger's elbows were on his desk and his hands together as if in prayer. "I started this paper with nothing but an idea, Mercer. There was only one other paper in Philadelphia at the time. What are there today, seven, eight? We made this market. People paid attention to what we had to say."

"It sounds like you're writing your own obituary, T.P." Carlton reached across the desk and cupped his hands over Grainger's. "People still pay attention. I don't want to hear your farewell address. I want to hear how you're going to run McComb through as though this story were a bayonet."

Carlton stood and made the slashing motion of a soldier in battle. "A long, sharp bayonet. You said there are eight other papers in Philadelphia. If Cooke starts one there'll be nine. But the *Courier* will still be the one the people are reading because we'll be the paper with the courage to expose the stench in whatever is going on with the railroad."

Grainger didn't sound convinced. He leaned back in his chair. "Five thousand dollars is an enormous sum of money for a few desks and a rickety old press."

"You know that's not what you're selling, T.P. The *Courier* is a living, breathing being. It has a pulse and a soul. You might as well negotiate with McComb to sell him your right arm."

Carlton reached into one of the pockets of his coat and retrieved two cigars. He offered one to Grainger, who declined. Carlton fumbled for his blade and then cut the end. He toyed with the flame of his match until the cigar was lit to his satisfaction.

Smoke swirled around his face as he spoke. "I've never known you to run from what's right, T.P. Do you remember the heat you took for giving Frederick Douglass such a prominent voice? Do you remember when people threatened to burn you in effigy after you spoke out on Brown's defense after Harper's Ferry? You came back with the same message day after day for a month."

"That was easy. Slavery was a cancer on the nation. There was a clear wrong to be righted. It was easy to be principled in the face of that."

"I never told you this, T.P., but your so-called decent competition couldn't promise me enough to abandon ship and to join their papers every time you took a stand that got the *Courier* into more hot water."

Grainger smiled, a bit painfully perhaps, but a smile nonetheless. "I'm flattered you stayed, Mercer, but from our current vantage point it appears you might have been better off taking one of those offers."

"Pish posh, Grainger. There may have been days when I was coming into work where I didn't know if you were going to be tarred and feathered or have a statue built in your honor on Independence Square by the time the paper went out, but I knew the *Courier* was the only God damned paper in this town where I wanted my byline. McComb's threat is no different. Sometimes we're asked to stand up in the face of a foreign enemy. Sometimes the enemy is on our shores, as it just was in the war. This new crop of wealthy men who think they can buy their way into the government is every bit as much an enemy as anyone we've ever faced. If the press doesn't call them on their thievery, who will?"

Grainger looked toward Benjamin with a wan smile. "I presume you're in Mercer's corner on this one." Benjamin nodded and Grainger continued. "Why is it that it's always so much easier to have the certainty of your convictions when you're young?"

"Because by the time you're our age you know what fear tastes like." Carlton picked a piece of tobacco off the end of his tongue. "Stare it down, T.P. We're right to expose these men who are trying to buy Washington brick by brick. You know that as sure as you're

*Chapter 21*

sitting there. That's why you need to keep this paper. That's the story the *Courier* was destined to tell."

# 22

STEPHEN CARSON WRIGHT weighed seven and a half pounds. He came out of Susanna all screaming mad and red and covered with syrup, but he cleaned up nicely and by the time Benjamin first laid eyes on his son, the boy had fallen asleep at Susanna's breast.

Benjamin kissed Susanna on the lips, as tenderly as the circumstances would allow, the room being occupied at the moment not only by Susanna and Stephen, but by Rachel and Gwendolyn Nicholson as well. Benjamin paid the doctor his seven-dollar fee—four weeks' worth of rent, but worth so much more than that—and tiptoed up the stairs in case his new son was sleeping.

"You look tired. The doctor said everything went fine." The shades were drawn so the sunshine didn't hurt Stephen's eyes. The walls glowed around the window where there was enough room for the light to slip through.

Susanna kissed Benjamin back. "I'm a bit sore right now. Giving birth is a bit like pushing a watermelon through a knothole, but women have been doing this for thousands of years so I'll be fine. What's more important is that Stephen is alert and already nursing. I've given you a fine young son, Benjamin Wright."

Benjamin wasn't a man who cried easily. He wondered in fact if he had any tears left after those he shed for his brothers had dried. But his eyes were pools as he looked at Susanna and Stephen. "This is what life is all about, isn't it, Susanna?"

Benjamin looked at Rachel, gently moving back and forth in the rocking chair in the corner of the room. She had taken Susanna's hand in hers when they both prayed silently for Susanna's mother, and now Rachel was back to her task of knitting a pair of deep blue booties for the baby. Seeing Rachel at peace took Benjamin back to a gentler time, when Matthew and Willie were still young boys and Benjamin was the baby. Rachel showered him with such affection, such grace. If only he could turn back the clock, stepping over the madness that set in after Jacob left the two of them alone, wounded and fearing the future.

Stephen shifted in Susannah's arms and then let out a small burp. Rachel leapt from the rocking chair. She hugged Gwendolyn Nicholson and the two of them giggled and waited for another message from the boy. His gurgles brought about squeals of delight from the women. When he passed gas you would have thought St. John the Evangelist himself had spoken.

Benjamin touched Susanna's hair and then, for the first time, Stephen's skin. He had never felt anything as soft. When he put his hand over his son's chest, his tiny heartbeat was like that of a bird, only deeper and more purposeful.

"We've done a wonderful thing, haven't we, Benjamin, bringing Stephen into the world? There is so much going on around us he'll be a part of, so much possibility for our son."

The *Courier* seemed a thousand miles away. The evils of Washington and Henry McComb's greed might as well have been on the moon. "Can I hold him?"

Susanna passed him the baby. Benjamin didn't know how he was supposed to feel at the first touch of his son. He was awed, fearful of the boy's vulnerability and overtaken by responsibility and tenderness. Stephen was less than two hours old, but he had the power of a shaman to summon emotions from places within Benjamin even Susanna hadn't reached. It was magic, pure magic, that they had created this child out of their passion and commitment to each other.

Benjamin looked again at Rachel. She stared at him in a way he hadn't seen before, as though she were acknowledging his transition, his completeness. Susanna stirred on the bed and then touched both Benjamin and Stephen with the same finger. Benjamin felt himself grow warm to the touch, to the celebration of their unity.

When Stephen opened his eyes, Benjamin was sure the boy recognized him. When Stephen's lips turned upward in what Benjamin was certain was a smile, Benjamin felt as though he had entered a holy place.

# 23

BUT WHILE BENJAMIN AND SUSANNA were marveling at the wonder of Stephen's birth, the harsh reality of the threat to the *Courier* was playing out in the Brandywine Inn, a small roadside tavern that had been a meeting place for merchants who traveled between Philadelphia and Wilmington since long before the Revolutionary War. Henry McComb suggested he and Grainger meet there because it was far enough away from Philadelphia to give them privacy.

Grainger's note rejecting McComb's offer to purchase the *Courier*—delivered by one of Grainger's copy boys, a lanky Negro child with a broad smile and a loping gait, who simply handed the envelope to David Kimberly without waiting for an acknowledgment—prompted a response from McComb within the hour.

"You're making a terrible mistake, Grainger. I have powerful friends. They're not the kind of men you want as your enemies." McComb rarely delivered his threats in person. He had aides for that, clerks and runners whose only job was to allow McComb to equivocate and to deny the message if ever confronted. But he wasn't often confronted. A man who could drop Jay Cooke's name into a conversation with the certainty he could carry out any threat he delivered didn't customarily have his views challenged.

While McComb was dressed in his city lawyer's finery, Grainger wore his more casual boots and light field jacket. He refused McComb's offer to send a hackney and instead rode his old chestnut gelding to give them both some fresh air and exercise. The bar room was sparsely populated in the middle of the afternoon. Grainger ordered ale. McComb chose brandy.

There were no introductions beyond a handshake, no inquiry about family or weather or the state of the world or any other small talk. Grainger wouldn't have wanted that in any event. "Henry, I appreciate the offer and I understand even more the context. But the *Courier* is my life's work. I suspect if you cut me my blood would be as black as the ink I buy by the barrel."

Grainger sipped at his beer. He ran his finger around the wet circle the glass had left on the table. "Beyond that, I have thirty men who report to me. Those men have wives and children. I can't simply ignore their interests."

"If it's a question of price, T.P., I'm certain we can talk things through."

Grainger found the comment offensive. His back stiffened. He couldn't remember a time in his life when the *Courier* hadn't been at the center of what he stood for. Other papers came and went, but the *Courier* had endured two wars, the battle over slavery, and more work stoppages by disgruntled pressmen than Grainger could remember. It would endure this as well.

"You're defining it as though we were having a business negotiation and the only question was one of price. I don't see what we're talking about in those terms, Henry. You may as well ask me to sell one of my children. It's just not something I can do."

"Don't take my willingness to negotiate over price as a lack of resolve, Grainger. The message you received from Kimberly was quite accurate." McComb paused for a moment, as if to emphasize what he was about to say. "Cooke is completely serious about pursuing this acquisition. He wants to take over the *Courier* and he's not a man easily denied."

"And if it's not for sale, what then? How can even Cooke's millions buy something that isn't on the market? I can't stop him from opening a rival paper. Men do that all the time. I can't even stop him from hiring all my men, if that's his plan. But he can't have the soul of the *Courier* at any price."

McComb sniffed. "Don't be naïve, Grainger." McComb saw no point wasting time with either first names or false civility. "Everything in life has a price. I never saw you as a man who craved wealth. If you were, you would have picked an occupation other than the news business. But, for the love of God, Grainger, I never took you for a fool, either. You have no idea what it means to cross Jay Cooke."

Grainger scoffed. He'd been threatened by bolder men over issues of far greater urgency. In the run-up to the war, two crosses were burned on the lawn in front of his house. When the *Courier* published an editorial praising Lincoln's courage for signing the Emancipation Proclamation, someone shot a hole through his living room window. He responded to each attack by increasing the next day's run and by putting an even bolder anti-slavery statement on the *Courier's* front page. Carlton said there wasn't a general in either the Union or rebel armies with more spine than T.P. Grainger.

"Will he send men to have me murdered? Will he burn my building down? Does what I have to say in my four daily pages strike such fear into Cooke he'd resort to that? You're his errand boy, Henry. Tell me what the great and powerful Jay Cooke sent you here to say."

Grainger was surprised by the anger that was welling over. He wasn't sure any longer why he'd bothered agreeing to meet McComb. They really had nothing to discuss. McComb found Grainger a stubborn old fool, blind to the stark reality of the few options he had, as if Jay Cooke were some sort of a clerk who sat behind a desk all day entering names in a stock trading book and not more powerful than the President himself.

"I never knew much about you, Grainger, except what I read in your penny paper. You hated slavery and were a strong voice for the cause, I'll grant you that. You seemed delighted with the out-come of the war and of the Johnson trial. I read now that you think the President has hung a for sale sign outside Washington. From my vantage point you strike me as a man of principle, a man who gives voice to an element that seems to view that government can be mocked and criticized no matter what it does."

"As someone schooled in the law you should know the Constitution gives the press that voice, but why quibble the point?" Grainger didn't bother even looking at McComb. He knew this conversation was over.

"Well, so be it, Grainger." McComb stood and pushed his chair to the side. "Cooke is far more powerful than the Constitution you so revere. How he delivers the message to the *Courier* will play itself out."

McComb threw two coins on the table. "Finish your drink, if you like. I've got business in Wilmington and I'll take my leave." Grainger was as pleased with the morality of his position as he was curious about the next steps.

It took him, in fact, only until the middle of the next afternoon to learn what they would be.

The fire started in a shed behind the *Courier's* offices where Jesse Greene stored old papers and boxes. It wasn't more than ten feet on either side, barely protected against the elements. By the time an alarm sounded and a group of men armed with buckets and shovels assembled, the building was gone. A crowd of fifty men, women, boys and girls surrounded the ash pile, poking at it with sticks or watching their spit boil the moment it touched the embers.

Veterans were likening the smell to cannon fire. The air tasted both acrid and a bit sweet. An ashy residue coated the street.

Benjamin felt responsible for the damage. A small part of him felt nine years old again, wanting to run away and hide in the hay loft, to hold his breath so the horses wouldn't stir and wait for Jacob's anger to subside so he'd avoid a beating. Jacob was a hard man, unforgiving, quick to anger, and sure to hold a grudge. Benjamin was surprised when the drumbeat of the war grew louder that his father would play the role of patriot, rallying the men and boys of Grayton to Lincoln's cause. Benjamin didn't think of his father as a man who took bold strides. He certainly didn't have Grainger's courage to stare down the likes of Henry McComb and Jay Cooke.

He walked next to Grainger and Carlton. Both men were watching Greene sift through the wreckage for anything that might be salvaged. It was a wasted effort on his part, but one he felt he had to undertake. A man in a black coat and a top hat had set up a camera on a wooden stick with a brass foot on it for stability. He was adjusting the lens, ready to take a photograph of the mess.

"I see McComb's hand in this." Grainger had reported on the Brandywine Inn meeting when he came into the offices in the morning. He wanted the men working on the story to be able to put it into the proper context. Benjamin was certain of the connection, ready to offer an apology if Grainger asked for one. Grainger spoke before Benjamin could say anything. "This was meant as a warning."

Neither Benjamin nor Carlton said anything before Grainger continued. "On the other hand, Benjamin, the wind might have blown the door open and a spark from one of the dozens of chimneys around here may have ignited the paper inside the building." Grainger spoke softly. He saw no need in stating the obvious, no need in trying to excite a young reporter into blowing something out of proportion. He knew he was up against powerful enemies, knew he had to measure his response.

Carlton pointed to the man taking the pictures. "We need to figure out a way to get photographs into the paper, T.P.. That will bring in a whole new age to the newspaper business. We need to keep evolving, T.P., always giving our readers more."

Benjamin was taking notes, forming a story in his head, as though the fire had happened somewhere other than right outside the back door of the *Courier* and it was his job to report it to his readers

He detached himself from the cause of the fire and concentrated on the facts in front of him. He walked off the dimensions of the building. He asked questions of the few men who lingered, pouring the occasional bucket of water on any sparks that dared to fly up, the details of both the fire and of the attempted rescue. One of the men looked familiar, although Benjamin couldn't place where he'd seen him before. There was nothing particularly distinctive about that man that would cause Benjamin to know where they'd met, but he was certain their paths had crossed.

Carlton waited until Benjamin was out of the range of what he was about to tell Grainger. "The boy is right, T.P. I've never known you to be blind to the truth."

"This is the wrong fight to pick, Mercer. You and I both know that." Grainger didn't want any of Carlton's antics stirring the pot or giving McComb any leverage. The stakes were too high, the outcome too uncertain.

Benjamin turned away from the men who had been dousing the fire. He returned to where Grainger and Carlton were standing. "At least no one was injured. The flames didn't jump to the main building. We're fortunate in that. Shall I begin preparing the story of the fire for tomorrow's paper?"

Grainger's expression was one of gratitude for Benjamin's commitment and for his focus.

Carlton stopped fussing with the end of a cigar and spoke before Grainger. "No more than fifty words, Benjamin. It was a small rubbish fire, nothing more. No news in that." He'd been at Grainger's side long enough to understand his message.

Grainger paused, as if he were summoning an internal strength. "There's no sense poking around these ashes looking for clues that will lead nowhere. Your time will be better spent, Benjamin, continuing to gather the facts that tell the story of why men would go to this degree of trouble to scare us away from looking too deeply into the Credit Mobilier. That's where the fire is."

# 24

SUSANNA WAS NURSING STEPHEN when Benjamin made it home. She lifted her face. "What's that smell? Your clothes reek of nothing but smoke."

She waved him away with her free hand. "Get away from the baby." She put a towel over Stephen to shelter him. It was the first time since he and Susanna were together that Benjamin felt he didn't belong.

While he was changing into other clothes and scrubbing his skin with a cloth over a bucket of water, Benjamin reported on the day's events, the Delaware meeting, the rejected offer, the fire, Grainger's direction to dig even deeper into the story. He spoke for ten minutes without interruption.

He pulled a chair to his family. His voice was animated, his words tumbling out. "You should have seen Grainger today, Susanna. Carlton, Grainger and I are convinced that as much as McComb wants the Credit Mobilier shares, he wants to keep their real value hidden from the public. The company has to be inflating its costs for the building of the railroad. It's no wonder Peter Dey was reluctant to talk on the train."

Stephen was restless in Susanna's arms. She stroked the top of his head while Benjamin continued, "We're now certain the Credit Mobilier is stealing from the government. There could be millions involved, tens of millions. And I'm at the center of the investigation. I'm responsible for uncovering the facts. Can you imagine what this will do to my career?"

Susanna had a blank expression, but if Benjamin noticed that she either wasn't paying attention or was uncomfortable with his story, it didn't stop him from prattling on with his story. "The piece I wrote about Ross will be nothing compared to this. We'll be able to write our own ticket to any newspaper in this country, Susanna. This will put my reputation over the moon."

Susanna placed a cloth over her shoulder, held Stephen against her and gently patted his back. Her voice was melancholy. "I want to be happy for you, Benjamin, but there's something about this that frightens me. These men don't seem the type who will stop at a small trash fire. This isn't the impeachment story. What you did then was wonderful. You energized your readers. You recognized the remarkable bravery and decency of Senator Ross, and hopefully defined how he'll be remembered for the ages. Your writing was like poetry, Benjamin, only stronger."

Benjamin was silent. Stephen finally burped. Susanna shifted him to Benjamin and got out of her chair, as if she needed to distance herself from Benjamin. "But this is different. You watched the impeachment from afar. You reported what you saw, but you weren't making the news. Here, you're putting yourself into the middle of something you don't understand, in the gun sights of men who are far more powerful than you are. You mentioned Jay Cooke. I've read about him. He rules the world. You and I may think we're sophisticated because we're living in a fancy city instead of the farms where we grew up, and I adore seeing the *Courier* come out with your stories in it, but what do you know about congressmen and millionaires? What do you know of men who can hire hoodlums to burn down another man's property as a way of getting their message across?"

Benjamin adjusted Stephen on his lap so he could take one of Susanna's hands in his. "They're people, just like you and me.

Certainly, they have more money and schooling, but I have the power to be heard, to expose them for the frauds that they really are. I have the *Courier* behind me."

"And what if they continue to prove they don't want to be exposed? What then? They've already tried to buy the paper. What if they try to stop the paper or to stop the men who are trying to bring the story to light? Will you leave me a widow with a tiny baby and nothing to live on? Have you thought about whether you're putting yourself into danger? You talk about truth. Have you thought about the price you're asking me to pay for that truth?"

Susanna's eyes filled. Benjamin wanted to hug her, but she had thrown a shawl around her shoulders and moved to the other side of the room.

Benjamin was unable to move without waking the baby. His voice lost the urgency, the anticipation it had when he was telling her about his meeting with Grainger and Carlton. Susanna's words disappointed him. He didn't understand and certainly didn't share her fears. "I'd never do anything to hurt you and Stephen, Susanna. You know that. These men may be hard in business, but they're not ruffians or criminals. They wouldn't risk harming me or anyone else associated with the paper. The law would come down especially hard on them."

"I suspect men like Jay Cooke never get their fingernails dirty." Susannah's voice was filled with fear. "They hire others for that."

"But exposing government corruption wherever it exists is the very purpose of the press," said Benjamin. "We have a duty to pursue the claims that the government can't or won't."

Susanna stood. "Duty? To whom? You used to talk about your desire to write as a way of exploring what was interesting and good about people, about what possessed them to live outside themselves. You're changing, Benjamin. I fear the change isn't for the good. You're beginning to sound like a lawyer advocating for some client and not someone interested in elevating men's souls."

## Chapter 24

"The fact of the matter, Susanna, is that these men are robbing the government. I'm merely exposing that truth to the light of day. I see no contradiction in that." Benjamin had never before raised his voice in anger at Susanna. But the woman talking to him wasn't the woman with whom he'd fallen in love.

"The fact of the matter, Benjamin, is we now have a son who needs you more than the *Courier's* readers need you. Think of him, Benjamin. Stephen is your flesh and blood." Susanna had never seen Benjamin as so out of touch, never before believed his priorities were so completely wrong. But she now had a son to protect, and his interests had to be considered above everything else.

Benjamin reached his hand out to Susanna. She stiffened. "Susanna, I understand that. But that's exactly the point. This is entirely about Stephen. This is about whether the government that took my brothers and that one day may call Stephen to duty will be honorable and true and decent. Tens of thousands of men died for that ideal, Susanna. All I'm doing is writing a story."

"That's right, Benjamin. It's only a story." She swept her arm around the room. "What you're doing outside is only creating stories. This is where your life is, Benjamin. All of us. Our lives are here."

"If you're not happy with the idea of my doing what is right, be selfish, Susanna. Think of what that story could do for us. This could be the story of a lifetime."

"I am selfish. I want you for *my* lifetime, Benjamin."

Benjamin was without words for a moment. "You know I love you. You know I adore Stephen."

"This goes beyond love, Benjamin. Maybe it's because I've seen how dependent Stephen is, how much he needs me. How much he needs us." She wiped away a tear. "Maybe his being so vulnerable makes me feel the same way. We need you, Benjamin."

Susannah moved the baby away from Benjamin, as if to say both she and her son needed to put some distance between the life they were forming and the story Benjamin was pursuing.

As Benjamin moved toward the two of them, Susannah bent her body over Stephen and covered him with her arms. Benjamin froze at the image and the idea of his wife protecting their child from his father.

# 25

IN ALL HIS TIME at the *Courier*, Benjamin had never seen T.P. Grainger in such battle mode. In ordinary times (assuming the impeachment of a sitting President and a raft of government scandals can be considered ordinary), Grainger was the conscience of the paper and Carlton its heart. It was Carlton's booming voice that sent men and boys alike scurrying. Even Jesse Greene, who reported directly to Grainger because his job was to count the number of papers sold and not to write or even to read them, got out of Carlton's way when he had a head of steam up about how a story should be told.

Grainger was more the patriarch. It wasn't that he was aloof. His job was to let other people do their job.

But Grainger was taking the McComb story personally. He wanted the right direction and the right timing. It was as though McComb's twelve-thousand-dollar offer woke up a long sleeping passion in him, as if he recognized the importance of prevailing in this battle.

"We'll smoke McComb out. We'll describe the lawsuit, tell about the Credit Mobilier's contracts with the government and see how he reacts."

"He'll either offer twenty-five thousand for the *Courier* or burn the place down, T.P. How much do you think he'll pay for my desk?" Carlton laughed so hard at his own joke he missed the spittoon by at least eighteen inches.

"Is there any real risk in this?" Benjamin wanted to retract the words as soon as he said them. He loved Susanna, he really did, but she was frightened over what he hoped was nothing. She was being protective of Stephen, of course. That was her job. He regretted that he lacked Carlton's willingness to stare down his enemy.

Carlton barked. "Risk? One risk is that Henry McComb gets exposed for being part of a corrupt group of men who are robbing the government right under its nose. The only other risk is that Greene has to order more ink because everyone in Philadelphia is going to want to read this story. My God, boy, don't you understand what we're sitting on? Don't you understand the power you have in your hands?"

Grainger was more reserved, but his message was the same. "You say risk, Benjamin? I don't doubt McComb will get Cooke to put up the money for the paper he threatened to start. I doubt he'll send men over to bloody us, if that's your question. That's not Cooke's style." Grainger paused, lowered his voice. "But if you have concerns, I'm not going to ask you to involve yourself any more in this battle."

Benjamin reddened. He shouldn't have listened to Susanna. He certainly shouldn't have let her fears enter his thinking. "I'll have your story within an hour."

"Give me the pages as you write them, Benjamin. I'm going to have them set as the story is being written. This will be tonight's lead." Carlton leaned out of his office. "Greene, double tonight's run. We're onto something big."

At four in the afternoon, the first issues of the *Courier* began rolling off the presses on the first floor of the building. By seven that evening, three thousand copies of the paper had been gobbled up in every part of the city. There wasn't a man in Philadelphia who wasn't reading or talking about Benjamin's story.

It isn't often that members of Congress get sued, which is why the action Henry McComb of Wilmington and

Philadelphia brought against Oakes Ames of Massachusetts is so intriguing to this paper. Mr. McComb is seeking to have Mr. Ames turn over several hundred shares of stock in a Pennsylvania company known as the Credit Mobilier.

While all readers know a railroad line is being built from the Atlantic to the Pacific, not many details of the construction of that line have been made public. This paper has learned that the Credit Mobilier is responsible for the line's construction and is being paid no less than forty-two thousand dollars for each mile it builds.

We are continuing to look into this affair, but the fact that Mr. McComb is pressing so hard to recover these shares suggests to this newspaper that the Credit Mobilier is making unusually high profits for its efforts. We trust our readers share this curiosity in that regard. It is, after all, their money these men are spending. We call on the Credit Mobilier to make its affairs public. We will print this demand, Mr. McComb, every day until it does just that.

Grainger was so pleased with his paper's efforts he bought Carlton and Benjamin a drink—imported rum, no less—to celebrate the fact he'd shown McComb what he could do with his threat in such a bold and convincing way.

"We're onto something, boys. This will be big. If they're stealing from the government to build the railroad, by God, we'll nail them all. This is why the Founding Fathers wanted freedom of the press. This is what a newspaper was destined to do. By exposing wrongdoing in the government, we're serving the people as much as if we'd been elected ourselves. Maybe more so."

Carlton lifted his glass. "T.P., I toast your courage and your instincts. By God, man, I can't imagine another place I'd rather be than shoulder to shoulder with you in a battle."

He turned to Benjamin. "Wright, my investigator extraordinaire, I toast your ability to ferret out the truth. We are a remarkable team."

It wasn't the rum, although certainly that contributed to what Benjamin was feeling. He was warm from the room, warm from the fact that every man in the tavern and on the streets of Philadelphia was debating the very words he'd put on paper. Carlton talked about battles. Benjamin wondered if Willie and Matthew felt the same sense of commitment, the same devotion to the rightness of their cause that he and Carlton and Grainger were feeling at that moment. He assumed as much. The brotherhood that had formed between the men, the common purpose of the path they had set themselves on, made them inseparable.

Benjamin never experienced such a complete and undiluted sense of commitment to the cause to which the three men dedicated themselves. His love for Susanna and Stephen was pure, of course, fulfilling in the way that only family can be. But this sensation was different. Everything about the moment surged with nobility and purpose. Benjamin looked at his compatriots. If asked, he would pledge his fealty to them in an instant. They were knights on an historic crusade.

Benjamin noticed a man among the crowd who looked familiar. Wasn't he the man he'd seen at the scene of the fire behind the *Courier?* Or had he seen him behind one of the desks in McComb's office? Or was it both? The room was dark, filled with smoke. He couldn't be certain, but as drinks were being passed among the well-wishers, the man put out his hand and congratulated Benjamin on a job well done. Perhaps he just was an innocent, one of those men drawn to the excitement of the moment. Benjamin saw no purpose in trying to ask the man whether and where they'd met before. He quickly became just another face in the crowd. It was as though the man, and all of the others drinking Grainger's liquor, needed to feed off their celebrity as much as the newspapermen needed its readers' validation.

Susanna was awake when Benjamin tiptoed up the stairs. He was pleased she had waited up for him, certain she'd want to celebrate his success in breaking the Credit Mobilier story. She was standing in the middle of the room, next to a rock and some broken glass. She was holding a crumpled copy of the front page of the evening's paper in her hand. Susanna had been crying. Her eyes were dark red—but there was no sadness in them, only anger, the anger of a mother protecting her young. Benjamin didn't have to ask what was wrong.

"Stephen was on his blanket on the floor around half past six, Benjamin. I was in the kitchen making us supper. Something shattered the window. Glass was flying everywhere. A piece caught Stephen's leg. The rock landed on the floor about a foot from my baby's head. It was wrapped in this, Benjamin. It was wrapped in your words about Henry McComb and the Credit Mobilier. You've all chosen to weigh into the battle, haven't you, Benjamin? Well, your son almost became a casualty of that war. I hope you're pleased with yourself, Benjamin. I hope you're happy to know your wife and son have been drawn into this fight."

Benjamin reached out to Susanna. She turned away from him. He looked into Stephen's crib. The boy was gone. Benjamin had the dread feeling he'd been taken to the hospital. But if that had been the case, Susanna wouldn't be here. She'd be with the baby.

"I'll be at the Nicholson's for the evening. I've left the mess you made for you to see what you've put us through, Benjamin. Think about the next article you're going to write as you pick through the pieces of glass that almost killed our son. Think long and hard about that, Benjamin."

# 26

MERCER CARLTON PARADED AROUND the newsroom of the *Courier* holding a rock wrapped in a piece of the front page of the paper as though it were the Holy Grail and he were the most fortunate man in Philadelphia to have been chosen as its target.

"We've got McComb's attention now, by God. The bastard had one of his goons wait until around two in the morning to throw this through my window." He was as animated as he'd been in the run up to the impeachment, his face lit by that spark that sends newspapermen off to the crusades.

"Whoever he put up to the task couldn't even throw straight. He missed the first time."

Carlton laughed at his own story. "I was in bed. Darling Sophie was snoring softly, the way the old girl does. I heard this thump on my wall." Carlton slapped the top of the desk where he was standing with the palm of his open hand to mimic the sound. The others in the room—save Benjamin, who remained silent—laughed and smacked the tops of their own desk, relishing the show as much as Carlton.

"I looked out and saw some pathetic little turd picking through my rhododendrons to find the damn thing. He finally did. He took a few steps back from the house so he'd have a clear shot." Carlton was going through the winding and twisting motions of those new-fangled baseball pitchers playing on the weekends in Germantown everyone seemed to be talking about.

"Weren't you afraid?" Jesse Greene sounded genuinely afraid for his friend, or at least, for Sophie.

"Afraid? Hell no. I opened my window, pulled down my pants and stuck my blooming arse right out. I shouted to the little fart he should aim for the crack in the middle of my buttocks." Carlton started to unbuckle his pants but the crowd shouted him down. "He was so frightened the little scoundrel missed again." Carlton laughed at his valor. "It took the weasel three attempts to do it right."

"My Lord, Carlton. I'd have run straight away at the sight of your bum staring me in the face." Grainger was enjoying the story as much as anyone.

Carlton fished through his desk for matches. "T.P., maybe we should write an editorial suggesting to Henry McComb he hire himself a higher class of stooge."

Grainger smiled. "At least stooges with better aim." He pulled a rock out of a small satchel. It too was wrapped with the front page of the *Courier*. "Whoever he sent to my house either had a better arm, or better luck. He not only broke one of my leaded glass panes but the rock then hit one of Abigail's mother's plates from Andrew Jackson's White House that was hanging on the wall."

"There will be hell to pay for that, I'd say."

"Actually, Mercer, Abby took it in stride. She said the last time one of her mother's things was broken was when we sided with the abolitionists and the pro-slave boys fired their guns into the house. She said things couldn't be too bad this time around if they're resorting only to rocks."

Carlton roared. "By God, man, we're onto something this time. McComb doesn't know where to turn. If he clams up about the lawsuit he knows we'll keep coming at him. If he opens up the facts we've got him there as well. I swear, T.P., I don't need to go any-where for entertainment. You've got the best damned show in town right here."

Benjamin remained somberly quiet. At another time he would have danced around the newsroom with Carlton and Grainger showing off the rock used as a weapon against his family, and boasting about his courage in the face of the threat. It would mark him as one of the chosen, one of the select few at the *Courier* whose words were so feared McComb and Cooke would target him as well. But he was afraid. Afraid for Susanna and Stephen. Afraid if he opened his mouth he'd only show those fears. After Carlton finished showing his trophy to everyone in the newsroom like a returning general, Grainger walked to the table where Benjamin was working. He pulled a chair close to Benjamin so they wouldn't be overheard.

"Is everything okay at your house, Benjamin?"

"Of course, sir. Why wouldn't it be?"

"Benjamin, I had my hackney drive past your lodgings on my way in this morning. I noticed one of your windows had been boarded over. I presume you received the same gift Carlton and I did last evening."

Benjamin said nothing. Where Carlton and even Grainger looked at what had been thrown at them as something to be ridiculed, Benjamin wanted to discard every bit of evidence of the destruction of his sanctuary as quickly as possible. He swept all the glass, washed the floor and then went over it on his hands and knees with his cheek pressed against the floor boards to assure not even the smallest remnant of glass would harm Stephen. He found some old boards in the shed behind the Nicholson's and covered the window. All the time he could hear Gwendolyn Nicholson comforting his grieving and frightened wife.

When he was finally done with his chores, he poked his head inside the Nicholson's' front room. Gwendolyn Nicholson looked at him and shook her head. That was all the counsel he needed not to invade the room. For the first time since they'd been married, Benjamin spent the night alone in their bed. He missed Susanna's warmth, the gentle stirring of her breathing. But most of all he regretted the empty space that had opened between them. And he alone was to blame.

What could Benjamin say to Grainger that wouldn't lay out Susanna's fears? He wanted to appear brave. He wanted to show Grainger and Carlton he was cut from the same cloth, but all Benjamin could see when he looked at the front page of the *Courier* wrapped around the rock that Grainger set on his table was the sight of the weapon landing within inches of his son's head.

Grainger lowered his voice. "Listen, son, I understand what you're going through. Carlton doesn't have young children to worry about. I talked about how Abigail could laugh about these things. What I didn't tell you was when she was Susanna's age with a baby on her breast we had a cross burned on our front lawn. She looked out the window at the men who assembled there and saw the guns in their hands, the hatred in their eyes. She scooped up our daughter and took her to her mother's house in Lancaster until the troubles passed. She was gone for months. I hated it. We both hated it, but we saw no other way to both keep our family and the paper intact. We simply refused to let our fears overtake us."

The thought of giving up his wife and his new son for more than a moment tore at Benjamin. Still unable to respond to Grainger, he remained silent. Grainger continued. "We'll understand if you want to step away from this matter. I don't want to ask you to work on something that could put you or your family in further danger. The *Courier* is going to move forward on the investigation of McComb and the Credit Mobilier. I'll understand if you choose not to involve yourself in any of this work. I'll understand if you don't want your family in the crosshairs because your name is on the byline."

Benjamin couldn't find the words to do more than to mutter thanks to Grainger for his compassion. As he watched Grainger walk back to his office, stopping along the way so others could touch the crumpled paper and to feel the weight of the rock in his hand, Benjamin felt something he'd never experienced.

It was the sense that rather than freeing him to explore the heavens, Susanna was a weight on his chest.

# 27

BENJAMIN WAS AWARE Grainger was looking at him. He couldn't imagine why. He couldn't tell what Grainger was holding in his hand, except that it was a paper of some sort. Grainger kept reading it as though he had difficulty believing it. He looked at Benjamin and then at the letter again. Grainger's hesitancy to approach him was making Benjamin nervous about whatever he was holding.

Grainger walked over to Carlton's desk. He showed Carlton the paper and then bowed his head close to his. Benjamin pretended not to notice, but he had nothing else on his mind. Finally, Grainger came to Benjamin's table. He pulled a chair close to where Benjamin was sitting. "Benjamin, we've had an interesting break in the Credit Mobilier case. My hesitancy in not showing you this immediately comes from my concern about not drawing you deeper into this controversy. I know how upset Susanna was about the rock incident. I don't even know if Susanna mentioned this to you, but Abby called on her to see how she was."

Benjamin was ashamed Susanna put him in this position. Yes, she was his wife. Of course he loved her and adored Stephen. But what did that mean? Was his tie to family meant to lash him to her as though he were a pack mule? He'd done so much at the *Courier* in such a short time. People knew him. People knew his stories. His words shaped the public discourse. Certainly he'd captured Ross for the ages. When historians looked back at the vote to save Johnson, to save the nation, they'd mime Benjamin's words. What was Grainger holding in his hand that was so intoxicating that he was certain it would expose them to danger? Had it to do with his time with Ames? Did McComb rise to the level of his threat?

"Susanna is fine, sir, as is my boy. Your concern is appreciated. I'm curious, though, about whatever it is that you're holding. Could you share it with me?

"Always the reporter, asking the necessary question." Grainger smiled. He unfolded what he'd shown Carlton. It was written on lined paper, the sort of paper Jesse Greene used to keep the *Courier's* account books. If it came from a booklet, it had been cut precisely with a knife. The handwriting was small and detailed, as if the note had been written by an accountant or an engineer. Benjamin read the letter twice before saying anything to Grainger.

Sirs:

I read your article about Mr. McComb's actions against Mr. Ames regarding the Credit Mobilier stock with great interest. I believe I am responsible for that story, for I recall discussing the Credit Mobilier with a young couple on their honeymoon on a recent journey, although I must confess to have forgotten their names until I saw Benjamin Wright's name on the byline. Benjamin and Susanna.

I was the Chief Engineer of the Union Pacific Railroad until my recent resignation. Seeing the words in print made me realize we have many more details to discuss. Ours are the only voices questioning what the building of the railroad is costing the citizens of the United States. The courage you have shown in exposing this story makes me realize it is important that we talk. I can be reached at the address below.

Yours sincerely,
Peter A. Dey

## Chapter 27

Benjamin felt as though he was too close to a fire. He wanted to shout what he'd just read across the room. But he wanted even more to have Grainger's dignity and poise about the remarkable gift this letter represented. He opted for a bit of humor. "The Chief Engineer of the Union Pacific? Well, that would explain the fine handwriting. Mr. Dey is accustomed to technical drawings. This is one more." And then Benjamin couldn't contain his excitement any longer. "Of course I remember our time together. Would you like me to arrange a meeting with Mr. Dey? I don't know if he'd like us to meet him in Baltimore or to invite him to Philadelphia."

"I was thinking of the latter, but I'm not sure yet whether I should involve you in this enterprise."

"Susanna will be fine, Mr. Grainger. She was talking about visiting her father in Grayton in any event. This might be a good opportunity for her to get away for a couple of weeks." Benjamin was lying. He thought about what Grainger said about his wife in the early years of their marriage, when the troubles with the pro-slavery crowd brought the danger of his position into the midst of his family. He hadn't talked to Susanna about this. He hadn't talked to Susanna about anything in the weeks since the rock broke open the chasm in their lives.

Susanna busied herself with Stephen. In the rare times she ventured out of their house, it was only to go to the store, and only then when Gwendolyn Nicholson was doing her shopping so she'd have a companion. Susanna had either no time for Benjamin, or worse, no desire. At night, when the baby was asleep, Susanna would wait until Benjamin had fallen asleep before getting into their bed. It was as if she preferred not talking about what was missing in their relationship to trying to understand what it would take to bring it back together.

"I can't imagine there's any danger involved in any event."

Grainger paused. He didn't want to see his young protégée stepping into dangerous territory. And yet, that was how he made his name. He threw himself into the fight against slavery when other voices were muted and his family was young and vulnerable.

"Why don't you write Mr. Dey and invite him up to see us? We'll send him his fare. He might enjoy visiting our fine city now that he seems to have some time on his hands."

Benjamin waited until Stephen was asleep. Susanna was gathering up the baby's clothes. The dinner dishes had been put away. "Susanna, we need to talk a bit. Can we sit at the table?"

Susanna became rigid. "I know what you want to talk about, Benjamin. You want to know why I'm avoiding you. I'm not. My mind is full with the baby. I'm tired all the time. Gwendolyn told me that every time she had a baby it took months before she was able to think about her husband, and that all women go through this period after they have a baby."

Susanna was answering questions Benjamin hadn't asked, but desperately wanted to ask. He touched her hair. He rubbed the top of her hand. "Please listen, my beloved. This isn't about how we've been for the past month. I understand how hard it is to adjust to a new baby. This is about something at the paper."

Susanna's body jerked, as though she was trying to relax at the tenderness of Benjamin's comments only to have a spasm of anxiety that took control of her. "No, Benjamin."

"We've been approached by Peter Dey, the man we met on our trip to Chicago. He seems to have been influenced by my story to share details with us we might otherwise not have access to. This opportunity might blow this Credit Mobilier story sky high."

Benjamin so wanted a hearty reaction from Susanna, for it was her probing questions that had been responsible for creating this story in the first place. But she was quick to throw cold water on the idea. "Benjamin, no. Who knows what these men who threw the rock through the window are capable of doing?"

"I hoped you might not react that way. You were as enthusiastic as I was about meeting the man."

"We have a son, Peter. We have men threatening us. This no longer is a game. I intentionally did not allow the Nicholsons to repair the window so you would never forget what your passion for this story did to our family."

"Susanna, I've thought of little but that window since it was broken and of the rock that almost hit Stephen since that night, but I can't live my life in fear that the people I write about will be upset about my stories. I may as well quit the newspaper business if that's how I'm going to have to live my life."

"I'm afraid, Benjamin. I'm afraid for me and for the baby. Doesn't that count for anything?"

"We have to strike a balance, Susanna. It's fine to be cautious, but we can't let our fears overtake us."

Susanna began to tear up. "Do you think I like to feel this way? Do you think I enjoy being cooped up here all day with Stephen wondering if someone is lying in the weeds to attack you and to leave me a widow with a small baby? You've known me since I was five or six. I could ride a horse and climb a hill better than any boy. Have you ever known me to be afraid of things? I just worry so much about Stephen, about how I would take care of him if you weren't here to provide for us. Look at all those women who lost their husbands to the war. Look at your own mother. Do you propose to leave me like that?" Susannah had to stop to catch her breath.

"Do you want me to give up the paper?" Benjamin's voice was tinged with anger and frustration. "Do you want me to take a job as a bricklayer or as a clerk somewhere and hate what I'm doing and hate you for making me do it against my will? Is that the future you see for us?"

Susanna was frightened by the starkness of the choices that Benjamin presented and by the indelicacy—no, the hostility with which he detailed them. She buried her head in her hands. "I don't want that, Benjamin."

"What do you want?"

"I want to stop being afraid of the dark. I want to stop being afraid of the light. Isn't there another story you could pursue? Why must you bell the cat when the cat is so much more powerful than you'll ever be? Why create enemies of people who are capable of destroying you?"

"This is the biggest story since the impeachment, Susanna, maybe bigger. These people are under contract to work for the government and they're stealing it blind. The whole world will be interested in this story. This will solidify my position as one of the most prominent reporters in the entire country. These opportunities don't present themselves every day, and no, I'm not prepared to turn my back on this one."

Susanna had no response so Benjamin continued. "Grainger told me that the same thing happened to his family years ago. He was writing unpopular stories against the slave trade. People threatened him. His wife was as afraid as you are. She didn't get in his way. She sheltered his children by taking them to her mother's house away from the city until the troubles passed."

"Abigail Grainger called on me. She told me the same thing, although she didn't use the phrase you just did about getting in her husband's way. Is that how you see me, Benjamin? Am I now an obstacle because I am concerned about our son? I am prepared to leave if that's what you want, Benjamin. It will be hard, but I am prepared to leave you to your newspaper if that's what you'd prefer."

Benjamin's silence hurt them both.

# 28

PETER DEY WIRED he'd be on the train scheduled to arrive in Philadelphia at 2:30. He'd spend the afternoon with the representatives of the paper and then take dinner and spend the night at his sister's, so accommodations weren't necessary. He was grateful to the *Courier* for sending his fare. Benjamin arrived at the station at 2:20, only to be told that the train was thirty minutes late.

The station was teeming with passengers and well-wishers. A group of black bellmen was off to one side, sitting on their empty carts, playing cards while they waited to gather up the passengers and the new quarters they might make for helping with their bags. Those porters who already found passengers stood patiently as the smartly dressed men and women waited with their luggage, hoping to board the train to New York or Boston. A man walked through the crowd selling sandwiches and cold drinks out of a handcart. Benjamin gave him three pennies for a small glass of lemonade. He sat on one of the benches under the clock in the center of the station and reviewed the questions he'd prepared for Mr. Dey.

Benjamin heard the train before he saw it, broadcasting its arrival with a great blare of its horn. When he looked in the direction of the sound, Benjamin saw the broad plume of smoke being thrown up from the engine and then, finally, the glistening black locomotive, its wheels turning ever slower as it neared the station point.

Peter Dey suggested that rather than try to find each other in the crowd of people getting off the train, they should meet at the base of the clock. He'd have only a small satchel, so he wouldn't waste time looking for a porter.

"Mr. Wright." He put out his hand. "I admire both your tenacity in following the story we discussed and your paper's courage for publishing it. When I read what you wrote I was embarrassed I hadn't said more when we met." Benjamin assured him that no apologies were necessary. Dey inquired about Susanna. Benjamin assured him she was fine, and talked about what a fine boy Stephen was.

"I'm looking forward to talking to you at length, sir," Benjamin said. "Needless to say, we're all pleased you reached out to the *Courier* as you did."

"We seem to have a common cause, Mr. Wright." Dey spoke as if they were colleagues.

"The Baltimore papers reprinted your articles about Senator Ross. Your story about the matter between Mr. McComb and Mr. Ames was quite polished as well." Dey looked at Benjamin with some admiration. "You write as though you have a great deal more experience than a man your age might have."

"I accept your compliment, sir, with honor." Benjamin made a small bow. He wished Susanna could witness this exchange. He wished she could understand the future he was building for their family.

"Shall we find a hackney, sir? The offices of the *Courier* are about four blocks from here. I don't know whether you'd enjoy stretching your legs after all that time on the train or whether you'd prefer to ride."

Dey opted for the walk. Never one for small talk and too interested in what Dey might have to offer to waste time on chit-chat, Benjamin plunged right into his list of questions. Dey was as interested in talking about the Union Pacific as Benjamin was in absorbing what the man had to offer.

"I'm afraid you'll be asked many of these same questions when we get to the *Courier*, Mr. Dey. I know Mr. Grainger and Mr. Carlton are as eager as I to learn about the workings of the Credit Mobilier."

"I really can't speak to the inner workings, Mr. Wright. I can't tell you with any specificity who owns the entity, although I gather from Mr. McComb's suit that both he and Mr. Ames claim shares. Beyond that, I was never made privy to the details behind the ownership of the organization. I only can tell you that when a decision was made to enter into a contract with a man named Hoxie to build the first hundred miles of the road for fifty thousand dollars a mile when I knew that it would cost only slightly more than half that, I wanted no part of what was going on. I'm now told Mr. Ames himself has a contract to build several hundred miles more of the road for forty-two thousand dollars a mile while my colleagues who are still employed actually overseeing the construction tell me that the section was already built for around two-thirds of that cost. I may be a simple engineer who knows nothing about high finance, but that strikes me as fraud. We'll have a great deal to discuss, Mr. Wright. You needn't worry about my repeating myself."

To say Benjamin was surprised to see David Kimberly in T.P. Grainger's office is a massive understatement. Grainger, Carlton, Kimberly and another man—the man from the fire scene, from the bar—the man who Benjamin couldn't place in those contexts but who he now recognized as one of McComb's clerks the minute he saw him with Kimberly, was the fourth man in the office. They stood when Benjamin and Peter Dey entered.

Kimberly spoke before anyone had a chance even to make introductions. "Mr. Dey, I am formally serving you with papers on behalf of the Credit Mobilier and its investors. You will be held personally responsible for anything you say about the organization."

Kimberly handed Dey a wreath of foolscap paper tied in a blue ribbon. He turned to his colleague and asked that he make note of the time of the service of the papers.

"Mr. Dey, you hereby are put on legal notice of the possibility—no, of the probability that you will be named in a libel action and sued personally for stealing corporate secrets for anything you say about the organization or about the construction of the railroad while you were under its employ. I'm prepared to stay a minute if you have questions about these papers with which you have been served, although as I understand you have a dinner engagement with your sister this evening. It might be best if you accept my invitation to use the hackney I have downstairs to take you to her home."

Dey reddened, but said nothing. Benjamin began to speak, but Grainger put up his hand to silence him. "Mr. Dey, my deepest apologies. We made the mistake of believing the arrangements we made for this meeting over the telegraph would be kept between us. They were obviously leaked to Mr. Kimberly's employer and, well, you see the results. This hardly is the welcome I had planned for you to my newspaper. Under the circumstances, I'll understand your reluctance to do more than to take your leave."

Carlton began to bellow as soon as the three men left. He stormed around Grainger's office, but Grainger sat motionless. He knew he'd been bested. For his part, Benjamin went to his table and began writing. Within twenty minutes, he returned to Grainger's office and asked that he consider redoing the front page of the evening's paper to find room for what he'd prepared.

*An open letter to Henry McComb from the people of Philadelphia:*
*We know you are one of the owners of the firm building the transcontinental railroad. You are discharging a public trust, spending our government's dollars in that effort, and yet you will not answer our questions about the cost or the method of your work. Mr. McComb, it is time for you and your cronies to let the sun shine into the room. What*

*was the actual cost to build the first hundred miles of the road? What were you paid for that work? Was any portion of the road let on contract after the work already had been completed? You cannot hide from these questions forever, Mr. McComb. Make a clean breast of it now.*

"You got everything you needed out of Dey on the way over, didn't you, Benjamin? By God, Grainger, I've trained him well." Carlton was screaming to Jesse Greene to hold the presses because the paper was being redone. "I know it's going to cost money, but this is big, Greene, bigger than anything you can imagine.

Grainger simply smiled at Benjamin's initiative. "You remind me of what it was like to be young, Benjamin. Thank you for that." But then, before Benjamin could say anything, Grainger lowered his voice. "I like this piece, Carlton, but I think we need to wait a few days before running it. We need to let passions subside. We need to let Mr. Dey return to Baltimore. He's had enough of a shock without burdening him with a letter tonight. I doubt his sister wants or deserves rocks through her window. Beyond that, Benjamin, this might be a good time to have your wife and son visit her father. I'm not at all sanguine about where all this will lead."

# 29

BENJAMIN WANTED TO CARRY Stephen to the station. Susanna said it was too cold. She insisted she take him in her papoose. It was a great swath of red fabric Gwendolyn Nicholson fabricated to carry her babies around when they were little. Stephen was swaddled to her chest. He was beginning to hold small objects in his hand, so to occupy his attention Susanna gave him the brown wooden bird Benjamin's Uncle Curtis had carved.

Susanna's decision to visit her father came with almost no discussion between them about whether it was the right thing to do. Abigail Grainger paid another visit. Susanna was packing when Benjamin arrived at their rooms.

"You might have had the decency, Benjamin, to tell me you'd gotten yourself deeper into this Henry McComb story. I had to learn from Mrs. Grainger that you actually met with Peter Dey and pumped him for information about the way the owners are over-charging the government for their work. Was I supposed to learn of that meeting when I unfolded the paper wrapped around another brick through our window?"

Benjamin reached out to touch Susanna, but she turned and continued folding her things. "Susanna, it's not like that at all. McComb intervened before we could talk to the man. We haven't decided what we're going to do. There's no need for you to go." Benjamin didn't know whether to be grateful or angry that Grainger had made his decision for him. Benjamin had struggled for two days with the question of whether to raise the point with Susanna. He owed her that much, but she had been so fragile of late. He feared what the very conversation itself would do to them. That Abigail Grainger had done so meant that her husband had decided to plunge even deeper into the battle. Seeing Susanna pack her things, Benjamin wished he'd been the one delivering the message. That, at least, would have saved the scene he was about to endure.

"Don't ask me to believe that, Benjamin. Mrs. Grainger would hardly suggest I spend some time at the farm with our son unless something was afoot. As bad as anything was that I had to hear it from her and not from you. Choose your work over your family if you must, but at least show me the respect I deserve. We've known each other since we were children. I bore you a son." If Susanna had tears for their parting, she had used them all up. Her face was rigid. Her eyes solidly dry.

"I don't want you to leave, Susanna. There's no danger."

Susanna sighed. "Benjamin, let's not start down that path again. We both know where it will lead. You're not prepared to give up this quest you're on and I'm not prepared to risk my child's safety over it. Do what you must do. I'll be at my father's. You know where to find us once." Susanna stopped. "I should say if. You know where to find us if you figure out what's important in your life. The train leaves within the hour. We'd better go."

It was bitterly cold, unusually so a couple of weeks before Christmas. Susanna bundled the baby close to her body. She didn't knock on Gwendolyn Nicholson's door, didn't look back for one last memory of the house. Perhaps the visit to her father's really was intended to be only temporary. Whatever its intended duration, as they turned onto Grace Street for the four-block walk to the station, Benjamin's pang of separation was genuine.

"Is there any talking to you about this? I thought we were going to discuss balance in our lives, not that you'd just walk out like this."

"Benjamin, please. I've already wired my father. He's expecting us. It will be two weeks, perhaps three. Candidly, you could use a little loneliness right now. It will help you think about what it would be like not to have us around forever. Your choices will be clearer, Benjamin, unless you're so intoxicated by the life you've built for yourself at the paper your choice already has been made."

"Can't we talk about this as man and wife?"

"We have, Benjamin. I've talked but you haven't listened. This is the right thing for us at the moment."

They walked quickly, but quietly. Stephen fussed. Susanna pulled his hat around his ears, adjusted him in her sack. Benjamin wanted to help, to have some bit of contact with his son, but his hands were full with their bags.

Of all the people he expected to see on this walk to the station, Henry McComb's clerk was the last person he wanted or anticipated. But there he was—the one whose name he still didn't know although he'd seen him at both the fire behind the *Courier* and the other day with Kimberly—and Benjamin moved close to Susanna to avoid the awkwardness of the need to feign any introductions or even an acknowledgment. It was early evening. The streets were crowded with people and wagons.

They turned right on Potter's Lane. Stephen was complaining. Susanna fished through her fabric cradle. "He's dropped his bird."

"I'll go back for it."

"No. You go buy the tickets and find someone to deal with the bags." She turned in the direction from which they'd come. Benjamin waited, assuming she'd be back in a minute or two. He thought about what to say when she returned. Susanna couldn't leave, even for a week, with this cloud hanging over their head. He wanted to somehow find a word to assure he understood her concern, that he acknowledged what she was going through and they'd be together soon. *Susanna, listen to me for a minute. I love you and know that you're always going to be part of my life. I know how hard it is for you to deal with this. Most importantly, I know that we'll get through this and that we'll be together forever. Think of that in the week that we're apart.* They'd kiss, and there would be a promise of renewal. That's the best that he could hope for. He was certain—hopeful perhaps was a better choice of word—Susanna would accept his message as the love offering he wanted it to be and they would at least be left with the sense that better times lay ahead.

The small chestnut bird was on the sidewalk. It was no more than thirty feet from the corner. Susanna crouched to pick it up. She was holding Stephen's head with her other hand. Her back was to the street. If she heard the wagon she certainly couldn't see it. A man shouted. Then there was a woman's scream. Two horses had broken loose from their hitching post. They were charging down the street. The load of bricks they were hauling was being thrown from side to side. The raging animals were heading from the part of the street Susanna and Benjamin had left, from the direction in which McComb's clerk was going when he passed them. Despite the load they were carrying, the horses were moving too fast now for anyone to stop them.

Benjamin heard the crash from around the corner, a great explosion of falling bricks and the screech of the wagon's side against the pavement. The wagon broke free from the horses and splintered into a wall. The horses furiously charged down the street.

Benjamin looked for Susanna and Stephen but only saw the mass of bricks and the wagon on its side. He didn't know how far she'd walked to retrieve Stephen's bird. His view behind the pile of debris was obscured. He presumed they were just beyond his vision. He waited for her to walk around the pile in the direction of the station.

A thick, red pool of liquid stained the pavement. It was pouring onto the street from under the bricks and shattered wood. A woman screamed, "There's someone trapped under here!" Men began throwing bricks off the pile. Benjamin and another man righted the wagon. Benjamin looked across the street and saw McComb's clerk. He was standing with his arms folded.

Susanna had cradled herself around Stephen. A man who had been throwing bricks off the pile cried out, "There's a child. Is he alive?" The witnesses' screams were frenzied and filled with fear. "There is a woman under there who appears to have been crushed by the bricks, and she was holding a child. Hurry. In the name of God, move all this debris. Is the baby alive?"

Benjamin approached the policeman who was holding the baby. He looked at Susanna's body, still wrapped in a fabric now soaked with her blood. He could barely get the words out. "That is my son. That is my wife."

"My God, man. What a horrible accident. You were fortunate to have been spared." Benjamin was silent, numb. Stephen was fussing. Benjamin looked at the ground. He bent to Susanna. The bricks were off her now. She was still. He brushed away the hair from her face. He took his handkerchief out of his breast pocket and rubbed some of the dust off her skin. She was as lovely as the morning he awoke to see his new wife for the first time. The policeman put his hand on Benjamin's shoulder. Benjamin touched Susanna's cheek.

"We'd better go, son." The policeman was whispering, but his grip on Benjamin's shoulder was firm. Benjamin knelt and kissed Susanna. She was still warm. He wondered when she would awaken. He began to shake. He felt so cold, so terribly frightened. The policeman again said Benjamin needed to get his son into a place where it was warm.

Benjamin opened Susanna's hand and took the small bird for which she died.

# 30

THEIR ROOMS SMELLED OF THE LIME in the cream Benjamin bought Susanna to rub on her chapped hands and of the soap she used to wash her hair.

Benjamin had no idea how he had gotten to his quarters after the accident, only that he was surrounded by a cluster of people. Gwendolyn Nicholson was holding Stephen to her chest and wailing about his mother's untimely end. The Reverend Nicholson had his hand on Benjamin's shoulder, whispering how God has a plan for us all and Benjamin must find the purpose of the tragedy and to build something good upon it. The police officer who picked up Stephen from the sidewalk, the Nicholson children, neighbors who Benjamin had seen in his daily comings and goings. Jesse Greene. People were eating and then saying things to Benjamin he could barely hear. Strangers talked among themselves and then left, only to be replaced by others. The sound of dishes being washed in the background, the smell of coffee. Someone put a plate of food on Benjamin's lap and then the plate was gone. Carlton was there and then he wasn't. And then he was again. T.P. and Mrs. Grainger came and went. Abigail Grainger said something about how awful she felt that she suggested Susanna visit her father. Or was that something Gwendolyn Nicholson said when she wasn't blubbering about losing someone as close as a sister, even closer? The room was crowded with people and then food and then there were fewer people. Stephen was awake and then asleep. It was light outside the window and then dark and then light again. Benjamin got himself dressed and cleaned and changed Stephen. There was a carriage ride to Grayton where Blaine Michaels led a service. Susanna was placed in a hole in the ground. There were more people at her father's home, more food, and mercifully, some quiet. One day smudged into the next, as though someone had put a potion in Benjamin's eyes to obscure his vision.

There was one image that Benjamin couldn't shake. It haunted him in the daylight, when he walked past the spot where Susanna had been trampled. He left a flower there each morning on his way to the *Courier*. Some mornings he'd leave a rose. On others, a tulip or a morning glory. He knew that not long after he left the memorial it would be stepped on or thrown into the street, but it didn't matter so long as Susanna's spirit knew he was remembering the short time they'd had together.

The image returned to Benjamin in the evenings, when Stephen was fussing and he would take him from his crib and walk him around the rooms they still occupied. Gwendolyn Nicholson cried constantly at the thought Susanna was lost, but she treated Stephen as though he was one more of her children. Rachel came at once and stayed with Benjamin and Stephen for weeks on end. But it was clear in time their lives were separate and they didn't belong together.

It wasn't the picture of Susanna beneath the bricks, or even of her grave in the fields around her home in Grayton. It was the image of McComb's clerk, standing across the road while the frenzied citizens tried to save the poor woman who'd been caught in the wrong place at the wrong time. It was the picture of the man with his arms folded as if to say that he'd accomplished what he'd set out to do. The man now had a name. Ansel Parker. The same Ansel Parker who stood in front of Grainger's office, holding an envelope with Grainger's name on it.

Parker was perhaps twenty-five. He was dressed in a gray suit coat. His pants didn't match. His shoes were surprisingly dirty for someone who frequented the rarified atmosphere of Henry McComb's office. If Ansel Parker were training to be a lawyer, he was beginning his apprenticeship as a common delivery boy.

Parker's calling card identified him as a clerk to the law offices of Henry McComb. He referred to himself as McComb's second assistant. His voice was high, almost comically squeaky at times, when his nervousness showed through. "I've been asked to deliver this package from Mr. McComb and to await Mr. Grainger's response, if you don't mind."

"You'll get a response in good time, young man." Mercer Carlton didn't bother opening the envelope before filling his spittoon.

"My instructions, sir, are to wait for a reply. Unless you forcibly remove me from the premises, I'm going to do just that."

"We lock the door at seven. You'll be on the other side of it, I can assure you of that."

Carlton barked to Benjamin to come into his office. "Find a spot for this lad to stand where he won't touch anything. His employer asked that he wait for a response for whatever is in this envelope." Carlton put the unopened envelope on his desk. "It's addressed to Grainger, who won't be returning from New York until this afternoon." Carlton looked toward the messenger. "Mr. Parker, you're not welcome to sit, or to talk to anyone, to drink our water or to use our privy. But if you want to stand in a corner like a coat rack for the next seven hours, it's not my province to stop you. Benjamin, please escort—" Carlton paused and fished the business card from his desk, to show the man his name meant so little to him that he'd already forgotten it, "—Mr. Parker over to the corner. Ask one of the Negro boys to keep an eye on him so he doesn't fish through anyone's pockets." Carlton laughed at the opportunity to tweak old Henry McComb by treating both his message and the messenger with such disdain.

Benjamin spent the morning watching Ansel Parker with some bemusement, first that Carlton would tether him like some animal and then that Parker would allow himself to be treated that way. His anger began to rise, however, as he watched the man stand in the same spot for over four hours without moving, his arms folded as they had been the evening of Susanna's death, mocking the *Courier* as he mocked Benjamin.

For weeks after the accident, Benjamin had been certain he'd seen Parker that evening, certain he was the man with the self-satisfied smirk on his face, but in time (and it had been four months now; Benjamin had eventually settled into a routine of leaving Stephen with Gwendolyn Nicholson in the morning so he'd have time to work) nothing seemed certain. Once the flood of visitors and tears had subsided, once the fog began to lift and the reality of Benjamin's loneliness and of Stephen's complete dependence settled in, Benjamin talked to the policeman who first held Stephen. He wanted answers, wanted to be told why the horses had become unleashed, why the police hadn't arrested someone for creating a dangerous and deadly situation, or worse, why someone had intentionally set the horses on their destructive path. Benjamin was told only that he lived in a dangerous world where terrible things can happen and that he should be grateful his son survived the misfortune.

When Benjamin left for lunch he had to brush past Parker to get his coat. When he returned to the room, the man still was there, rigid as a statue.

Benjamin fidgeted at his desk, unable to delay any longer for fear that Grainger might return, and answer whatever message Parker had brought before they might have a chance to speak.

"I saw you, you know."

## Chapter 30

Parker seemed more surprised than annoyed. He hadn't spoken in hours. He hesitated. It was as if he had to relearn how to speak. "Excuse me?"

"I saw you. You were across the street from where my wife was killed. You untethered the horses. I'm certain of it. You watched your handiwork and then reported to McComb that your effort to silence me, to end my investigation into his dealings with Ames, had accomplished its goal. I'm certain of that."

"You're wrong, sir. I don't doubt you're heartbroken. It was a terrible thing that happened. I wouldn't wish something like that on my worst enemy. But, my God, man, to suggest I would be responsible? That's blasphemy. I'd never in a million years think of doing anything remotely like that and I'd challenge any man who even hinted I might."

"Don't hide behind your threats, Parker. You will answer to God for what you've done. Of that I'm certain." Benjamin didn't let Parker interrupt what he was saying. "I don't look at my child without thinking about what you did to his mother. I don't reach out to the empty space in my bed without knowing you killed her. Don't underestimate me."

Benjamin walked away before Parker could respond. He was certain of his purpose, his conviction. "Let McComb come after the *Courier*. Let him try."

He found himself outside the *Courier* in the damp and relative cool of an early April afternoon, without a coat or hat almost before he realized what he'd done. His hands were shaking, his throat parched. He began walking, first turning left and then right. The only thing of which Benjamin was aware was the need to keep moving.

Benjamin made it to his home. Gwendolyn Nicholson was surprised to see him. "Are you feeling well, Benjamin? You look ashen."

Benjamin realized how odd he must have seemed, his coat wet, his hair down matted to his forehead, standing in front of the woman in the middle of the afternoon without any apparent purpose. "Thank you. I'm fine, really. A bit stressed from work, perhaps, but fine. I was hoping to see Stephen."

"The darling is sleeping. I just put him down. I'm reluctant to wake him. He was fidgeting all morning with his teeth coming in. The poor boy needs his rest." She put the back of her hand on Benjamin's forehead. "Perhaps you should lie down yourself, or let me get you some water."

Benjamin resisted being treated like a patient. He made his exit. He walked back toward the *Courier*, but found himself almost instinctively drawn to the spot where Susanna died. The tulip he'd placed along the wall in the morning was largely intact, a bit faded and partly chewed. Benjamin picked it up. He sat on the curb. The street was filled with wagons and horses and people moving in all directions. No one even noticed him, or if they did, they passed him by.

The great sea of time washed over this place. The world moved on, shed its memory of that morning. There were lives to be lived, commerce to be conducted. It was as though Benjamin was the only person in Philadelphia still frozen in the horror of that moment.

What is the life of one woman—however unfulfilled, however tragic in the way in which she left the earth—when there is progress to be made?

# 31

HORACE GREELEY STOOD about a half a head taller than Benjamin. His handshake was firm, for a man older than Benjamin's father by a great deal, older even than Grainger. He wore a high white collar and black silk tie. His small wire-rimmed glasses and fringes of white hair curling out from behind his neck gave Benjamin the impression he was greeting Benjamin Franklin himself. He might as well have been. To anyone in the country calling himself or aspiring to be called a newspaperman, the founder and editor of the *New York Tribune* was descendent from Olympus.

"Wright?" Greeley cupped his hand over his ear to be certain that he picked up Grainger's introduction. "I admired your piece about the Omnibus Bill. Damned fine journalism."

Benjamin blushed. "Thank you, sir, but I should be the one complimenting you on the ability to write in a way that inspires men to think beyond the narrow space of dirt we occupy. *Go west, young man, and grow up with the country.* I can't set foot on a train or watch the sunset without repeating those words from your editorial."

Greeley nodded. "Then from one newspaperman to another, Benjamin, feel free to follow that advice. It's an amazing place out there. Mountains. Rivers. Valleys so deep and fertile they'll feed the entire nation. And it's waiting to be discovered."

Benjamin smiled, nodded, and wished this conversation could go on forever. Greeley, however, wasn't about to let Benjamin forget who was in command. "You were one hundred and eighty degrees wrong, of course. Johnson was a drunk and a fool who deserved to be impeached, but you certainly can write. I even liked your piece on Ross, although I can't for the life of me understand what the man was thinking when he voted the way he did." Greeley spoke in dogma rather than in sentences.

Greeley stopped and extended his hand to Carlton, who had entered Grainger's office. "Mercer Carlton, my God, man, with all the demon rum you've put through your plumbing since I've known you it's a wonder you're still alive." They both chortled, and embraced like the old friends and friendly adversaries they'd been for years.

Grainger closed the door to his office. He spoke directly. "Horace asked a few of his old anti-slavery newspaper cronies up to New York to see if we'd support his running for President. Hell of a meeting. Nichols, Kingsley, Miller. It was as though it was 1856 and we were fighting the battle over how the new states treated slavery all over again."

Greeley laughed. "But the liquor was better this time and it washed down caviar."

"Listen, boys. I've decided to throw the *Courier's* voice behind Horace's bid." Grainger was animated. Benjamin shared his enthusiasm and hung on his every word. "Grant has proven to be so deep in the pocket of the special interests he can't see the light of day."

Greeley interjected. "He's surrounded himself with sycophants so busy praising him for saving the Union that he's unable to focus on the fact the government is being sold out from under him."

Grainger jumped in, "Or worse, maybe he knows what's going on and condones it. Either way, he's putting this country in a real pickle."

Carlton wanted to ask whether Greeley wasn't a bit of an odd duck for the public's taste, what with his publishing of Karl Marx and of his absurd notion that citizens should move into communes.

*Chapter 31*

But it was Grainger's paper and wading into the fray with the leading newspaper in the United States on a brass knuckles Presidential campaign would be too much fun to miss.

"Grant's vulnerable in the South, although it will be a question of which one of us they detest more down there. The real challenge will be to find enough mud to throw at Useless to get the Northern and Western states to turn on him."

Grainger turned to Benjamin. "Benjamin, this is where you come in. Horace is down here to meet with some supporters for a couple of days, but I thought you could spend a bit of time explaining what you learned about Henry McComb and the Credit Mobilier."

Benjamin was delighted to have another outlet for what he was learning about the whole affair. He looked forward to educating Greeley. His reverie was short lived, though, broken by Carlton's voice. "McComb? Great Jesus, that reminds me. Do you see that scarecrow standing by the coats, T.P.? He's been there since early this morning. He's waiting to deliver an envelope and to take your response back to McComb. Let me go find that damned envelope."

"McComb's the fellow who sued the Congressman from Massachusetts, right?" Greeley turned to Benjamin. "I'm going to need a list of the players, young man. Grainger tells me you're onto something big here. He also told me about your precious young wife. I'm so sorry to hear about that horrible incident. I understand you have a very young son. You are both in my prayers, Benjamin. Sincerely."

Benjamin was falling under the man's spell. He reminded him of Edmund Ross, at least in the certainty he had that a man could become an essential part of the government without bargaining his soul.

"Do you know of the Credit Mobilier, sir?" Benjamin paused but then continued when Greeley shook his head. "We believe it was established by the trustees of the Union Pacific Company to build the rail lines the railway itself was charged to construct. We have every reason to believe it is being used as a vehicle to steal money from the United States government."

"And the excess is going into the trustees' pockets. Is that where this story is heading?" It didn't take Greeley more than a few seconds to grasp the narrative of Benjamin's story. He continued speaking, "Greedy bastards. And I'd bet if I turned the page I'd find Grant's not doing a damned thing to stop them. Wouldn't surprise me to find his hands in the cookie jar as well."

Greeley had a high pitched laugh that didn't quite fit his body. "Prove that for me, Wright, and I won't stop at President. They'll make me the God damned King."

Greeley took Benjamin's right hand in both of his. He stared intently at Benjamin. "It's time the average citizen learned in minute detail what's really going on in Washington. Did all of those poor men on both sides of the Mason Dixon Line really die so the President can make his cronies even richer? If this story can help us get elected, by God sir, you will have done wonders for the reform cause."

Benjamin was careful not to blush. He felt himself getting warm. "I can't speak to the President's involvement, sir. We have no doubt the trustees are pocketing at least some of the money, but we have no proof of that as yet."

"We'll smoke that out."

"Likely we will. All we know as of now is that McComb is claiming that several hundred shares of stock that Oakes Ames was given belonged to McComb. They must be quite valuable or he wouldn't have gone to the trouble of suing a member of Congress."

"Do you know what Ames did with his shares? Did he sell them at a profit?"

"That hasn't been established. McComb hasn't been cooperative."

"I should tell you, Horace, McComb is backed by Jay Cooke. They offered to purchase the *Courier* to stop my investigation. They even threatened to start a rival paper to put me out of business." It was odd to Benjamin that Grainger didn't mention either the bricks that had been thrown at them or the fire behind the *Courier*. Benjamin was unable to think of anything other than the weapon that shattered his life. He held himself back, concerned about showing fear.

"You'll all have jobs at the *Tribune* if that happens, T.P.. Any man with the backbone to stand up to slavery with as powerful voice as you did is a friend for life. Even Jay Cooke's millions can't silence the *Tribune*."

Carlton returned. He handed Grainger the envelope Ansel Parker had delivered when the *Courier* opened its doors. "Shall we open the envelope or drink until closing time and then throw the boy out, T.P.?"

"Perhaps both, Mercer. Let's see what McComb has to say that it was necessary to have his boy wait all day for a reaction."

Grainger slit the envelope with his knife. There were two pieces of paper inside. He read silently. He passed the papers to Greeley without comment. Greeley read them once. He wiped his glasses before reading them a second time.

"My God, T.P., I think I've just been handed the keys to the White House."

# 32

"STEPHEN, YOU'LL NEVER BE ABLE to imagine the day I had."
Gwendolyn Nicholson had just bathed the baby and put him into
his sleeping gown. He smelled of the same mint soap Susanna
used. Benjamin closed his eyes. He imagined she was just in the
next room.

Benjamin was carrying his son in his arms, talking to him at
a thousand miles an hour. Stephen looked at his father with large,
smiling, dark brown eyes.

"Horace Greeley, of the *New York Tribune* came to the *Courier*,
Stephen. *The* Horace Greeley. He's an old friend of Grainger's. I sat
there and listened while they talked about his running for President
against Grant. He's going to do it, Stephen, and I'm going to be
involved. The Credit Mobilier is going to be smack in the middle of
the campaign for the office of the Presidency and I'm going to blow
the story sky high. Every man in the country will know the Wright
name, Stephen. Yours and mine. Every man of every color. And
we're going to take a strong stand for a cause that will help restore
some decency and honor to Washington, Stephen. You won't have a
chance to know your uncles, but you'll grow up knowing they died
for a purpose, Stephen."

Stephen looked at Benjamin with what Benjamin assumed to
be tenderness. He had his mother's eyes. They were beginning to
shut, so Benjamin whispered. "I'm so sorry, Stephen. I've only been
talking about myself. I should have asked about your day. Soon

enough, you'll have stories to tell. If your mother were here she'd tell me all about it." Benjamin kissed his son. He held him against the warmth of his body.

"I'm so sorry for taking your mother away from you, Stephen. She never would have left if I hadn't been so involved in this story. She was so afraid for your safety. But you understand I'd never do anything to hurt you, don't you, Stephen? If you were older you'd understand why this story is so important. You'd understand what the information I've been uncovering can mean for the country. These men are stealing from the government and there's no one lifting a finger to stop them. They'll pay for their lies, Stephen. I owe it to your generation to expose them for what they're doing."

He put the baby in his crib. Stephen yawned, but was too tired to complain much and soon enough was asleep. "Your mother was excited about the story, Stephen. She loved the idea."

The windows rattled, as if to criticize Benjamin on that point. He reached into Stephen's crib to adjust his blanket around his back. "I didn't mean to leave you without a mother, Stephen. I didn't mean to drive her away. Believe what I'm telling you. She was so young, Stephen, barely twenty. We had our whole life in front of us. You would have been surrounded by brothers and sisters, but now, who knows? Will you ever forgive me for that? Will you forgive me for being so selfish I denied you a mother?"

Benjamin took the baby's things Gwendolyn Nicholson washed and folded and put them in the drawer of the cupboard. Susanna's clothes still were there. There were so many needy people in Philadelphia who could use them, but Benjamin wasn't ready to let go. He needed to be reminded of what he'd done to the woman. "Stephen, my mother wrote I should take you out to the farm. She thinks this is no way to live. I've been spoiled by Gwendolyn Nicholson, but I can't ask her to look after you forever. That's unfair to her. Mother said you'd be around my Uncle Curtis's children. You'd have room to run around, hills to climb, streams to fish. She said the city is no place for a boy to be raised. She's unhappy I'm working at the paper. She wants me to come back to the farm. I can't do that, Stephen. You understand that, don't you? I can't give up my writing. We'll figure something out, boy. Maybe you can visit the farm for a while. You wouldn't think I'd abandoned you if you went there for a few months, would you, Stephen? I'd come see you all the time. Mother could bring you to the city."

*What kind of father will you be to our children, Benjamin? The kind that doesn't abandon them.* Benjamin caught himself. His father must have gone through the same rationalization before leaving him alone with Rachel. He was about to do the same thing. He was about to leave the woman with a child who couldn't fend for himself to pursue some crazy notion that it was his responsibility to save the country.

*This is different.* Benjamin poured himself a drink from one of the bottles of whiskey left behind by someone in the crowd that called on him after the accident. He hadn't been accustomed to doing that before Susanna left, certainly not alone. But he wasn't alone. He had Stephen in the room. The liquor warmed his throat, at first. It was reassuring to feel its touch, to be aware of something other than Susanna's absence from the rooms. Eventually, Benjamin knew it would dull his pain enough to let him sleep for a couple of hours before Stephen again would be awake and demanding his attention. Susanna always had gotten up with him, but then she was nursing. Benjamin would be half asleep listening to Stephen coo as she rocked their son back to sleep after his feeding. When it was truly cold outside (when the night was seeping through the boards Benjamin nailed to the window), Susanna would put Stephen between them in the bed and Benjamin would put his hand on his son's chest, to feel his breathing.

Benjamin knew that whatever was in the bottle would make his justifications easier both to articulate and then to accept, so he poured himself another drink. *I'm not abandoning Stephen as my father abandoned me. He's just too young for me to take care of him all the time without Susanna. I'm not prepared to marry again just so someone can raise the boy. I can't go back to the farm. There is nothing for me in Grayton. I belong in the newspaper business. This is only temporary. The story will run its course and I'll be reunited with Stephen. I'm not abandoning Stephen as my father abandoned me. This is different.*

A week later, Benjamin turned for one last look at his son in Rachel's arms as he headed east on the same road his fathers and brothers had taken to march into battle.

# 33

THE LIBERAL REPUBLICANS wanted to make a statement. They were unhappy with the way Grant turned Washington into a Turkish bazaar, offering what it had to sell to the highest bidder, so instead of throwing their support behind the leader of their party, they nominated Greeley for President. The Democrats couldn't quite figure out what they wanted, so after a fractured convention, they threw their weight behind him as well. In June the Republicans nominated Grant and the race was on in earnest.

By August, it was clear to anyone paying the slightest bit of attention (or to anyone simply skimming Thomas Nast's editorial cartoons tying Greeley to Boss Tweed so tightly Greeley was choking) that the prize was Grant's for the taking. On August fourth, desperate for the spark that would ignite his campaign, Greeley brought together a group of anti-Grant editors to the *Tribune*'s office in New York.

The heat was stifling, both inside and outside the building. The ice vendors were fortunate if half their cargo was left in the wagon by noon. There never seemed to be enough straw or sawdust to insulate the wagon against the blistering temperature or enough men to keep young boys from trying to steal what they could.

Benjamin was accustomed to seeing people sleep in the park to get out of the still air in their rooms; he'd even done that himself in Philadelphia. But there were so many people laid out in Reservoir Square the night he arrived with Grainger and Carlton that when they had to walk to Greeley's offices (the heat being far too taxing for the horses) he thought the mayor had ordered all New Yorkers to attend the same picnic.

Of the twenty men in the room, only Greeley kept his coat on. Greeley hired four Negro boys to stand in each corner pulling ropes he'd attached to ceiling fans, but they did little more than push the smoke from the men's cigars into whorls that gave the room the feel of a séance. Benjamin was younger than all the men in the room by a good ten years, maybe twenty. Grainger made the introductions, but they were a blur of papers he'd read and of names he'd seen on mastheads. Kittinger of Boston, Edwards from Chicago, Johnson from Kansas City. Anyone who could shape opinion, anyone who could scratch out a few votes for Greeley's faltering campaign, had been summoned.

Greeley spoke first, thanking people for their time, reminiscing about the dragons they'd all slain in the past. His voice was a bit hoarse. He explained he'd given a speech in Buffalo and then had traveled all night on the train to get to this meeting. "We have our work cut out for us, gents, I'm not going to run from that fact, but who in this room hasn't reveled in a good fight before? Everyone says I'm so far behind the old man I can't smell the back of his horse. To that I say the voters won't even pay attention to this race until the weather breaks in October. And when they start paying attention, we have just the sort of information they're going to want to hear.

"You all know T.P. Grainger of the *Philadelphia Courier*. T.P. stood shoulder to shoulder with us on all the important issues before the war and he's still there. There's a bit of a dust-up going on in his courts our friend Ulysses isn't going to like one bit."

Grainger went to the front of the room. He motioned for Benjamin to join him. Benjamin's throat was so dry he was afraid that he might not be able to get any words out. Greeley's staff set out ice water, but almost as soon as they refilled the pitchers the ice melted. The glasses were sweating as much as Benjamin. However, warm, the water at least freed Benjamin's voice.

"We've discovered a theft from the government of epic proportions. Millions. Tens of millions are involved." There wasn't a bit of hesitancy in Grainger's voice. "It involves the transcontinental railroad construction project."

"Where else could someone find that kind of money to steal?" Benjamin didn't recognize the speaker, a man with a pinched face and generally sour disposition. His face was beet red, either from the heat or from the life he'd lived up to the point of this meeting.

"Horace, you don't propose to turn this election around because someone overcharged for railroad ties, do you?" Benjamin recognized Charles Dana of the *New York Sun*. Dana had congratulated Benjamin for what he'd written about Senator Ross. "This is a matter of contract. It's been what, three years since the line was finished? Pilots touching head to head. Every school child in the country knows that poem. The American people are damned proud of this railroad. People are rushing out to California to build new lives for themselves and are thrilled with the opportunities they're finding out there. The voters aren't going to throw out a President who gave them the future itself over a few dollars."

Greeley spoke. "We're talking about tens of millions, not a few dollars."

"Horace, you're challenging destiny itself. This isn't going to move anyone to vote for you or against Grant unless the money ended up in his pocket. You didn't bring us here in this Godforsaken weather for this, did you?" Asa Wood of the *New York Daily News* waved his cigar in his right hand like a flag of surrender.

"Calm down, boys." Greeley gestured with both of his hands. "Don't let the heat get to your heads. This is more than some construction company cheating on a contract. Benjamin, take the floor. Let's talk about your friend Mr. McComb's lawsuit and what you've turned up about it."

Benjamin opened his satchel. He removed a folder, put it on the table in front of him, and one-by-one took out three pieces of paper. The gesture struck him as corny, but he was following the script Carlton had devised and Greeley had approved. If the editors of the leading Democratic papers in the country didn't find the energy in the report Benjamin was about to deliver, how could their readers?

"Gentlemen, I'm about to read from a letter that Oakes Ames, a congressman from Massachusetts wrote to Henry McComb, an attorney. The letter is dated Washington, January twenty-fifth, eighteen sixty-eight."

Benjamin paused for a moment. The editors were as silent as Greeley predicted they would be. Even the Negro boys who were supposed to be moving the air in the room stopped to hear what Benjamin was about to read.

"Dear Sir: Yours of the 23d is at hand, in which you say Senator Bayard and Fowler have written you in relation to their stock. I have spoken to Bayard but not to Fowler. You say I must not put too much in one locality. I have assigned as far as I have gone to four from Massachusetts, one from New Hampshire, one Delaware, one Tennessee, one Ohio, two Pennsylvania, one Indiana, one Maine and I have three to place, which I shall put where they will do us the most good. I am here on the spot, and can better judge where they should go."

Benjamin looked up from the paper. "There's more in this letter, which you all can review at your leisure. In the portion I just read, Mr. Ames is explaining the method by which he decided to deliver shares of stock in a company established to build the railroad at inflated prices to various members of Congress. The company was named the Credit Mobilier. We'll explain the workings of that entity in a short while."

Benjamin put the first piece of paper on the table and retrieved another. "I'll now read portions of a second letter Mr. Ames wrote to Mr. McComb approximately one week after this first letter. Dear Sir: Yours of the 28th is at hand. I don't fear any investigation here. What some of Durant's friends may do in New York courts can't be counted on with any certainty. I have used this where it will produce the most good to us."

The men in the room stirred. *Bribery? Who would be so foolish as to put into writing a plan to buy votes from a legislator?*

"I have one more piece of information to impart. I'm about to read a list of names prepared by Mr. McComb during a meeting with Mr. Ames where the latter was identifying those representatives who had been bribed. The list includes Blaine of Maine, Patterson of New Hampshire, Garfield of Ohio, Kelley of Pennsylvania and most interestingly from the perspective of the Presidential campaign, Schulyer Colfax. We have made photographs of all of these documents for each of you so that you can review the complete list."

For men who trafficked in words, the editors were surprisingly silent, almost painfully at first. Benjamin took a degree of pride in the reaction he'd obtained. He heard the sounds of the horses on the street below. Moving from the front of the room, he gave a tug to the stilled ropes, causing the Negro boys to jump to the task of once again moving some air through the room.

Finally, Todd Kittinger of the *Boston Beacon* broke the silence with a deep New England baritone. "The public story about why Grant dropped Colfax as his running mate this time around was that he didn't like it that Colfax threw his lot in with the Liberal Republicans. Are you implying, Horace, that Grant knew Colfax took some of this stock when he was his Vice President and that he dumped him as insurance in case word of this ever got out? Are you suggesting the President is trying to cover this up? My readers certainly would be interested in knowing the answers to those questions. Mr. Wright, how did you come into possession of this material? Did McComb authorize its use?"

Benjamin looked to Grainger, then to Carlton. It was Greeley who answered. "What I'm about to say stays in this room." He lowered his voice, as if to underscore the need for discretion. "It's completely legitimate. McComb wanted some of the stock Ames was passing out to go to the congressmen and senators to whom he'd made promises, but he wasn't successful in getting Ames to deliver it. He made T.P. a business proposition. He elected to sell his letters and notes."

"Good God, T.P., you can't be serious. You didn't take him up on his offer."

"Grainger's hands are clean." Greeley spoke calmly. "There are people close to my campaign who understand the importance of such a charge in the last weeks of the election. They acquired the materials and allowed us access. It's very clean and very proper."

"Dare I ask the price?" Charles Dana was the first editor to ask the question, but several others nodded.

"Thousands. Let's just say several thousand and let it go at that." Greeley had lowered his voice.

"But surely there are records, trails of checks that can be followed, banking documents." Todd Kittinger led the request for details.

Greeley wasn't disturbed. He responded simply, "The men we're talking about had the resources to reach into their pockets, gentlemen. Greenbacks leave no footprints."

"And McComb, what is his story?"

"He'll deny the whole affair, of course. He'll say he's not a Greeley man and accuse some ruffian of breaking into his office to remove some papers. McComb is of no consequence, gentlemen. His reaction is little more than a sideshow. Let me show you something."

Greeley passed around copies of the afternoon edition of the *Tribune*. Ames' letter to McComb took up the entire first column.

Greeley used two full columns to highlight the words *Put Ames on the Stand.*

"Gentlemen, here's the issue that's going to get us into the White House. Is everyone on board?"

# 34

IT WAS STILL WARM in the middle of September. Fruit trees were ready to be harvested. Crops were still in the ground. Horses were in the field, cows in the milking barn and chickens scratched at the grain Stephen threw out for them. But with his mother gone, his first birthday hardly seemed time for celebration.

He was a happy enough boy, bright dark eyes hiding whatever sadness he felt for being without his mother, pulling himself up by grabbing on whatever he could to stand, pounding away at anything that might sound like a drum, fussed over by Curtis's three children as though he was their baby brother. He had Susanna's light color and the disposition she had as a girl, charging into things without fear. Benjamin strained to see himself in the boy, but Susanna's presence was so close and so vital it pushed aside all other possibilities.

Rachel baked a cake for the occasion and knitted Stephen a winter sweater. It was a bit big for him now, but by the time of the first snow would fit him just fine. Curtis mended one of the rocking horses his children had broken, painted it and presented it to a wide-eyed Stephen who took to the gift as though it was the most precious thing in the world.

One of the chickens pecked at Stephen, a rooster Rachel had named Joe. He was too aggressive to be around people and Rachel talked to Curtis about having him killed off, but Joe didn't let himself get caught all that easily and hid in the tall grass every time

Curtis came around. Stephen ran into the place where Joe was standing in the sun. The bird raised his wings and lunged after him. Stephen was more startled than hurt, but when he fell on his behind, the shock of it all frightened him and he let out a wail. Benjamin rushed to him.

Stephen squirmed. He resisted his father's touch, his squeals, as if a reproach, were saying, *who are you that you're picking me up when I need to be protected? I don't even know why you're touching me.* The boy screamed. He reached out for Rachel. She waddled slowly to Benjamin's side, her steps becoming more deliberate and more at risk, as though something was eating away at her limbs. She held the baby close to her cheek.

"There, there, Stephen, it's all right. Joe didn't mean anything by that. You know he's dumb as a bale of hay." Stephen gulped for air as he began to stop crying. He leaned his head against Rachel's shoulders. In a moment, he started to breath normally. Benjamin began talking to the boy in a soft voice. Stephen turned his head away from his father. Finally, Rachel put Stephen on the ground. He scooted off to join Curtis's kids in whatever mischief they were up to.

"I guess he doesn't know you all that well at the moment, Benjamin." Rachel barely tried to avoid sounding judgmental. She sat on a nearby bench and gathered her breath before speaking once again. Whatever illness was devouring her hadn't slowed Rachel's capacity for criticism. "You've only seen him what, three or four days in the past few months? He changes constantly, Benjamin. You can't expect him to know you or to react to you simply because you ride up and announce that his father is here. It takes time to nurture a relationship with a child, Benjamin. What did you expect would happen to Stephen while you were spending all of your time parading around the country with Mister Horace Greeley? Stephen grew. He became attached to those who are there for him."

The Credit Mobilier story had rocketed its way into the battle between Greeley and Grant. A day didn't go by without some newspaper reprinting Benjamin's articles about Ames' acknowledgment to McComb he was buying influence in Congress—including, most particularly, the vote of the Vice President—with the stock McComb was claiming. Almost every pulpit in America resounded with Sunday morning calls for Ames' ouster from Congress and for an investigation into how it was that matters had gotten to the point in Washington where votes could be so openly bought and sold. Town meetings and legislatures in every state were passing resolutions as fast as they could be printed demanding that Congress investigate the allegations.

And Benjamin was in the center of it all, giving speeches on Greeley's behalf or writing speeches and proclamations for others to deliver. New York one day, Chicago three days later, then St. Louis and Kansas City and then on to New Orleans. The campaign to see who would be sworn into the office in March of seventy-three consumed Benjamin with a passion he'd known only in the earliest days of his time with Susanna.

But what did Stephen know of such things? What did he know of political aspirations or mudslinging or whatever purpose was being served by all of this frenzy? He was a little boy who had been startled by a rooster who needed the comfort and assurance of someone he knew and most of all, trusted.

"I'll be here more often as soon as the campaign winds down, Mother. This separation isn't easy for me, either. But what I'm doing is important and ultimately will be for the best."

The disgust in Rachel's voice matched the expression on her face. "Men always say what they're up to is either critical or in the public interest when they want to justify ignoring everything that really is important in their lives."

She threw her arms into a big circle to emphasize how offended she was that Benjamin was following almost precisely in Jacob's footprints. "You're going to help Mr. Greeley change the world. He'll bring in his own broom to sweep the city of Washington clean after the mess Grant created. I can read the newspapers, Benjamin. But I don't have to. I've heard this all before."

"You needn't mock me, Mother. Respectfully, the stakes have changed. Government contractors stole millions of dollars from the American people. Someone has to hold them accountable."

"Benjamin, listen to what you're saying. You just buried a wife. You have a son who desperately needs a father. But like your father before you, you're abandoning him just at the moment he needs you the most in the name of some greater good that won't amount to a handful of spit. I'm hardly mocking you, Benjamin. I'm only trying to get you to see the world through my eyes because yours are too blinded by the sunlight surrounding your Mr. Greeley to see clearly."

"It will be only a short time, Mother." Would Benjamin have accepted the truth if it came from someone other than Rachel? Wasn't she saying the same thing Senator Ross had told him at Polly Fisk's?

"Your father said the same thing in the early days, Benjamin. I'll be back soon. I'll just be in Washington, which is no more than a two-day ride. That was several years ago, Benjamin. I long ago stopped asking if he'd be coming back."

"Rachel, Benjamin, let's light Stephen's candle and have some cake. It looks too delicious to wait any longer." Curtis's wife was a gentle woman. Her invitation was too right to ignore.

Curtis put a paper hat on Stephen's head. One of his children (Katherine, a bundle of charm of seven) tickled Stephen and made him giggle. Benjamin watched from a distance, careful not to frighten the boy at such a happy moment. He wished someone were here with one of those cameras that could capture the image. He wanted to keep this picture forever, of his son as bright and as joyous as he was at that instant.

More than that, he wondered if he should step into that picture, return to the land where he was raised, take another wife and give Stephen his own brothers and sisters. The image tempted him in a way, but then so did the life he'd be leaving behind. He looked at Rachel. She was kneeling next to Stephen, cutting his birthday cake, absorbed only in pleasing her grandson, showing the devotion to the boy she wasn't able to show Benjamin after she'd buried his brothers.

Rachel kissed Stephen. She began sharing pieces of the cake with those who had gathered around the baby. She seemed to have found a purpose for her life that was keeping her vital.

But at that very instant, Benjamin thought about Jacob. Did he have the same ambivalence Benjamin was wrestling with the morning he left Grayton forever?

# 35

"WELL, WE AT LEAST SHOULD TOAST the old man for a game fight." Grainger lifted one of the three glasses of bourbon he'd poured on his desk.

"Game fight? Great Jesus, T.P., he carried Maryland and six Southern states. Geronimo could have beaten Grant in the South and he's my collie." Carlton loved to laugh at his own jokes. This was a time when he had to see the humor in something.

It was almost a week since the votes had been cast. The final count at last was coming in. Grant was returned to the White House in a landslide.

"Listen to what the *Post* said. The Presidential election is over at last; and the nation breathes free in the security of its delivery from Mr. Greeley and his galvanized democracy."

"Galvanized? Greeley certainly could do that to an issue. Nobody had any doubt where the man stood, even if he had his head up his behind half the time."

"Let me go on. General Grant has saved the Union a second time, not from rebellion and dissolution as before, but from an uprising of office-seekers under the lead of an erratic, unstable and ill-advised philanthropist, from confusion and corruption and absurdity and babble and ink shed no end."

"Christ, T.P., that pretty much describes Washington any day of the week." Carlton picked a piece of cigar off the end of his tongue and spit.

"It's hardly a wonder Horace has taken to bed. The criticism of the man has been relentless."

"Relentless, but not entirely unwarranted, T.P. Horace is a bit of a utopian for the public's taste. And a bit of a nag, if you ask me."

"Not entirely unwarranted, perhaps, but unnecessarily cruel. I hate to think the election of a President turns on such half-truths and innuendo. The American people deserve better."

Carlton took the paper from Grainger. He peered over the top of his glasses. "The *World* doesn't seem to approve of Grant all that much either, although that doesn't surprise me. Marble never liked the man very much. He calls him the choice of a lesser evil. A Republican paper turning on its own before the final votes have been counted, taking him to task for not properly respecting the office and for allowing scandals like Ames passing out stock under the Capitol dome right under Grant's nose."

Carlton handed the paper to Benjamin. "Now you know we've hit a nerve with our story, T.P.. The Republicans are no more interested in reform than is the part of me that looks out for our profit. Honest government doesn't sell papers and doesn't make politicians rich. But they can't run from what we've uncovered. Henry McComb has put the *Courier* in the center of the universe, by God. Smack in the middle of the action." Carlton's voice gave away his enthusiasm.

"You're right on that, Mercer." Grainger nodded in agreement. "Word is that as much as the Republicans want this issue to go away they know it won't. The Democrats already have called for a Congressional investigation into the bribery as soon possible."

Grainger turned to Benjamin. "Do you have an appetite for another month or so in our nation's capital, Benjamin? There's no one more deserving in the entire country to see this story through to its conclusion. Your name has been on every byline so far."

Grainger looked toward Carlton. Carlton nodded and suppressed a smile, as if they were schoolgirls unable to hold a secret. "Benjamin, there is another reason we'd like you to go to Washington. Mercer has been talking for some time about how the *Courier* needs to do a better job of keeping up with what's going on down there. We've been relying upon the locals, but their allegiance is strained. With the telegram, having one of our own men sitting in Washington wouldn't be much different from having him in this very room. We'd like you to consider opening that office for us, Benjamin. You've certainly earned the right to do so."

Benjamin hesitated. He wanted to be certain his response had the same gravity and dignity of Grainger's question. It represented a remarkable step for the paper and even more so for Benjamin. "On one level, T.P., of course. I accept both the challenge and the responsibility with alacrity." Benjamin was proud he'd earned the right to address Grainger by his initials.

Carlton spoke. "It sounded as though there's another part to that sentence, Benjamin. Spit it out."

Benjamin was stirred by his doubts about whether he wanted to be part of this business much longer. Certainly, Grainger was a decent man. For all his bombast about being the guardian of the truth, though, Carlton was as relentless in the pursuit of his vision as any man who claimed to be conducting the people's business for the greater good and filling his pockets in the process. But there was no point raising any of that, as it would only invite endless debate that would resolve nothing.

"I'm worried about my boy. I've barely seen him in months. I've got to begin shaping a normal life with him."

"Take him along."

Benjamin laughed. "Take him to Washington? I doubt the smoke in the committee rooms will do him much good, even if I thought I could get any work done under those circumstances."

Grainger smiled. "It's likely the hearings will take place before the new Congress settles in. Mercer's right. Nobody will risk ignoring these charges. Pig-Iron Kelley has been implicated in the scandal. Our readers will want the details involving a Pennsylvania legislator as the story unfolds." The idea that Jacob worked for the man and might himself be drawn into the scandal depressed Benjamin.

"I am flattered by your confidence, T.P. Truly so." Benjamin bowed to Carlton. "And in yours, sir. But I have no quarters there. Housing is scarce in Washington and extremely expensive."

Grainger addressed Benjamin's concern with ease. "My sister has a townhouse on Nineteenth Street that's always empty around the holidays except for her house staff. She's off in her place in Louisiana where it's warmer."

"Oh, to have the good sense to marry money." As always, Carlton couldn't resist putting in his two cents. "And not even cotton money, where she'd now have to battle for those tariffs we've spent the past three months criticizing, but good, solid timber."

"Her husband's a decent enough man, Mercer." Grainger seemed sure of himself. "We maintained relations even during the war, although it hardly could be said we saw eye to eye on the issues. As for his money, he keeps a roof over my sister's head."

"Benjamin, wait until you see the roof T.P.'s describing. By the way, be sure to ask old Schuyler Colfax what it feels like to be labeled as a harlot who'd sell his office for a few shares of stock. It will be good to see such a pious bastard of a Vice President sweat a bit on the witness stand. Maybe the teetotaler will even start drinking."

Carlton emptied his glass and reached for Grainger's bottle.

"And if he did, it would do him some good."

# 36

Luke Poland had been a judge in Vermont before getting elected to Congress, so he seemed a natural choice to head the House investigation. The Republicans wanted to get this behind them as quickly and with as little fuss as possible. They needed someone above reproach to quiet the whispers and worse than that, the constant drumbeat of the newspapers demanding the facts be laid bare. They wanted the whole thing out of the way long before Grant took his second oath of office, so they even started their work well before their Christmas break. Even the name of his committee, the Select Committee to Investigate the Alleged Credit Mobilier Bribery, was enough to send Republicans into apoplexy.

If the Republicans thought the public would be distracted by their preparation for the holidays, though, they were terribly wrong. When word got out that Henry McComb would be the first witness, at ten o'clock on the morning of Friday the seventh of December, people lined up outside the Capitol at six to be sure to get a seat. Benjamin had the luxury of showing up just as the hearing was about to begin, having secured one of the few and coveted seats reserved for the newspapers for the duration of the hearings. Washington hadn't seen such crowds at a public meeting since Johnson's impeachment trial.

Poland was a tall man, slight of build, with an open face surrounded by short-cropped white hair and a neatly trimmed white beard. Four representatives joined him behind a long table that, like all the others in committee meetings, had been covered with green felt. Ten feet in front of them the table for the witness had two chairs. McComb was in one of them when Benjamin arrived. Benjamin didn't recognize the man next to him. McComb didn't seem surprised to see Benjamin enter the room.

Luke Poland had a soft voice barely heard over the hum of the crowd outside the door. "State to the committee what knowledge you have in regard to shares of Credit Mobilier stock disposed of by Mr. Ames to members of Congress."

McComb was too skilled a lawyer to risk getting caught giving statements to the Poland Committee that might conflict with or undermine his claim against Oakes Ames. "If the committee please, I would prefer to have them ask me specific questions and let me give direct answers. I have with me my sworn testimony in the suit in Pennsylvania which has been instituted on this subject, which, if the committee desires to examine, will give them all the information I have." The horse trading of using the marginal players to build a case against the real targets, the ones with title and power, had begun.

Poland began reading from one of the pages in the pile in front of him. "You stated in your testimony that three hundred and forty-three shares of the Credit Mobilier stock were put in the control of Oakes Ames and were given to members of Congress. You then were asked where you got that information and you said from Oakes Ames."

"Yes, sir. I repeat that answer."

Benjamin looked around the room. None of this was news to him. It was all background about the Credit Mobilier Benjamin had heard a dozen times before and had spoken or written about even more once the papers had been made public during the Greeley campaign.

There were perhaps sixty people sitting in four rows of chairs and another twenty or so standing behind them. Most were men, but the women in the crowd were dressed in winter finery that Benjamin was coming to expect as one of Washington's spectacles. Large, ornately decorated hats were all the rage among the prosperous women of most of the cities up and down the coastline and Washington was no exception.

Poland showed McComb the letter Ames sent him on January 25, the same letter Benjamin had read to the editors in the *Tribune* offices a few months before. There wasn't a person in the country who hadn't seen that letter and the others that followed, but Poland wanted no criticism of the manner in which he conducted his hearing.

He walked McComb through the steps of identifying Ames' signature, of the way in which the list of those representatives who received stock from Ames came into being as though he had to lay the foundation for their admission into evidence at the most formal of trials.

"Have you other letters from Mr. Ames?"

A clerk walked to the witness table. He took a single piece of paper from McComb and handed it to Representative Poland. "This letter purports to be from Mr. Ames. Do you recognize his handwriting?"

"I do. I have a photographed copy of the letter in front of me."

"The letter refers to the desire to have more friends in Congress and to the need to assure the Credit Mobilier's business will not be interfered with. What do you understand that to mean and did you ever have a discussion with Mr. Ames on this subject?"

"We had a discussion on that topic in New York in the first part of January of eighteen sixty-eight. The meeting was in Mr. Durant's office at the Union Pacific Railroad at the corner of Cedar and Nassau streets. We discussed the status of the stock. Mr. Ames said he had divided it among members of Congress."

"How did the list of names of the recipients of the stock from Mr. Ames come about?"

## Chapter 36

"I was taking notes as he was speaking. He was reading from a small green leather notebook he eventually put in his pocket. I recognized some of the names, such as that of Speaker Colfax, because they were men of some prominence."

"And the numbers next to their names of two and three, to what do they refer?"

"I understand that to mean the value of the stock in thousands of dollars."

"Did you ever discuss these letters with Mr. Ames?"

"I visited Washington earlier this year. We met at the Arlington House. His attorney was demanding I produce these letters. I offered to give him the letters and to deny their existence if asked, so long as I could get the shares that were rightfully mine."

"Did Mr. Ames respond to that entreaty?"

"He exhibited some petulance of feeling and told me I could publish any letters I had received from him and that everybody knows that members of Congress are bribed and everybody does it."

"Have you spoken to Mr. Ames since the publication of the letters?"

"I met him in New York at the Fifth Avenue Hotel. We had a little spat between us at the time. He and I have not spoken since."

The testimony ran on for well over an hour. One by one the other committee members asked McComb for further explanation of his intentions, or of Ames' motives. Benjamin wrote in his notes that the genie now was out of the bottle. Ames was implicated. Colfax was identified as using his power as Speaker to thwart a request by one of the members to investigate the railroad, which led Ames to comment on how their investment had paid off. Brooks of New York, a representative with great power over the railroads because of the committees of which he was a member, was shown demanding that fifty shares be placed in the name of his son-in-law so his own name would never be linked to that of the Credit Mobilier.

McComb the lawyer was at his skillful best, slowly dismantling and laying bare the wall Ames had built around his endeavors.

Benjamin was only partly disappointed Ames declined the opportunity to cross-examine McComb. It promised to be great theater, but Stephen would be awakening from his morning nap soon. If he hurried to Grainger's sister's house, Benjamin might be able to have lunch with his son.

# 37

McComb was the only witness of the day and the Credit Mobilier committee was the only business scheduled for the day, so Benjamin and Stephen had the luxury of having the Capitol almost to themselves. The building was empty except for a few guards and a large number of Negro women washing the floors. Congressmen, Senators and their staffs were out doing their holiday shopping, or heading home for the weekend.

A light snow was falling, so instead of spending the afternoon in the park, Benjamin decided to show Stephen the building where he spent his time when he left the house in the morning.

Rachel accepted Benjamin's request to take Stephen to Washington for the hearings with some reservations. Clearly, the boy needed to be with his father. Isn't that what she had protested? She was hard-pressed to argue when he telegraphed to say he'd made temporary arrangements for Stephen's care and that he'd be home in three days to pick him up. But at the same time, having Stephen around—and, more to the point, having him need Rachel's care and affection—gave her a focus so badly needed in her own life. They bargained that Benjamin would take Stephen for a week or two and that in all events they would spend Christmas at the farm.

Benjamin was ready to leave after Stephen had explored the building for well over an hour, but Stephen wanted one more chance to stare into the dome. Benjamin was lying on his back with Stephen's head on his stomach when they heard a woman's footsteps coming in their direction. Benjamin cupped Stephen's head in his hand and began to right himself when he heard a woman's voice.

"Don't stop what you're doing on my account, sir. I often do the same thing, occasionally at first light, when only the top of the dome is visible. I watch the sun sweep down the sides of the dome until the whole building is bathed in morning light."

Benjamin looked at the woman walking toward them. She had a white tunic over a long black skirt and a white beret. Her sleeves were bunched at her wrists. Long black curls fell out of her cap down her back.

Although the woman hadn't recognized him yet, Benjamin knew her at once. "Miss Ream? Vinnie Ream? We were introduced by Senator Ross. I'm Benjamin Wright. We met at one of Polly Fisk's parties." He stood and brushed the dust off both himself and his son.

"Mr. Wright? Of course. I'm sorry I didn't recognize you. I hardly expected to see you in the Capitol on a day when very little business is being conducted." Vinnie laughed. "And I certainly never expected to see you horizontal."

Vinnie knelt down and put her face close to Stephen. She reached out with her hand and touched his cheek, as though she were examining a piece of art. "And who is this handsome young man? Might he be your son?"

"This is Stephen Wright. Stephen, say hello to Miss Vinnie Ream. She's a very famous sculptress, Stephen. She fashioned the toes of President Lincoln that you were touching not long ago."

Vinnie looked around. "If my memory serves me correctly, your wife's name is Susanna. Is she here with you or is lying on the floor of the Capitol a treat reserved for the men in the family?" Vinnie smiled, and looked around the room, expecting to see Susannah exploring another part of it.

Benjamin paused. His voice softened. "I'm afraid that Susanna has passed on. There was a terrible accident in Philadelphia just over a year ago."

Vinnie gasped and drew her hand to her mouth. "Oh, I'm so sorry. I've been in Europe. I was working on the Lincoln statue, actually, in Italy. I'm so sorry to hear what you just told me."

"It's unlikely the news would have reached you in Washington in any event." Benjamin shifted Stephen on his lap as he spoke.

"You poor darling boy, to have lost your mother like that." Vinnie chose not to dwell on that topic. She touched Stephen's cheek and then leaned close to him. "Are you having fun looking at all the men's faces here?"

Stephen nodded. Then he smiled at Vinnie. Her skin was as smooth as the marble with which she worked, her eyes more hazel than brown. The idea she could just pick up and head to Europe fascinated Benjamin. He envied Vinnie's freedom to pursue her art wherever she was, but Vinnie was so transfixed with Stephen it was the wrong conversation to have at this point.

"Would you like me to show you where those faces get made, Stephen?"

"I was going to ask you, Miss Ream, what it was that brought you to the Capitol today. You weren't planning on looking up into the dome, were you?"

"I've been working. Mr. Mills' studio is just at the end of the hall. I'm in a competition now for a commission to create a memorial to Admiral Farragut. I've been working on my design. Come, let me show you the studio while there's some good southern light.

"The Lincoln piece really is quite magnificent. Stephen was admiring it earlier."

"Before you got flat on your back? Stephen, you have wonderful taste."

Vinnie fished for a key as they walked toward the end of the hall and then down a flight of stairs. "Have you corresponded with

Senator Ross at all? He was gracious enough to come to my wedding but I'm sad to say that we've lost touch."

"The poor man. He voted his conscience and they hounded him no end. I understand he's back in his native Kansas in the newspaper business. Candidly, Mr. Wright, I was happy to be in Europe for some time following the whole impeachment business. People were saying the nastiest things about the two of us."

"I heard no such rumors. They never made it as far as Philadelphia."

"It was scandalous. Senator Ross was a boarder in my mother's rooming house, so of course people presumed the worst about what I was up to behind closed doors. There was a whispering campaign that I took him to my bed to convince him to vote for the President."

"How unkind."

"At least I was able to obtain a commission that took me to Europe. I had the comfort of an ocean separating me from the gossip mongers." Vinnie sighed. "Washington, I fear, is a city where people can only express their disappointment in the outcome of an issue by destroying anyone they can find to blame for their failure. Things were quite unpleasant around here for some time. I hope whatever ill will still lingers doesn't get in the way of my being rewarded the Farragut commission."

"They're going to get more unpleasant for a while, I'm afraid. I'm here because the House is investigating an allegation that one of its members bribed others with shares of stock in a company building the transcontinental railroad. The implications could be quite severe."

"I've heard stories of that, of course. This is a very small town in the way gossip travels. This time, at least, which is almost refreshing. And of course I'm in this building all the time. My work brings me into regular contact with the prominent men of the day, who often pose for over an hour or more. Of course, we talk during those sessions. The Credit Mobilier business was quite the talk of the recent election, *n'est pas?*"

Vinnie opened the door to the studio. Benjamin never saw such a place. A long workbench ran along one side of the room. It was filled with partially completed busts, of clay and a few of other materials. A shelf above the table was filled with life masks and death masks of plaster. The floor had been swept, but it still felt gritty beneath his feet. The air tasted of dried plaster and clay. Bags of plaster lined another wall. There was a dry sink with a basin on top and behind it a curtain that blocked off a clean area where men could sit for their sessions with the artist.

Benjamin pointed to a mold above the table. "Is that Horace Greeley? I'd swear that's his exact likeness."

"You know Mr. Greeley?"

"I was the reporter who uncovered the claim the bribery committee now is investigating. Mr. Greeley has been acquainted with my employer for years. I was quite active in the portion of the campaign that publicized the scandal."

"What an odd coincidence. What a small world we live in, Mr. Wright. What are the chances of people our ages not only knowing men of such prominence as Senator Ross and Horace Greeley, but of playing roles in their histories? I read your stories about Senator Ross. I was impressed by the way you captured the man's decency and courage."

"And I'm impressed by the way you have captured Mr. Greeley. That's a perfect likeness of the man."

"Thank you for that. I sculpted Mr. Greeley several years ago. The bust now is in New York. He was a charming man. A bit eccentric, perhaps, but a delightful conversationalist. It's a shame the Presidential campaign drove him to his death bed. Politics has become such a ruthless business."

Vinnie took a mound of clay and began kneading it with her hands. "Stephen, would you like to sit next to me and to help me make something?" The boy scooted to her side. Benjamin rolled up his son's sleeves. Vinnie took his hands and began working with him to shape the clay. She whispered as her hands began to pull a small horse out of nowhere. It was no more than four inches high, but it was as real to Stephen as any horse he might have seen at his grandmother's farm in Grayton.

"Do you see the horse, Stephen? Can you see the nose, the ears?" Vinnie took a small wooden knife and began shaping the finer lines of the animal.

Stephen put his own clay down. He had no space for anything in his life at the moment except Vinnie's magic. "Horse." Stephen pointed and whispered the word, as if he were afraid if he said it too loud the animal might run away.

Benjamin marveled at the boy's openness to Vinnie. Stephen was far too young at the time of the accident to have interacted with Susanna in any meaningful way that was obvious to Benjamin. He only saw Stephen with Susanna as a frighteningly small object that might break if he was held too hard.

But here the boy was completely relaxed with a woman he'd never met, laughing and talking and most of all, trusting her. For her part, Vinnie seemed as natural with Stephen as she was with the materials in the studio, as able to draw a sense of wonder out of him as she was to draw the body of a horse out of a pile of clay.

"Would you do me the honor, Mr. Wright of allowing me to sculpt your son in clay? He has such a lovely and open face that I'd like to capture. I've been considering a bronze of a boy's head as a small project. I saw so many wonderful pieces in Europe. Here, the statuary is all of generals and statesmen. There should be an interest in the common man as well. What better way to start than with such a handsome child? Will you be in Washington next week? I'd only need a couple of hours."

"Actually, Mr. Ames will be in front of the committee Tuesday. I'm hoping it will be quite the confrontation." He wanted to talk to Vinnie as though she knew the whole story of the spat between McComb and Ames. But this was Stephen's moment.

"Then perhaps we could meet Wednesday afternoon? We'll have the studio to ourselves. Mr. Mills is away for the holidays."

It had been over a year since the accident. Benjamin had thought only of Susanna during that period. Was it time to move past his mourning for her loss? How do you measure the propriety of such a step? There certainly were no markers along the way that told Benjamin when it was appropriate to move onto the next phase of his life, but however this instant felt it wasn't as though it was an act of infidelity to Susanna. To the contrary. She was part of this scene, her warmth, the way she taught Benjamin how to want someone else—a woman in Stephen's life, and in his.

How could Benjamin be criticized for thinking of such things?

# 38

HOWEVER RELUCTANT Henry McComb wanted to appear as a witness, Oakes Ames relished the fight. His lawyer, R.C. McMurtrie of Boston, walked into the committee room on Tuesday morning with fifty printed copies of Ames' statement to the committee. He even distributed it to the newspapermen in the room before the hearing so the story could make the afternoon papers.

Whatever Luke Poland had in mind for the man, it was clear Oakes Ames had no intention of going gently into the night. Ames even bought a new cloak for the occasion, as if to flaunt the fact this investigation would not get in the way of his enjoyment of the good life.

Poland opened the meeting with some stiffness. He asked Ames to raise his right hand so he could be sworn in. McMurtrie interjected, saying that before the committee posed any questions, Mr. Ames had a statement he wanted read into the record. Poland granted the privilege.

"The charge is that Representative Ames distributed stock in the Credit Mobilier for the purpose of corrupting members of Congress. The charge is that while Mr. Ames paid the company the par value of the stock he gave to various members of Congress, the actual value of the stock when he delivered it was so much above what he paid that the difference was meant as a bribe."

McMurtrie paused, to be certain every eye in the room was on him. He waited until the room was entirely still, as if he'd rehearsed for this moment from the first that Ames retained him. "The charge is a complete fabrication."

McMurtrie wasted no time boring in on Ames' accuser. "Consider the character of the men involved. The allegations are based solely upon conclusions Mr. McComb chose to draw from letters Mr. Ames wrote to him and from statements Mr. Ames allegedly made to him."

He looked at his client as the victim he was trying to make him out to be. He then looked directly at Poland. "If those charges are even partially true, if Mr. Ames truly sought to subvert the workings of the Congress, then Mr. McComb was duty bound as a citizen and as a man schooled in the law to report those charges to the proper authorities."

McMurtrie slapped the table hard enough that the men in the room reacted to the gesture. "Did he do that? To the contrary. You will learn, gentlemen, that Mr. McComb's only interest was to profit from this venture, either from the earnings of the stock itself or from his efforts to coerce Mr. Ames into paying him to keep the papers secret."

He paused, gathered his papers. "That, gentlemen, is the matter you have before you. A passel of lies sponsored by a blackmailer."

Luke Poland interrupted. "Mr. McMurtrie, the committee gave you the right to read a statement of facts from the witness into the record. This is beginning to sound like your closing argument. I must ask that you constrain yourself to the fact gathering portion of this proceeding."

McMurtrie proceeded as if Poland hadn't spoken at all. "The evidence will be irrefutable that Mr. McComb only went public with the charge after Mr. Ames refused to buy Mr. McComb's silence This whole investigation rests on the word of a man who tried to blackmail a member of Congress. It wouldn't surprise me if the fact came out in these proceedings that the only reason that the charge even saw the light of day was Mr. McComb then sold his story to the Greeley camp, which was so desperate to find a way to deflect the public's admiration of the President that it would pay anything to get its hands on these allegations."

"Mr. McMurtrie, I will warn you only one more time."

"Gentlemen, to understand the totality of Mr. McComb's fabrication you must understand the history of the effort to raise funds to build this most noble of public works projects."

McMurtrie had a deep baritone voice. He began reciting the difficulty of raising capital in the early years of the project, the enormity of the task at hand. Benjamin had no need to write down anything McMurtrie was saying, as it was all in the text he'd circulated. Benjamin already hired a boy to run the text to the telegraph office so Carlton would have it in time to print it on the afternoon paper's front page. He had the luxury of watching the committee members react, of watching the curiosity seekers in the seats around him take in the event.

Ames was a popular figure around the city, spreading some of his wealth on lavish entertainment. To his delight, Ames' friends rallied to his side. The hearing was delayed by close to twenty minutes when those wanting to shake the man's hand didn't take their seats until Poland threatened to clear the room if some order wasn't obtained.

Benjamin began writing the story he knew would grace tomorrow's front page.

The die has now been cast. Henry McComb stands at one pole and Oakes Ames at the other. Ames doesn't deny making the Credit Mobilier stock available to certain members of Congress. In his defense, he contends his intentions were benign. Ames claims that as Congress had passed all of the legislation needed to bring about the building of the railroad, there was nothing he stood to gain by parsing out stock to members of that body. Why, then, distribute the stock at all, and why did he pick the particular men that he selected for his largesse? Ames claims capital was still necessary and he was seeking goodwill. The defense rings as hollow to our ears, as we trust it will to our readers'. We eagerly await the stories of the powerful men such as Vice President Colfax and Pennsylvania's own Mr. Kelley, who were among those on the receiving end of Ames' bounty. We can only hope the spirit of the Christmas season will cause them to look into their hearts to find the truth.

# 39

STEPHEN SENSED BENJAMIN'S EXCITEMENT as they prepared for the visit to Clark Mills' studio. He reacted with giggles and smiles to the lightness in his father's voice and to the gentleness of his touch.

"You'll be good for Miss Ream, won't you Stephen? We want her to invite us back to the studio, don't we?" Stephen nodded and clapped his hands, eager to spend time with a father who for once in Stephen's short memory was both buoyant and as bright as the sun.

Benjamin bought a small box of chocolates. He wanted to appear grateful for Vinnie's time, but not too forward. She blushed ever so slightly when he handed them to her.

"You're right on time, Stephen. I like a man who doesn't keep me waiting. That's a woman's prerogative." Vinnie smiled at Benjamin.

"Are you ready to let me make an image of you?" Stephen nodded. He liked the attention, liked the smell of the room, liked being the center of Vinnie's universe.

Vinnie had Benjamin sit on the chair behind the curtain. She put Stephen on his lap, moving him from side to side and tilting his head to capture the light just as she wanted it. She was whispering because her face was so close to the baby's. She smelled of peppermint. Vinnie gave Stephen a small cloth doll to occupy his hands.

Vinnie stood behind a podium that came to her waist. A square block of clay and some wooden utensils were the only things in front of her. A basin of water and several towels were to her left. She looked at Stephen, then came to his side and knelt beside him. "Can you show me your nose, Stephen?" Benjamin leaned in and smelled her hair.

Vinnie's hands never stopped moving around the block of clay. She worked in almost total silence for close to an hour, only talking to ask Benjamin to move Stephen in one direction or another. Stephen was so taken by the way she seemed to be pulling a little boy out of a block of clay he barely spoke until he saw an ear emerge from one side.

"Ear." A bit later he whispered, "Nose, dada."

Benjamin hadn't felt this relaxed since the rock came through his window and sent his life spiraling down the path it had taken. His son on his lap was smiling and engaged in the magic unfolding in front of his eyes. A woman was creating something that never before existed, a small child Benjamin would cherish for the rest of his life. Vinnie was so like Susanna in that. There was nothing that mattered in the world except Stephen, Vinnie, and the young boy she was modeling. There were no Congressmen with dirty hands, no stories to write, no night after night loneliness without Susanna, no criticism from Rachel or from anyone else about the way his life had turned out. There was only the three of them, family, if only for this most precious of afternoons.

Vinnie washed her hands in the basin and then dried them with a towel. "Let's break for a few minutes. Stephen is being so good I don't want him to get restless. I'd like him to play with some clay while I sketch some images of him."

She put one of Benjamin's chocolates in her mouth and offered the box to him. "Delicious. Thank you. Tell me a bit about the hearings, Mr. Wright. Do you find them of interest?"

"May I talk while you work, Miss Ream? And, please. I prefer that you call me Benjamin.

"Then you should call me Vinnie. Tell me, is Mr. McComb or Mr. Ames prevailing at this point?"

"Do you know either man?"

"I've never had the pleasure of meeting Mr. McComb. I've been at several parties where Mr. Ames was in attendance. He's very well known in Washington social circles." Vinnie put Stephen's chin in her hand before continuing, "I do hope the stories about him are unfounded. He seems like such a nice man and he's been so instrumental in getting the railroad built across the country."

Benjamin was quick to respond. "I wasn't terribly impressed with his defense, frankly. The idea he'd pass out valuable stock to a select group of Congressmen and Senators for no reason other than to generate good will strikes me as preposterous. Men of commerce don't act that way as a rule. From the expression on his face I doubt Congressman Poland was terribly impressed either."

"I know many of the men involved, Benjamin. Mr. Colfax sat for me. Mr. Brooks made the loveliest speech at the unveiling of my statue of President Lincoln in the Rotunda. He is one of my primary supporters in my effort to get the Farragut commission. I hope what they're saying about him isn't true. I feel very kindly towards him."

"We'll know soon enough. They're both scheduled to appear before the committee in early January."

"Oh, good. That means you'll be able to bring Stephen back here to the studio." She touched the boy's hair. "You're such a handsome boy. You're being so good, Stephen. Would you look at me for a minute? I want the two of us to look straight at each other."

Stephen wouldn't move his eyes away from the clay occupying his attention. "Benjamin, please stand behind me for a moment and call your son. I want to see his face directly."

*Chapter 39*

Benjamin was only too happy to oblige. He was several inches taller than Vinnie, so he had no trouble seeing over her. He called Stephen's name and held up one of the plaster masks from the shelf above the table. He started dancing with the head and singing a silly song. Stephen looked up. "Perfect. Keep him looking in your direction if you can." Benjamin could feel the warmth of Vinnie's body. She had large and powerful hands for such a small woman. They were rough from working with the materials that were her stock and trade. Her nails were cut short, not in keeping with the new fashion of long and colored fingernails women were sporting in New York and Philadelphia and Washington. She had her work to consider.

Vinnie turned her head. Benjamin hadn't moved. Their faces were closer than either had expected. Her eyes were filled with the small amount of light that remained. Her skin was a pale pink. Susanna's skin was darker, always tanned from being outdoors. Vinnie's was the skin of a woman who kept herself from the sunlight. Vinnie's cheeks reddened. She pulled herself back. "Could you sit Stephen on your lap a bit longer, Benjamin?"

The mention of his son's name reminded him they were not alone, that he could not pull her toward him for an embrace. That was the only thing that constrained him. Propriety be damned. This was a woman of the world. Look at the experiences she'd enjoyed at such a young age. She hardly could take offense at such a gesture. January would bring more testimony, more time in Clark Mills' studio. Who knew where this all would lead?

# 40

"THE LAST PIECE OF LEGISLATION involving the Union Pacific Railroad was passed three years before Mr. Ames and I discussed the possibility I might buy some Credit Mobilier stock. After inquiring about the propriety of such an investment for a man of my limited means I agreed to buy several shares. As my resources were limited at the time, I paid Mr. Ames five hundred dollars in cash and agreed to pay the balance over time."

Schuyler Colfax spent his entire public career delivering speeches in favor of temperance and the virtues of living a God-fearing life. That didn't change when Grant picked him to be his Vice President. He was known around Washington, and indeed, around the entire country, as a bit of a prig. What a delicious moment for his political enemies to see him appear before the committee as a man accused of a crime that brought his character so deeply into question.

"Before I took possession of any stock or any dividend, I learned of the unpleasantries among the shareholders of the entity. As I loathed the idea of being drawn into any litigation, I told Mr. Ames to forget the small amount of money that had passed between us and to withdraw my name from those receiving the stock."

Colfax leaned forward on both elbows. "I state categorically I never received either stock or bonds or dividends from this entity. Gentlemen of the committee, I will now answer your questions."

"Mr. Vice President, please tell the committee what you knew about the ownership of the stock by other members of Congress." Luke Poland was polite to the man who was second in command in his party. He hoped for the sake of the Republicans that Colfax's appearance before the committee would be quick and clinical. The Democratic papers were already having a field day with the idea that a sitting Vice President was implicated in this scandal and having to testify like some mere scoundrel.

"I know, sir, only what I have read in the newspapers."

William Merrick of Maryland was a Democrat. As such, he didn't particularly share Luke Poland's concern about saving the reputation of the Republican Party. He drilled in immediately on what the Vice President knew about the enterprise.

"Did you know the stockholders and officers of the Union Pacific Railroad Company were to contract with themselves as shareholders of the Credit Mobilier to build the railroad and to derive for themselves the profits of the construction?"

"Not quite as strong as that. I considered the project a natural one." Colfax spoke with confidence.

"Did it occur to you at the time whether there was any moral or legal impropriety in the stockholders of a railroad company making a contract with themselves to build the line?"

"I do not like to be called upon to settle moral questions for others."

The crowd tittered. Colfax spent his entire public career making moral judgments about others, and earning a decent living doing so. Colfax was with Lincoln the afternoon Lincoln went to Ford's Theater (declining an invitation from the President to accompany him), as he had been at the signing of the Emancipation Proclamation. He spent the summer after the assassination touring the mining region between the Rocky Mountains and the Pacific and made over seventy speeches that started with reminiscences about the President and ended with long discourses sprinkled heavily with Biblical quotations to support his positions about temperance and the virtues of clean and sober living. If anyone made a public spectacle of himself passing upon moral questions for others, it was Schuyler Colfax.

Luke Poland silenced the crowd. He asked Oakes Ames if he would like an opportunity to cross-examine the Vice President.

"I would indeed, Judge Poland, but I ask the committee's indulgence in deferring the examination for a day or two so that critical facts can be obtained and brought to the committee's attention."

"Facts?" Judge Poland seemed doubtful. "You'll have to educate me, Mr. Ames. We've heard nothing in the testimony thus far to suggest any contradiction in anyone's recollections that justify a delay."

"The Vice President just swore under oath he received no dividend from the Credit Mobilier stock. That statement is false." The crowd seemed to inhale in unison, as if on cue.

Mr. Merrick spoke up. "He did indeed, Mr. Poland. That is the position he's taken publicly since the story broke during the election campaign. Do you have evidence to the contrary, Mr. Ames? The committee would be most interested in receiving such evidence. Most interested, indeed."

Colfax looked uncomfortable at being called out in such an aggressive and ugly manner. He loathed being discussed in the third person unless people were praising his virtue or perhaps his ability as an orator.

"It is not in my possession at the moment, but it certainly is obtainable."

"How so? Where are you proposing this committee look for such evidence? We're not in the business of guessing about such things, Mr. Ames." Luke Poland was as angry as he'd been since the beginning of the proceedings. He was supposed to run what could be called a balanced investigation, but he didn't see it as his responsibility to hand the Democrats evidence implicating the Republican Party's highest officials.

"My notes clearly say I presented Mr. Colfax a dividend check of twelve hundred dollars through his account with the Sergeant at Arms of the House. I suggest the committee call Mr. Ordway and ask that he verify that transaction by reference to the House of Representatives' books of account. The committee also might serve a subpoena on Mr. Colfax's bank to ascertain whether a deposit in that amount was made at about the time in question."

Luke Poland spoke before the Democrats on the committee had an opportunity to demand the subpoenas issue immediately.

"Mr. Vice President, Mr. Ames questions your denial of the receipt of any dividends. What say you? Is it possible that hearing what Mr. Ames just said about the topic refreshed your recollection on that point?"

Colfax lacked either the good sense or the mental agility to understand Poland was throwing him a lifeline. "I stand by my statements to the committee and to the American people."

"Mr. Chairman, the issue is joined." William Merrick pounced before Poland could maneuver around him. "I move that subpoenas issue immediately to the Sergeant at Arms of the House of Representatives and to any bank identified by Mr. Colfax as a bank where he had relations in the time in question. The committee will stand in recess for at least a week to allow the evidence to be obtained. The American people have a right to know whether their Vice President lied to both them and to this committee."

Luke Poland knew he'd been boxed in by Ames' statements and by Merrick's seizing of the point to give the Democrats a few days' worth of headlines attacking the Vice President's veracity. He hoped for the sake of his party Ames would be proven the liar. "Mr. Ames, the committee will not take lightly an attempt to refute Mr. Colfax's testimony that is not borne out by the evidence. You remain under oath whether giving your own testimony or cross-examining witnesses." Poland scowled at Ames as he continued, "You could be answering to this committee for perjury as well as for the other charges against you."

Ames was not impressed. "You will not find that I am the witness who has perjured himself, sir. I can assure you of that."

Benjamin thought to himself that as Carlton would say, this was going to be delicious. He certainly had his story for the next week's worth of editions of the *Courier.*

# 41

"BENJAMIN?" VINNIE REAM'S voice carried across the Rotunda. He hoped they might run into each other by chance. He was even more delighted it was she who initiated the contact. Benjamin stood where he was. He let the stream of representatives, lobbyists and their attendants work their way around him as he watched Vinnie move toward him.

She moved confidently, as if she belonged in the place. She had been standing at the base of her Lincoln statue, talking about her work with a group of children touring the Capitol. Vinnie always made a point of speaking to the young about her work, encouraging their interest in the arts. The greatest of presidents seemed to look over her approvingly as she made her way toward Benjamin. She kissed him on both cheeks, continental style, and put her arm through his.

"Is Stephen in Washington with you? I have something to show you. I was hoping you'd be here for the committee meeting. I was certain you wouldn't miss an appearance by the Vice President." Benjamin was on fire.

"Stephen caught something sleeping in a drafty room. I was reluctant to bring him out into this damp weather, so I'm afraid he won't be able to sit for you today. I trust your holidays are pleasant."

Benjamin hated himself for such a poor effort at small talk. He was nervous and afraid to say anything inappropriate. He barely noticed Vinnie was walking him toward the door to Clark Mills' studio.

"I don't need Stephen to sit for me any longer, although I would love to see him again. He's such a delightful young boy. I found myself so enthralled by his image I spent virtually the entire weekend in Mr. Mills' studio working on the piece. I used the time to complete the statuette. I worked from sketches and memory. Mr. Mills was so taken by the plaster he allowed me to cast a bronze for each of us. He's even thinking of casting several more for sale. I so want you to be pleased with what I've done. It was just finished yesterday. You almost can still feel the warmth from the molten bronze."

Benjamin let Vinnie's voice wrap around him like a winter scarf. He drank her enthusiasm like a fine wine.

"Close your eyes. Put out your hands." Benjamin loved the way Vinnie was teasing him. He loved the smell of the woman, the way she made his heart race.

He felt something heavy, so heavy it surprised him at first. "Open your eyes, Benjamin. Admire your son." Benjamin caught his breath. The image Vinnie created was flawless. She captured Stephen's eyes, the small pout of his lips even when he curled them into a smile, the curiosity in his gaze. It was as though she'd given birth to the boy a second time.

"It is perfect. Absolutely perfect in every respect. I don't know what to say."

Vinnie's smile was radiant. "There's no need to talk, Benjamin. The expression on your face tells me everything I needed to know about your reaction. Here, let me place the statuette into a satchel to keep it safe." She took the bust from Benjamin's hands. She set it on the table. She had to walk past Benjamin to get to the place where she stored the velvet bag she had purchased for the statuette.

He reached out and took her hand. She didn't resist. Benjamin pulled her face toward his and kissed her. Vinnie returned the gesture with neither hesitancy nor question. Benjamin felt her heart against his, lingered in the sweetness of her breath. The sound of a man's hand on the door to the studio and of his footstep on the top rung of the stairs that led to it were the only things that pulled them apart.

# 42

MERCER CARLTON COULDN'T STAY AWAY. The Vice President of the United States was about to be exposed to the country as a sanctimonious liar as well as a man who sold the integrity of his office for a few dollars. There were few things in life Carlton enjoyed more than watching men who spent their whole careers building a persona of a virtuous life being destroyed brick by brick.

Benjamin wasn't thrilled that Carlton traveled to Washington. He'd rather spend his time out of the committee room in Clark Mills' studio.

Luke Poland reminded the Vice President and Mr. Ames that they still were under oath.

Poland sat grim-faced as Nathaniel Ordway, the Sergeant at Arms of the House of Representatives, discussed the way in which he maintained the members' books of account. In response to the slow and methodical questions of Ames' attorney, Ordway cut the legs out from under Schuyler Colfax's denial of receiving any dividend.

"Mr. Ordway, explain to the committee your knowledge of any transaction between Messrs. Ames and Colfax involving the sum of twelve hundred dollars in the summer of eighteen sixty-nine."

"My ledger shows that at Mr. Ames' request, a check was drawn on his account to S.C. or bearer."

"And S.C. is whom?"

"I presume it was Schuyler Colfax, as I remember delivering a check to him at the request of Mr. Ames."

William Merrick interrupted. "Mr. Colfax, what say you to this point? Do you stand by your denial of the receipt of any dividend in the face of Mr. Ordway's testimony?"

Colfax seemed flustered. He elected to address the committee without the benefit of counsel and hardly could seek the protection of one now without appearing to be running for cover.

"I have no recollection of such a transaction. The fact a check was drawn to S.C. or bearer proves nothing. I trust there are other men in this city with the initials S.C., sir. It is altogether possible, perhaps even likely, Mr. Ames endorsed the check himself. Why otherwise make it payable to bearer, if it was intended for me? Even if Mr. Ordway is correct, and I know him to be a man of integrity, his testimony proves nothing of relevance to this inquiry."

"Lying sack of shit. What a ridiculous horse's ass. God, Benjamin, I love this town. We couldn't make this folly up if we tried." Mercer Carlton's aside was loud enough to generate laughter on his side of the room. Luke Poland gaveled for order.

"Mr. Vice President, would you like a recess to review the facts in more detail?"

Colfax denied the opportunity. He was so wedded to the certainty of his recollection (or so locked into his lie) he once again couldn't see the safe harbor Poland was offering. The man was a slave to the perception he'd built of himself as an arbiter of the public virtue and blind to the rocks in his path.

"Mr. Ordway, thank you. Unless the committee or the Vice President has any questions, I'd now like to call Mr. David Benson of the First National Bank to testify that at about the time of the check in question."

Ames' lawyer paused. He adjusted his glasses. He waited until every eye in the room focused on him and he didn't speak again until he had that concentration. "Mr. Colfax made a deposit of twelve hundred dollars to his account."

McMurtrie turned to the Vice President. He handed him a copy of the bank's ledger book for the month of August. "That is unless the Vice President is willing to stipulate to the committee that this entry accurately reflects the fact he made such a deposit."

For the longest time, the only sound in the room was the stirring of the crowd, as everyone moved forward at the same time. Colfax was silent, as if he was only now beginning to understand the depth of the hole he'd dug for himself.

Colfax's silence was that of a man stewing in his own juices. He regretted his decision not to be represented by counsel. It seemed like such an obvious decision at the time.

He was a man of unquestionable integrity. His standing in the eyes of the American people was above reproach. Men of virtue don't need to hide behind the machinations and theatrics that lawyers are only too happy to employ. But he now regretted he hadn't brought along someone who might distract the committee with card tricks or a rabbit in his hat. He wanted them to think about almost anything other than the facts that had been set before them with such precision.

Colfax spoke so softly his voice was barely audible, even in a room full of people holding their breath in anticipation of his response.

"Mr. Chairman, these events took place several years ago. I can hardly be expected to have committed every banking transaction in my life to memory." Colfax was laboring for air. "Perhaps a short adjournment to allow me to reconstruct my records is appropriate."

Before William Merrick had a chance to speak, Luke Poland gaveled the session closed.

"We had scheduled only one more day of testimony before the Christmas recess, gentlemen. I suggest we adjourn these proceedings until the first working day of the new year. I believe that will be January 6. Mr. Colfax, we'll resume with your testimony at ten o'clock that day. Ladies and Gentlemen, our best wishes for the holidays."

Poland was out of his chair and out of the room before the Democrats could do any more harm to the Vice President and, by virtue of his proximity, to Grant himself. The man was stained enough in his first term to destroy his reputation as the military genius who saved the Union. If Luke Poland couldn't save the President from himself, he might at the very least keep the Republican Party from falling apart around him.

"January 6? By God, Benjamin, we've hit the jackpot. We'll be in town for Pixie Carpenter's Twelfth Night party." Carlton was giddy with excitement.

"Pixie Carpenter? Twelfth Night party? Translation, please," Benjamin asked.

"Priscilla Madison Carpenter. Dolly Madison's granddaughter. She has all the charm and grace of her grandmother. She's married to a shirttail relative of mine, Daniel Carpenter, one of Grant's Brigadier Generals. He was in charge of the border states during the war. Pixie's been throwing a party on January sixth since just after the war to mark the end of the Christmas season. It's great theater, even by Washington standards. You're in for a treat, Benjamin. A real treat."

# 43

"Merry, sir, they praise me and make an ass of me. Now my foes tell me plainly I am an ass, so that by my toes, sir, I profit in the knowledge of myself."

Mercer Carlton bowed to one of the Shakespearean actors Pixie Carpenter had hired for the evening. It was a tradition of Pixie's to enliven her party on the last day of the Christmas season with the play named for the day.

"They praise you and they make an ass of you? Are you Malvolio or Schuyler Colfax?" The crowd around Mercer Carlton roared at his characterization of the Vice President. He bowed to his left, and then to his right, as though he was the one hired to entertain.

"If Malvolio, my friend, you had a better morning than the Vice President." Carlton turned to Dan Carpenter. The knot of people around him was lingering on his every word.

"Can you believe the stupidity of the man? To claim the twelve-hundred-dollar deposit he made wasn't from the dividend Ames gave him for the stock but was money that came from his father-in-law and from a campaign contributor?"

"And how remarkably convenient that both of those men happen to be dead."

Benjamin recognized the woman who spoke, but not her voice. She had attended every session of the Poland Committee. She was one of the well-wishers who greeted Ames at the beginning and at each break.

A small woman with a broad face and auburn hair that set off her lilac dress, she clearly was no fan of either Henry McComb or Schuyler Colfax.

"I don't understand why the committee is still bothering to call witnesses. McComb has been exposed as a man interested in selling whatever he can to the highest bidder. He doesn't care whether he's paid for his stock or his story."

Carlton tried to take her hand, but she resisted. Even the actors drew closer to the woman. She spoke in an ever rising staccato, as sure of herself as anyone in the room.

"The Vice President had two weeks to come up with some rebuttal to Mr. Ames' sworn declaration he gave him a dividend and the best he could do was to make up that nonsense we heard this morning? This investigation has become a mockery. No one has refuted Mr. Ames' statements that he never intended to curry favor with any member or that he had any improper motive. Bare knuckle politics is the only reason the Republicans are bothering with the charade any longer. They want to pillory some Democrats."

Benjamin should have resisted drawing the woman into a debate. It was such a splendid evening. The air outside the Carpenter home was cold and filled with stars. Inside, he was so lucky to be one of fifty or so elegantly dressed members of Washington's elite being served eel and caviar on tiny pieces of toast by silk-gloved waiters while stage actors enthralled them with the Bard. Why not simply take in the evening? If Susanna had been at his side she'd be pulling at his elbow, begging him to do just that.

Perhaps Benjamin was guilty of the same blind partisanship. He had lived with the story of the Credit Mobilier for so long and had sacrificed so much for it he measured a large portion of his own worth by how credible the whole idea that men stole from the government turned out to be.

"Surely, though, madam, you would agree that government corruption should be exposed and rooted out."

The woman's judgment was as quick as it was harsh. She looked at Benjamin as if he were no better than dirt. "You're the reporter, correct? I've seen you scribbling away at every session. I presume it's your slander I'm reading in the chorus of voices demanding what you label as justice."

"Is that such a terrible thing to be striving for?"

"Good luck finding justice in that room, young man. The Republicans have no more interest in listening to Mr. Ames than I do in knowing with certainty whether Schuyler Colfax is dishonest or merely a fool. From your writings it seems you are as predisposed as are the Republicans to find Mr. Ames guilty of corruption regardless of how obviously the facts lead in the other direction."

"I'm no more predisposed. . ."

The woman turned before Benjamin could finish his sentence, satisfied, no doubt, she'd stood her ground and defended Mr. Ames' honor. Benjamin reddened and felt his throat go as dry as the wine he was drinking. He was embarrassed by his lack of discipline, shamed he'd been reduced to the same banner-waving headline as had the woman. Where had the public dialogue gone, the reasoned discourse? This woman was as hard-headed and sure of her view of the world as Carlton was of his. Was anyone in government or the newspapers that followed it capable of listening to what someone else had to say?

As Benjamin turned to discuss the abrupt exchange with Carlton, Vinnie Ream came into his line of sight. He excused himself from the group around Carlton and walked to her side. He felt his pulse quicken. He hoped hers was quickening as well.

"You look lovely, Vinnie. I hadn't expected to see you here. My God, it's good to see you. I just arrived late last night and was at the committee hearing all day. I had to rent these clothes and get myself ready for this evening, so I had no time to stop by Mr. Mills' studio or to send a note to your home letting you know I'd arrived. Will you be in the Capitol tomorrow? I'd love to see you."

Benjamin was a running brook, but he was so happy to see Vinnie he lost all sense of anything other than the desire to wrap his words around her as a proxy for his arms.

"You're quite the dandy, Benjamin, in that frock and those white gloves. It's good to see you. Has Stephen's cold improved? I certainly hope that's the case." Vinnie was wearing a cream colored dress cut low across her breasts. An emerald necklace caressed her neck. Its sparkle set off the color of her eyes.

Stephen. The sound of his name reminded Benjamin of his son. "The bust you made is so extraordinary. Stephen's grandfathers are battling over who will get to keep it. I may have to commission more."

"Starving artists are always looking for work."

"God, it's good to see you. Have I told you how absolutely lovely you look?" Benjamin so wanted to kiss Vinnie a second time at that moment.

Vinnie smiled on hearing Benjamin's adoring words.

"Benjamin, shame on you. Did you think you could have this captivating woman all to yourself for the evening?" Carlton's voice startled Benjamin as though it was cannon fire."

"Will you introduce me or must I do all of the work myself?"

He took Vinnie's hand in his, bowed slightly and let his lips stay on her skin longer than Benjamin would have liked. Vinnie blushed when she saw the jealousy in Benjamin's eyes.

"Fair Olivia, I am Mercer Carlton, or for tonight at least, Antonio, this young Sebastian's protector."

Carlton loved to show off in front of beautiful young women. What better way to do that than to flaunt his mastery of Shakespeare? "I thought we had taught Benjamin how to communicate at the *Courier*, but in describing your beauty his words failed him. I am honored."

"She is indeed a vision, sir, but I'm afraid once the music begins this evening, my name will be on every line of her dance card." As he spoke, William Tecumseh Sherman looked at Carlton with the most piercing eyes Benjamin had ever seen.

General Sherman was a bit shorter than Benjamin, with red hair and beard and a perpetual scowl. He had walked up behind Vinnie so silently Benjamin barely noticed him. Others in the room had, of course. It was impossible in Washington not to know the war hero whose star was eclipsed only by Grant himself as the soldier who saved the Union. Unlike Grant, though, Sherman had the good sense to remain a hero and to avoid being drawn into the eddy of favor seekers and money grabbers that pull any President into the mud if he lets them. Sherman was dressed in an evening suit rather than in the full uniform his title as commander of all army forces allowed him to wear.

Carlton spoke first. "General Sherman. I truly am honored. Mercer Carlton. My brother Elliot served under you at Stone Mountain and Savannah. He remembers those battles as if they were yesterday, sir."

"Elliot Carlton?" Sherman paused. He was running through the mental files he kept of his officers. "Excellent horseman. Thrust his bayonet with his left hand leading as I recall. Left hand dominance creates an advantage on the battlefield. Where is your brother now, sir? I'm afraid after so many years I'm beginning to lose touch with my men."

"Raising dairy cows in upstate New York. Up to his ears in manure and loving it. Not my cup of tea, but he's a good man."

"He's a damned fine man and an able soldier, sir. Please tell your brother I send him my very best wishes." Sherman lowered his head slightly. Carlton did the same.

Vinnie put her hand on Sherman's arm. The gesture was so light, so comfortable, Benjamin was shot through with the sensation she'd done so a thousand times before. Sherman had a glass of champagne in one hand. His free hand rested on the small of Vinnie's back. Benjamin hated their familiarity, the easy way in which they let each other linger. He was powerless to do anything other than to let his body sag into his evening clothes.

"William, my dear, this is Benjamin Wright. Stephen's father. I told you about the boy I sculpted recently. You've yet to come to Mr. Mills' studio to see the finished work."

Sherman nodded, but kept his hand on Vinnie's back rather than extend it to shake Benjamin's hand. He moved her away from the two men with the slightest pressure on her back. He excused them and they moved to another section of the room.

Benjamin's world had fallen in around him in the three minutes it had taken him to walk across the room to Vinnie, only to have her snatched away from him by a veritable icon of the state.

Vinnie might have described Benjamin as a friend. Perhaps she'd even blush at the word, causing the war hero a moment of uncertainty. He'd raise an eyebrow and for that instant Benjamin would be his peer. But Vinnie had identified Benjamin only as someone connected to a boy whose image she had crafted. Benjamin so wanted Vinnie to feel for him the way he felt about her, but it was obvious he was nothing more than a party to a commercial transaction, and then only because he had accompanied Stephen to Clark Mills' studio.

Carlton noticed his colleague's disappointment. "It's painfully obvious, my boy, that you're smitten with her."

Benjamin paused. "I shouldn't be discussing a lady in these terms, but I actually thought she might return my feelings. She gave me a very clear signal of that intention in her studio."

Carlton put his hand on Benjamin's shoulder. "Love is a plague, Benjamin. I told you to read Shakespeare. Desire is a cruel hound. And you, my boy, are nothing but desire."

Benjamin watched as Vinnie and General Sherman moved through the crowd as the golden couple. She a noted artist who had sculpted Lincoln himself. He the conquering hero.

"I hadn't really thought about how lonely I was without Susanna until I met Vinnie. I perhaps let myself become infatuated with her over the interest she showed in Stephen. I feel quite the fool." There was no point pretending he wanted to be part of Pixie Carpenter's evening any longer.

"This is Washington, Benjamin. I wouldn't be surprised if she were using him as much as he's using her. Everyone here feeds off someone else."

"The man is more than twice her age."

"The man is the closest thing to royalty Washington has now that Lincoln is gone and Grant's been exposed as a drunk and a fool. Sherman won the war for Lincoln. Remember that. He may be the most hated man in Georgia, but around these parts he's revered. The man gave Lincoln the city of Savannah as a Christmas present the year before the war ended, for God's sake. He's one of the very few men in Washington on a pedestal who actually belongs there."

"So he's a hero. I thought generals were supposed to fade away. Why does Vinnie need heroes? She has her art. She's masterful at what she does."

"Statues cost money. The battle for the best opportunities is intense. Sherman can get Vinnie the commissions she wants. I hate to be so blunt about your feelings, Benjamin, but what can you do for her that can compare to that?"

The actors were ready for a small presentation. Malvolio was dressed in yellow garters. Carlton whispered to Benjamin. "The old fool has been told if he dresses like a canary and prances around the place he'll win Olivia's heart, so he's gone and done it."

## Chapter 43

"Are you warning me against such costumes, sir?"

Carlton put his arm on his wounded friend's shoulder. "We do strange things for love, Benjamin. And love does strange things to us."

# 44

BENJAMIN'S STORY APPEARED on the front page of the *Courier* and every Democratic paper as far west as Kansas City:

The investigation into the affairs of the Credit Mobilier is now into its third week. The New Year has brought no ray of sunshine, nothing other than the pathetic sight of men of prominence dissembling about their affairs. In the face of his damning letters, Oakes Ames, the man behind the whole sordid affair, at least had the good sense not to deny his delivery of the stock. He claims his motives were pure, but that judgment will be left to others.

Thus far, the pathetic image of the Vice President fabricating a story to justify the receipt of dividends from Ames is matched only by the oversized greed and stupidity of Mr. Brooks of New York. Brooks was a Government director of the Union Pacific Railroad. As such, he was charged with protecting the People's investment in that road. Surely, that responsibility meant he could not own stock in the entity with which the Union Pacific was contracting. But he not only demanded not one, but two large allocations of Credit Mobilier shares, and then channeled the graft through his son-in-law so his name wouldn't appear on any implicating records. Does that subterfuge prove anything other than he knew what he was doing was wrong?

While perhaps a matter of degree at best, Mr. Garfield of Ohio hardly has clean hands. The evidence has shown he received his stock without paying a penny, earned large dividends and then surrendered the stock at the first sign the transaction would be exposed to the sunshine. Is this all we can expect from our public servants? Perhaps we should take a closer look at the men we elect.

We now await the testimony of Pennsylvania's own Pig-Iron Kelley among the parade of men all too willing to have their hand in the public trough. As yet another of Ames' beneficiaries, we doubt he will fare any better than the rest.

"What you said about Mr. Brooks was cruel, Benjamin." Vinnie did nothing to hide her anger. "You're no longer reporting about the committee's investigation. You've stepped into the role of advocate. Beyond that, I felt that in attacking a man whom I told you was supporting my effort to get the Farragut commission you were striking out at me for having the temerity to attend Mrs. Carpenter's party with General Sherman."

Vinnie waited outside the committee room for a recess. She knew Benjamin wouldn't call on her at the studio and didn't want to be seen lingering in the Rotunda in the hope she might catch him by happenstance. Her voice was filled with disappointment.

"I have no right to question you about the men you choose to see, Miss Ream. Whatever their age."

"Benjamin, stop acting like a petulant child. There's no need to call me Miss Ream or to pretend you don't know why I'm here. Don't play such a wounded puppy that I walk away before I have an opportunity to explain myself." Her cheeks reddened. Benjamin felt himself deflate for wearing his feelings so obviously on his sleeve.

The woman's fortitude frightened him as much as it drew him to her.

They sat on a bench at the end of the hall.

"In hindsight, I shouldn't have kissed you that day in the studio, Benjamin. It certainly wasn't and isn't my intention to lead you on. But I had the same rush of feelings you did. We were obviously attracted to each other at that instant. Is that a crime?"

"I'm not sure you understand my feelings. I'm not sure I understand them myself."

"I was so happy with your reaction to Stephen's piece. I felt so wonderful about the moment."

"That hardly says anything about me."

"Benjamin, you're a young and vital and handsome man. Your gift for words is more impressive than my meager talents with stone."

"That hardly explains your attraction to General Sherman."

"Benjamin, you're naive about so many things. You cover these hearings but really aren't listening to what's going on. Nothing will come of those investigations. The Republicans control the process and the Congress. They're not going to let the members of their party get hurt. It doesn't matter who received the stock from Ames. I don't care what happens to Ames, but I told you how important Mr. Brooks is to me."

"For that I apologize, but the man hardly will be of much use to anyone now that his dealings have been spread on the public record. But in talking about Mr. Brooks we seem to have veered from the topic."

"To the contrary, Benjamin. The topic is precisely that in Washington people protect their own. You complain about the time I spend with General Sherman. There is virtually no one more highly regarded in this country than that man. He's going to help me get the Farragut commission. Do you understand what that means? The Lincoln was an extraordinary opportunity for me, but my best work is ahead of me. There's no more important commission in the United States at the moment. If I need to bat my eyelashes to one of the most influential men in Washington to garner his support for that prize, I absolutely will do just that."

So her kiss that day in the studio had meant nothing. How naive of Benjamin to believe otherwise. Vinnie continued when Benjamin was unable to respond. "Don't weigh me down with petty jealousies like some schoolboy whose heart has been broken. That only would prove you don't understand me any more than you understand Washington. I want you to respect me for what I am, Benjamin, but if you can't or won't, I'll accept that too."

The crowd was returning to the committee room after the short recess. Benjamin needed to return to his chair. It was just as well. He had nothing to say to Vinnie. He had nothing for her but a sense that for all he thought he had taken in during his time here, Vinnie knew more about Washington than Benjamin could learn in several lifetimes.

# 45

BENJAMIN CAME TO THE CAPITOL early the next morning, as much to collect his thoughts as to possibly see Vinnie studying the morning light sweeping the dome before heading to Clark Mills' studio.

His father's voice surprised him. "Benjamin."

"Father." It took Benjamin more than a few seconds to form the word.

"I'd like a moment of your time, Benjamin, if you have it. Perhaps we could find a quiet spot."

Jacob knew every space in the building. He led his son into a small antechamber large enough for only four or five people. The room was furnished with a sofa, two chairs and a cherry table. A small painting of George Washington was the only decoration. The bright morning light streamed through the window.

"Mr. Kelley asked if we might talk." Jacob cleared his throat. It was as if stating the purpose of his contact with his son under these circumstances made him uncomfortable.

Benjamin certainly took that as a sign this was not meant to be another step on the road toward their possible reconciliation. They met only once since their dinner at Bleecher's, not necessarily because that initial meeting ended without promise, but because their lives pulled them in other directions.

Benjamin wanted to question his father's motives in reaching out to him this morning, but he lacked time. He had the pressures of the Poland Committee, of Carlton's voracious appetite for dead-lines, of Stephen. And he wanted what spare time he might carve out of those obligations to be filled with Vinnie.

Jacob served at the pleasure of Pig-Iron Kelley. Of late, Kelley's pleasure was to tour the Reconstruction states begging for Union dollars to rebuild their ports, their bridges and roads. Kelley was all too happy to accommodate, but needed someone along for the trip to assure his elected hands were not soiled by cash.

"The piece you wrote the other day about Mr. Brooks and Mr. Garfield made Mr. Kelley very uncomfortable."

Benjamin became rigid. "I was doing nothing other than reporting what was presented in the committee room. Mr. Brooks hardly merits praise for what he did. He's a Democrat who made himself quite tempting prey by being so blatant in his effort to cloak his interest. Why are you speaking in his defense?"

"Brooks is of no concern to me, Benjamin. That he would be so stupid as to use his son-in-law's name to hide his ownership shows he lacks the good sense to hold a position that subjects him to the public's scrutiny. My loyalty is to Mr. Kelley."

"Mr. Kelley is a Republican. As the committee and the House are both comfortably controlled by Republicans, I presume he'll have no difficulties unless his behavior is as blatant as Mr. Brooks' or otherwise can't be explained away in a manner that allows his greed to be swept under the carpet. He should have nothing to fear of whatever the *Courier* may publish about him."

"The facts of his interaction with Mr. Ames are similar to those of Mr. Garfield, whom you chose to criticize. They are from other states." Jacob shifted in his chair. "The men who read the *Courier* are within Mr. Kelley's legislative district. There is a world of dif-ference in that fact alone, Benjamin. There is no need to adopt a patronizing tone. You know that as well as I do."

Benjamin refused to give an inch. "Mr. Kelley accepted stock in a company that benefited from legislation in which he was involved without paying for it. The *Courier's* readers would like to know their representative accepted a bribe."

"He paid for it. That's not a correct statement."

"Is this why you sought me out for dinner and talked about reconciliation? Were you planning for the possibility that some day you might need to use me to protect your benefactor?" Benjamin could not have been more insulted or bruised or distressed about how his relationship with his father might end.

Jacob ignored the question. "Let's stay on the subject we're discussing. Mr. Kelley paid for the stock. Anything you say to the contrary will ruin your career once the truth is uncovered. Grow up and face reality, Benjamin. Washington isn't a place for dreamers."

So be it. He would debate Jacob on the facts and walk out of the room knowing he no longer had a father in the genuine sense of that word.

"He paid for the stock, Father, only in the sense that when Mr. Ames gave him the dividend he netted out the price of the stock, apparently without charging interest on the loan. Mr. Kelley took no risk on his investment and yet he has been rewarded handsomely. I know you work for the man, but don't close your eyes to the obvious. Is what he did something our legislators should be doing? Shouldn't the people who elect him year after year know the character of the man they send here?"

"I may be out of line in saying so, but you're becoming as doctrinaire in your ways as your friend Mercer Carlton is in his. I know I have forfeited the right to give you any guidance, but open your eyes, Benjamin. You are becoming as preachy and small-minded as your mentor."

"The *Courier* prints what is in the best interests of our readers. You are correct in one thing, however. It is not your place to speak of such things." Benjamin made no effort to hide his distaste for either the man or his mission.

"Perhaps it's not my place to speak to you in these terms, but if I were you I'd get off that high horse. It's not your job to comment on the morality of other men. If you want that responsibility, give up the newspaper business and join the ministry."

How odd that Jacob would echo Carlton's first words to Benjamin. Had he done nothing in all of his time at the *Courier* other than to substitute one set of bias for another?

"That, sir, is what the press *should* be doing. The days of Congress conducting business in secrecy are over. That the people of your world hide behind curtains and smokescreens is abhorrent. Did my brothers really die so men like Pig-Iron Kelley can have envelopes stuffed in their pockets at the moment a vote is to be taken? Is that really why you left your wife and came to Washington?"

Jacob gathered his composure. "This has nothing to do with your brothers. My God, Benjamin, the war has been over for years. What happened to Willie and Matthew is unimaginably sad, but wounds must heal or we die of the poison that builds up in our system. I'm not asking you to endorse how business is done in Washington or even to condone it. I'm only asking for a bit of mercy for an old man. Mercy for your mother's sake. You've seen the woman more recently than I have of course. You know she doesn't have much time left. At least let me be able to continue to support her until she's gone."

"You're asking me to shut my eyes to what's going on in front of me. That hardly is in the best interests of the *Courier*'s readers. What of my duty to them?"

"There is a line, Benjamin, between duty and malice." The *Courier* is a Philadelphia paper. You know what I'm asking."

"You're asking that I abdicate my responsibility."

"I'm asking that you consider balancing your approach. I'm asking you to show some concern for others. If I were to lose my job, what would become of your mother? Are you willing or able to support her? Are you able to keep the payments up on the farm?"

"If the voters turn out Mr. Kelley it will be on account of his avarice, not on account of anything I write. I'm nothing more than a mirror."

"Benjamin, I beseech you. No matter how much you disdain Kelley or your own father, show mercy on Rachel. You have power in your words. You've developed standing in your community. People listen to what you say. People respect your voice. Show some decency. Show some kindness."

"People respect me because I tell them the truth. You're asking me to cut the very bond of trust I have with my readers. Wasn't it you who told me not to compromise on my principles? Was that just polite conversation you were making because you couldn't figure out what else to say after all those years without so much as a word to me? Is holding on to one's principles some platitude politicians and their acolytes espouse for everyone except themselves, especially when their reelection is at stake?" Benjamin imagined Mercer Carlton would give the same speech, word for word.

"There is a difference, Benjamin, between being principled and being so rigid you fail to see another man's pain." He held out his hand. "Look at that. I can't hold it straight out in front of me without it shaking like a leaf. I'm fifty-nine years old. If Mr. Kelley won't be able to keep me on, who will take on an aging cripple? Must I get on my knees to ask for your understanding?"

"I will hear out Mr. Kelley's testimony. I believe it is time to go into the committee room." Benjamin opened the door to the hall. The noise from the Capitol filled the room. The same fat lobbyists he'd seen before. The same whoring of the public's honor.

"If I can't appeal to your sense of family, then, or to any remote hint of feeling you might have for me, let me suggest this, Benjamin. It's an open secret Grainger has asked you to base yourself permanently in Washington. Mr. Kelley is a prominent mem-

ber of Congress. He has positions on a number of important com-
mittees and is close to men at the highest levels of the government.
The way to get ahead in Washington is to cultivate friendships.
That is particularly true of the press."

Jacob had reached out to Benjamin with words of both reconciliation and encouragement for his career before the scandal broke,
but what he now was saying seemed nothing more than an effort
to shield his employer. Benjamin felt himself harden. "What? How
could you possibly know of Grainger's plans?" Benjamin regretted
he wasn't able to hide what might make him vulnerable.

"We can open doors for you, Benjamin. If you will not show
leniency for me as your flesh and blood, or even for the sake of your
mother, then at least have the good sense to strike a business deal.
Don't do what I ask out of compassion or even pity for an old man
or even for what the loss of my position would do to your mother.
God damn it, Benjamin, just be selfish."

Jacob rose. He took Benjamin's arm so he wouldn't leave the
room without hearing his father out. He moved closer to his son
as he spoke. "Mr. Kelley and the men he knows can feed you
enough information to assure you'll be the preeminent journalist
in Washington within the year. Readers around the world will do
more than know your name. They will look to you as the defini-
tive voice for what is happening in this government. I've read your
work, Benjamin. I know how talented you are. Let me repay at least
a small portion of my debt to you by helping you ascend to the pin-
nacle of your profession, Benjamin. Think of the life you'll be able
to give Stephen from that position."

Benjamin stopped. He kept his hand on the knob of the door.
He was hoping the right words would form, but nothing came to
him to rebut what his father had said. Washington was built on
gifts and favors. Carlton's world depended upon attacking his enemies with whatever weapons he had in his arsenal. The two were

virtually impossible to reconcile. Benjamin left Jacob in the room and joined the throng moving through the Capitol.

When Benjamin entered the committee room, Pig-Iron Kelley already was sitting at the witness table.

# 46

SO MANY OF THE MEN CAUGHT UP in the scandal Ames created ran from the controversy at the first sign of trouble.

Henry Dawes of Massachusetts asked Ames to take back the stock and to settle all accounts between them at the first hint of McComb's lawsuit.

Ohio's John Bingham received only a portion of the dividends and then declined to accept the rest.

Pig-Iron Kelley's reaction was to slap the committee in its face for even daring to question his motives.

Jacob had taken a seat next to Benjamin. He gripped the sides of his chair until his knuckles were white as Luke Poland marched Kelley through the early round of his questions. Poland was exploring the nature of Kelley's relationship with Ames, the character of the investments Kelley undertook before the Credit Mobilier deal, and the same other territory he'd covered with all witnesses. Benjamin wanted to tell his father to stop fidgeting nervously in his seat, that Poland's questions were little more than one Republican protecting another with enough superficial detail to enable Poland to report how thorough he'd been in his interrogation.

The room was only half filled with the curious. The committee had shifted its focus from the star attractions to the marginal players in the Credit Mobilier story. Washington had moved on as well. Its residents were ready for something new to capture their attention. Even the woman who came at Benjamin with such unbridled passion at Pixie Carpenter's soiree stayed away.

Perhaps it was the half-empty room. Perhaps it was the knowledge there was nothing so blatant in his dealings with Ames that would cause the Republicans to break ranks and to try to pin something on him. Kelley hadn't been as obvious as Brooks, whose efforts to hide his ownership in his son-in-law's name was as much an admission of guilt as if he'd been caught in the act of robbing a saloon.

Whatever the motivation, Pig-Iron Kelley chose the moment of an otherwise benign question from Luke Poland to challenge the fundamental premise of the whole inquiry.

"You have asked all other witnesses and no doubt will ask me whether it was inappropriate for a member of Congress to hold an investment interest in the railroads when we were charged with their oversight. I have given a great deal of thought to that question, gentlemen, and have concluded most forcibly it was not and is not."

William Merrick would not let the comment pass. "Is it your view, Mr. Kelley, that as representatives of the people we should stand to gain financially from a vote we're asked to make? If that's your testimony, sir, the record should be absolutely clear in that regard."

"I cannot see that any member of Congress was precluded from making a purchase of Credit Mobilier stock any more than he would be from buying a flock of sheep, whose value could be affected by a change in the tariff on wool or woolen goods. To suggest otherwise would mean only the poorest of men ever could serve here, and only then on the condition they remain poor their entire lives."

Kelley pounded the table for emphasis. "If the Founding Fathers wanted the government to be run by a group of monks, they would have said as much."

Kelley leaned forward in his chair. "A number of years ago I bought a large amount of land outside Philadelphia. It was farmland and woods at the time, but it now is becoming part of the main portion of the city."

Kelley pointed his finger at William Merrick. "Let me ask you the same question you asked of me, sir, for surely the same rules must apply to both political parties. Is it your view I should be precluded from voting on matters regarding immigration because I will profit directly if new Americans want to live on the land I own? If the answer to that question is yes, sir, then I suggest you sell the forty acres you own outside of Baltimore."

Kelley waited for the small chuckles in the room to subside. "There is another matter that requires comment. I can assure the committee I have been extremely fortunate in my endeavors. I was able to enter public service precisely because of that wealth. My self-respect, gentlemen, will not permit me to believe Mr. Ames thought he could buy my vote for the measly profits I might make on an investment of a thousand dollars. The idea is so insulting to me personally it shows the utter folly of this committee's entire initiative."

Even if he saw an ounce of merit in Kelley's position, Benjamin knew the angle Carlton would demand in his story. With that mandate in mind, Benjamin began writing his story for the next day's paper.

*Mr. Kelley brazenly admits he knowingly took the stock but said he couldn't be bought for a price as small as one thousand dollars. What then is his price?*

*If the Poland Committee accepts this argument it will be opening the door to future generations of legislators, members of the Executive Branch, and even judges arguing we should overlook their obvious improprieties because to do otherwise would be to impugn their integrity. Where is the line Mr. Kelley draws? Is a congressman innocent if he accepts a gift of one horse and saddle but not if he accepts five?*

*To take Mr. Kelley's argument to its logical conclusion underscores its sophistry. If the Poland Committee accepts his argument, it will set the standard for the integrity required of those who would enter public service at so low a mark it will be meaningless.*

*The Courier believes the Poland Committee can and should send a clarion call for reform and stand up for the integrity of public service by recommending Mr. Kelley's removal from office. We did not lose a generation of men at places like Hoke's Run, Shiloh, and Gettysburg for spectacles such as this.*

Benjamin stopped writing. Kelley was explaining how he'd long believed in the expansion of the railroad to the Pacific and how he had supported every piece of legislation that furthered the cause since he entered Congress years before.

"Does the committee really think that if Mr. Ames was buying influence he needed to purchase the allegiance of someone who supported the very same cause for so many years? If the committee feels Mr. Ames was duplicitous enough to have an ulterior motive, at least credit the man with the sense of knowing where members of Congress stood on the enterprise and with enough judgment to put his shares to use where they might provide him support he didn't already have."

Benjamin leaned forward in his seat. He was certain the Democrats would pounce on Kelley's words with the fervor with which the hounds on the farm lunge at stray birds. But the Democrats were silent, leaning back in their chairs and looking as though they wanted to be anywhere else at the moment than across the table from Pig-Iron Kelley. William Merrick particularly seemed more interested in keeping any more references to his Baltimore property out of the committee's records than in dueling over the question of what it meant to serve the men who put him into office with integrity.

Jacob pointed to what Benjamin had just written. "No. Please, Benjamin. No. Think about what we discussed. You'll be throwing away a chance to become the leading journalist in Washington. Don't abandon that opportunity so lightly."

Benjamin twisted his body away from Jacobs's. His father leaned into him and continued to whisper. He was now so close Benjamin could smell the wet musk of his tweed coat. "At least join Mr. Kelley and me for coffee after his testimony concludes. Hear for yourself from him the kinds of doors he can open for you. I don't blame you for hating me, but for the love of god, Benjamin, don't throw your career away just at the moment it is poised to advance to a higher level. Hear the man out, Benjamin. Understand what he can do for you. Understand what kind of life he can help you offer Stephen. I know there's nothing I can do to heal the damage I've done to you, but at least let my ability to help your career be my legacy to my grandson."

Benjamin looked at his draft. Would listening to Jacob help or hurt the *Courier?* Would it help or hurt Benjamin's own career? Would he even want this sort of career? These were the types of questions he so needed to discuss with a friend or colleague over a long and thoughtful drink or a meal. But Benjamin's reward for his years of fealty first to the *Courier* and then to Greeley was that he had cut off himself from the world. What friends did he have? What allies?

Carlton? As the committee members dithered over what to do next, Benjamin could almost hear the man bellowing out his glee at bringing another politician down a peg, filling some invisible scoreboard with one more scalp as he pranced around the newsroom. *Another Washington whore exposed. That's why we sent you there in the first place, Wright. Jesse, print another five hundred copies. More, Benjamin. Now go find more stories just like this one.*

Vinnie? She'd be as convinced of the certainty of her position as Carlton was of his. *Leave those words in this room, Benjamin. The sun will still come up in the morning whether your readers believe Mr.*

*Kelley is a streetwalker or a saint. Befriend him rather than betray him.*

Stephen? If he could get his hands on Benjamin's inkwell, he'd spill it all over what Benjamin had written.

It seemed to Benjamin at that moment the boy would be more right than anyone else.

# 47

BLAINE MICHAELS HAD BAPTIZED BENJAMIN, comforted him when they buried his brothers, married him to Susanna, baptized Stephen, put his arms around both Benjamin and Stephen when Susanna was wrested from their lives, and now, on this stingingly cold early February morning, led a group of his parishioners and neighbors in a ceremony in which they sent Rachel on her way to the Lord Almighty. Her lungs had failed and her heart had slowed, but at least she went quickly. Mercifully quickly, but sadly alone. Curtis's wife found Rachel lying in her bed when she came to the farm with a plate of warm biscuits. Two inches of fresh snow blanketed the farm this morning.

The ground had been frozen for weeks. Benjamin and Curtis and John Henderson had to build a six-foot fire of peat and dry straw to soften the crystallized earth so their shovels would have a chance to give Rachel a place to rest near her boys. Stephen found the whole affair thrilling, running as close to the smoldering pile as he dared, and throwing on sticks and leaves with squeals of delight heard inside the house by the women preparing the macaroni and rice and kale soup and white beans everyone would eat when the service was finished. Jacob stayed inside, as if he'd forfeited the right to wish Rachel Godspeed, but then, of course he had. It was far too cold to sit on the porch, but he sat in the same rocker where he spent his days after bringing Willie and Matthew home, as if this were the seat of atonement. Beyond agreeing Jacob should deed the farm to Curtis because Benjamin had no intention of returning any more than did Jacob, the two of them hadn't really spoken during the forty-eight hours they'd been in Grayton. Their time together in the committee room had convinced Benjamin that Jacob's abandonment was real and his talk of reconciliation pretense.

The small service was drawing to a close. The cluster of men and women at the edge of Rachel's grave had been reciting the 23rd Psalm in one voice. *Yea, though I walk through the valley of the shadow of death, I will fear no evil.*

Benjamin picked up the shovel at his feet, walked with Stephen to the pile of dirt at the side of Rachel's grave, filled the blade and dumped it onto Rachel's casket, not once, but four times. Once for each of Rachel's sons and once for her grandson. He knelt by Rachel's grave for a moment, said his goodbyes and then whispered for only her ears, "Mother, we fought over what you said about Washington, but I must confess you were correct. On Stephen's behalf, I will not make that mistake again."

*For thou art with me; thy rod and thy staff they comfort me.* Benjamin handed the shovel to Jacob. They neither hugged nor gestured toward each other.

The brittleness of the air made the words of the psalm look like clouds of faith streaming up toward heaven. *Thou anointest my head with oil; my cup runneth over.* After Jacob threw his shovelful onto his wife's casket, he walked to Curtis's side and handed him the shovel.

As the rest of the group was finishing the psalm, Curtis's wife began singing a hymn she knew Rachel would want to carry her upward.

*How sweet the Name of Jesus sounds.*
*In a believer's ear.*

Her voice was soft at first, and then as the hole began to fill and the psalm had reached its end, louder and stronger and joined by the men and women now singing and wiping tears and holding hands and heading toward the house together.

*It soothes his sorrows, heals his wounds.*

*And drives away his fears.*

Curtis put his right hand on Benjamin's shoulder. Benjamin knew what the man was thinking. Curtis watched Benjamin pay the price of being the only child left in the house after Jacob left, the only target within Rachel's reach when she needed to lash out at someone or something to drive the demons from her soul. Curtis could only hope that in time Benjamin would let whatever resentment he had fade and instead remember his sister for the strong and righteous woman she was. But that was a conversation for another time. Jacob lingered at the fresh grave, perhaps finally giving Rachel the apology she deserved. It was his turn to speak to the dead.

*It makes the wounded spirit whole.*

*And calms the troubled breast.*

Stephen ran ahead with two of Curtis's children as though one of the parishioners had set them on a race to the front porch. Their laughter was the right and necessary accompaniment for the hymn.

*'Tis manna to the hungry soul;*

*And to the weary, rest.*

And the house was so deliciously warm. Men and women clutched their bowls of soup and pasta first to bring life back to their hands and then warmed their insides slowly. The room was quiet at first, but as vocal cords thawed, the house was filled with chatter and the serving tables overflowed with bread and cheese and steaming plates. Benjamin found himself sandwiched between Blaine Michaels on one side and Curtis on the other.

"It's a shame to see you leave Grayton, Benjamin, but it's hard for simple folks like us to compete with a place like Philadelphia." Reverend Michaels patted Benjamin on his left knee to lighten the mood. "But I'm still going to call you Grayton's favorite newspaperman."

Benjamin blew on his spoonful of soup and then swallowed before answering. "I'm not sure I'll end up there."

"Do tell." What made Michaels a successful pastor was more than his ability to render a stirring sermon. When he sensed something on the minds of his parishioners he had both the ability and the good sense to start a conversation allowing them to bare their souls and to get out of their way.

"I've been decamped to Washington for a while. There's an investigation going on by one of the House committees into all the shenanigans around the building of the railroad. As you know, I've spent the past two years monitoring that story."

"Exposing is the better word. Credit where credit is due." The pastor laughed at his choice of words. "Credit for the Credit Mobilier."

"Exposing. Monitoring. Getting fed up with. Whatever you want to call it. I need to be back there in two days to watch the Republicans finish up their whitewash. And then I'd like to be able to bolt like a bat out of hell, but I fear I'll be unable to." Benjamin dipped the edge of his bread into his bowl of soup. He seemed far more curious about what that was about to taste like than where the Poland Committee was headed.

"We expect to see you and Stephen back here with great frequency, Benjamin. You're family."

Benjamin stretched his back. "No question, but candidly, I'm thinking about putting some distance between us and what we've seen in both Philadelphia and Washington, so you may need to give us some leeway."

"Distance? You're considering leaving Philadelphia?" Curtis reacted to Benjamin's comment with both confusion and concern. "I may be nothing more than a simple farmer, but wouldn't most men who want to go into the newspaper business kill for the recognition you have? That's not something you can give up lightly."

"I hear what you're saying, Uncle Curtis, but the newspaper business is little more than one editor who believes in a particular side of an issue trying to shout louder than the editor across either the aisle or the street. I blame myself for expecting more from it. And look at the price I've paid." Benjamin couldn't look at Curtis without thinking of the small wooden swallow he'd picked out of Susanna's hand on Potter's Lane. He never returned the toy to Stephen. He couldn't bear seeing it in his son's hand. But he never put it far from his heart. Even now, even after nearly two years has passed, there were nights when Benjamin held the bird next to his chest and cried himself to sleep.

"But where will you go?"

"I don't know yet. Maybe San Francisco to see what all the excitement is about. Maybe the Dakotas to talk to the Indians. Stephen and I earned the right to have an adventure. And that part of the world is so fresh and so new that I want to see it through Stephen's eyes."

"Stephen? You expect to drag a two year old child around with you through Indian territory?" Curtis didn't hide either his surprise or his concern. "Isn't it better for Stephen to stay with us?"

Benjamin looked at Jacob and didn't try to speak softly. "We've had enough fathers from Grayton leaving their sons behind to last for some time." He wiped what was left in his bowl with the last edge of his bread and excused himself, explaining he wanted to ride to Susanna's resting place before it got too dark.

And when he got there, the snow was up to his knees, covering Susanna and everything around her with a blanket of solitude. A stranger wouldn't be able to find her grave, but Benjamin walked to the same western edge of the sycamore tree he leaned on for support the afternoon of her funeral. He knew exactly where he was. He knew exactly where Susanna was sleeping. Benjamin was quiet for several minutes, listening only to the wind. He wanted to be certain Susanna knew he was here.

"You can be so proud of Stephen, Susanna. On my way over here, I was thinking of the morning he was born. You said you'd given me a fine young son and it's so true. It was too cold to bring him here today, but you'd be amazed at how much he resembles you. He has your eyes. Your chin. And, most impressively, your passion to explore all manner of things. We both miss you so much, Susanna. We both hope you're okay."

Benjamin took out the handkerchief Susanna had embroidered six years ago. Frayed, bleached of its color, it was the one thing he always carried with him. Benjamin touched it to his lips and then to the snow on top of his wife's home.

"You will always be so much a part of Stephen. And so much a part of me. I will remember you always, Susanna."

And when the wind whispered past him, Benjamin was certain he heard it carry Susanna's voice as she whispered, *Always*.

# 48

Luke Poland served his masters well. The committee he chaired to investigate allegations that Oakes Ames sought to bribe members of Congress with stock in the Credit Mobilier heard all manner of implausible stories and outright lies from men in the highest positions in our government. In the most absurd display of sophistry the *Courier* witnessed in its coverage of every minute of the hearings, former Vice President Colfax even went so far as to say that money linked to Ames came from two campaign contributors who quite conveniently were dead. While less extreme, the stories of the others implicated in the scandal showed a systemic pattern of corruption and prostitution of the public trust.

Although every man who accepted stock from Ames could have been expelled from Congress, the Republican-controlled committee sanctioned only the two Democrats who stood before it. All others were exonerated from blame on theories defying both credibility and any semblance of respect for the interests of the American people. The Senate has begun its own investigation, but we expect nothing more from them.

By closing ranks and shutting their eyes to the millions—tens of millions—of dollars siphoned off by the proprietors of the Credit Mobilier in order to protect their own, Luke Poland and his fellow Republicans have opened the door to future generations of men to find ways to assure whatever contracts they secure for their businesses in Washington will serve them more than they benefit the American people.

Mr. Lincoln asked our fathers and sons and brothers to go to war on the promise that one day the better angels of our nature would prevail. The Republicans' closing of their eyes to the fraud and deceit taking place right in front of them cannot be what that kind and decent man had in mind.

Benjamin ran his fingers across the dust on her worktable while Vinnie read the copy of the *Courier* he brought her. Her tunic and hands and hair all were covered with grit.

"This is powerful writing, Benjamin, although I would have counseled a bit of restraint. The men whom you stand to meet through Mr. Kelley's good offices may feel constrained about opening themselves up to you. This will not help your newspaper gain its footing here."

"I will not either be recommending that the *Courier* have a formal presence in Washington or staying here on its behalf. It is far too partisan a paper to find any Republican friends in this environment. The *Courier* would be little more than the drum for the Democrats it already is. Grainger hardly needs to throw money away on a second office to do that." Benjamin thought Vinnie's body twitched slightly. "I wanted you to hear that directly from me."

"I am not happy to hear that, Benjamin." Vinnie walked to her water bowl, cleaned her hands and dried them on a white linen towel with blue piping around its edges. "I am surprised and not at all happy. Mr. Kelley could have done a great deal for your career."

"I wasn't interested in falling into the trap of reporters for the newspapers in this city who curry favor with the powerful just so they can be fed some tidbit of information the politicians want leaked to the public." Benjamin spread the fingers of his left hand on the table and used his right index finger to trace the image in the dust. "I'd spend my whole day feeling as though they were leeching my blood every bit as much as I was leeching theirs."

Vinnie took a step back. "You talk in such extremes, Benjamin. It is possible to befriend someone, and even have a rational discussion about positions, without, as you so crudely put it, sucking the blood out of that person. I find your words harsh and cruel and more than that, seemingly directed at me. You've never been comfortable with the idea I possess the skills to navigate Washington's very treacherous waters."

Benjamin rubbed the grit off his hands. "I don't fault you those skills, Vinnie. I just don't either share them or want to make them part of how I go about my business."

"And Grainger and Carlton, what say the two of them to this news of yours?"

"With the committee's work finally done, my next stop will be Philadelphia."

"You've made enough of a name for yourself I presume they'll keep you on the paper, but for the life of me, I don't know why you're planning to spend the foreseeable future under the thumb of a man like Carlton. He's as rigid and doctrinaire as the politicians you're so fond of castigating."

Benjamin smiled. "I'll see where our conversation leads. I'm not sure I want to return to the newspaper, for the very reason you stated."

Vinnie turned in Benjamin's direction. Her expression was more anger than disbelief. "What on earth are you saying? Take time to relax. Spend time with your son, but my God, Benjamin, why would you walk away from a career you've spent years building? That's just foolhardy."

"Let me ask you, Vinnie, why do you sculpt?"

She looked at Benjamin as if he were speaking in tongues.

"I'm serious. Please."

"To inspire, to create a sense of awe in my ability to capture a man's soul. To bring out what is unique and worth remembering in the men whose images I am capturing." She paused, as if wondering whether she needed to say more. "You might as well ask me why I breathe."

"You said we were alike and it's true. I write to capture that same spirit. But I can't do that here. And I can't do that at the *Courier*. The men who populate Washington and the men who cover its stories are little more than hungry wolves circling their prey. And all of them claim they're doing God's work."

"You have developed your reputation to the point where you will have your own platform soon enough, Benjamin. You've been through a great deal, but you are still a young man. We're both so young."

"Not more than four hours after I wired him the piece I just showed you, Carlton sent me a wire with a new angle on the Credit Mobilier story. He told me to write an editorial to run next week in every anti-Grant paper in the East demanding an investigation into the Poland Committee's work and labeling its cover-up of the scandal as nothing more than a way of protecting the Republican Party. He wants the cost of building the railroad to be the only thing men talk about until the next election."

Benjamin walked to the clay bust Vinnie was making of Pig-Iron Kelley. He ran his finger over the top of his scalp. "I sent him a return wire saying the American people are so enthralled with the idea of getting on a train in New York or Philadelphia and getting off in California they could care less about what it cost to build the line that gets them there."

Vinnie nodded in agreement while Benjamin continued. "I told him it was time the *Courier* moved on to other issues, but the man was relentless. I spent more on telegrams in the past three days than I did on lodging. Carlton said the issue could become the center-piece of the campaign for control of the Congress in two years and it was the *Courier's* duty to keep fanning the flames. I wanted to remind him our job is to report the news and not to make it, but there was no point."

Vinnie tried to reach for Benjamin's hand, but he stiffened. "I've already sacrificed Susanna and nearly two years of my life to the story of the railroad. It has taken everything from me I am able to give it."

Vinnie turned away from Benjamin. "I seem to have two choices, Vinnie. I either can give up any pretense of objectivity and turn into Mercer Carlton or I can become Pig-Iron Kelley's hidden spokesman. I prefer another path altogether."

Vinnie expressed exasperation. "Another path? What are you saying? Are you going to wander the earth like Diogenes of Sinope looking for an honest man? I don't pretend to have a head for busi-ness, but I doubt there is much of a wage in that."

Benjamin laughed. "You've studied the Greeks to master your work, Vinnie. I admire you for that. You've traveled the world for your art. Part of me wants to do the same thing." He swept his hand toward the western end of the studio. "There is a great big country out there. Stephen and I will find our place in it. The fron-tier is full of stories people will want to hear. Perhaps my destiny is to give people stories to inspire them and not merely to move them to resent one man or another. All that remains to be sorted out."

A single tear rolled down Vinnie's cheek. It made Benjamin realize everything about the woman was as stylized as her statues.

"With Rachel gone, I'm going to take Stephen with me. I doubt there's a father and son in the country who have earned the right of a ride on the railroad as much as we have. I must put some distance between these places on the east coast and the two of us for a while."

"A while?"

"A year. Perhaps two." Benjamin stopped before saying, *a lifetime.*

Vinnie put her hand to her mouth. "There's no talking you out of this adventure of yours, is there, Benjamin?"

He leaned in, took Vinnie's hand and squeezed it gently. He felt the itch of plaster dust on her fingers, "I'm going to worry about you, Benjamin. I'm going to worry about Stephen."

He took Vinnie's finger and pointed to the last paragraph of his editorial. "When I had dinner with my father he reminded me of the angels Mr. Lincoln invoked when he was inaugurated for his first term as President. I thought about them when I wrote this final paragraph and when I made my decision."

"You always play with words, Benjamin. But I don't always understand their meaning."

"As long as those angels watch over us, Vinnie, we have nothing to fear."

# 49

"WELL, T.P., at least this wasn't like the Greeley campaign." Carlton was fidgeting with his glasses. "We were on Nast's side on this one so he didn't come after either one of us. My God, if the man is going to put pictures of newspapermen in his cartoons, I'd better lose some weight." Carlton's aim was thrown off by his laughter at his joke, so the right side of his spittoon glistened.

"Let him that has not betrayed the trust of the People, and is without sin, cast the first stone." Carlton was out of his chair and standing over Jesse Green's desk with a copy of *Harper's Weekly* spread in front of him showing a scowling Justice, her scales in her left hand, her right hand pointing at the elected representatives who fed off the profits from their Credit Mobilier stock.

The men implicated in the scandal stood (and Grant's Vice President Henry Wilson sat) in front of the Capitol, under a sign saying they were disgraced in the eyes of the public for owning Credit Mobilier stock. Grainger pointed to Kelley. "Poor Pig-Iron looks as though he'd rather be anywhere than in this picture."

But the corrupt politicians certainly weren't the principal target of Nast's ink. Justice's face was pointed and her anger was directed toward those editors whose newspapers sat idly as the whole affair played out.

Carlton pointed to his friends and enemies at other papers who found themselves in the crosshairs of the nation's most famous political cartoonist. "Horace White, Jim Bennett, Charlie Dana.

Think of it, men, we smoked out this story. The papers owned by the men in this picture may be a lot bigger and more widely read than the *Courier*, but it was our article about McComb's lawsuit against Ames that started the whole investigation. And I don't care if *Harper's* and the *New York Tribune* now are running this cartoon on their front pages, this is still the *Courier's* story."

Carlton ripped the cartoon from the paper, tacked it to the wall next to his desk and then pounded the wall with the side of his right hand for emphasis. "And by God, men, we're going to continue to run with this story. Luke Poland's cover-up is only the beginning. This is way too big to ignore." Carlton shouted for Jesse Greene. "Jesse, you've got the best head for numbers in this place. Run the math for me. Ames had a contract to built six hundred and sixty-seven miles of track. For two hundred and thirty-eight of them, he'd already built the buggers for about twenty-seven thousand per mile. But he charged the government forty-two. Fifteen thousand times two hundred and thirty-eight, and that's just the beginning. I'll bet there's millions more. Tens of millions."

Grainger leaned into the picture. His nose was no more than three inches away from it. "Whitelaw Reid looks as though he's asking God to get him as far away from the man's inkwell as possible. I don't blame him. The last time I spoke with Nast he skewered me for working so closely with Greeley, but at least he didn't ask me to pose for a picture."

"Wright. Step up a minute, please. Carlton had been scribbling some notes.

It always started like this. Benjamin or one of the other reporters stood in front of Carlton's desk while the man railed over whatever set him on fire that day. Benjamin had taken to comparing Carlton's manner to a train leaving the station, slowly at first and then a flurry of noise and steam and debris flying everywhere.

"Before they adjourned, the Senate voted to expel Jim Patterson of New Hampshire, but now that they're in a new term, there's a movement to give the man a pass. We need to follow up on that."

"With due respect, Mercer, will our readers actually care about that?" Benjamin asked. "The issue seems pretty isolated and esoteric to me." How far Benjamin had come since that first morning at Carlton's desk, trembling, afraid to open his mouth.

But to Carlton, Benjamin was still an underling. He began rising in his chair, shifting his body so all of his weight would be behind what he was about to say.

Grainger stepped in, asked both of them to join him in his office. He'd spoken to Benjamin the day before and was aware of what was going through the young reporter's mind. He also sensed a confrontation was coming and didn't want it to play out in front of his staff. Carlton refused to sit at Grainger's request.

"Mercer, hear me out for a minute. Benjamin and I have been talking. He's been through a great deal. He and I agree he could use a rest, take a break from the Credit Mobilier story."

"What? Take a break from the news that's been on our front page for the past two years? Take a break from a story that fueled a presidential election, forced Congress to conduct an investigation and is now on the front page of every paper in the country? Do you think Thomas Nast points his pen at insignificant issues? For God's sake, will the two of you remember for a minute what business we're in?" Carlton's train was picking up its speed.

"I'm not saying the *Courier* can't continue in that direction, Mercer, although there are days I wish the whole newspaper business could take a breath or two and begin toning down our partisan rhetoric. That's not going to happen in my lifetime, though, but we're talking about Benjamin at the moment. After everything he's done for the *Courier* over the past few years, and after the tremendous personal price he's paid, he deserves a moment of our time. More than a moment. Hear him out."

Benjamin spoke with respect. "First, Mercer, I can't thank you enough for what you've done for me. The opportunity. The education. The support. But what T.P. and I discussed yesterday was the idea of my stepping away from the day-to-day grind of the paper for a while and exploring the possibility of writing a new kind of story. One with less of a partisan angle and more of an eye to the hope of encouraging men to better themselves."

"We're back to the preacher business. Where and how exactly do you see yourself doing this?"

Benjamin smiled. "I'm not sure, but I'm interested in learning about how our country is growing, whether the men and women now populating the west have learned anything from the mistakes we've made in this part of the country. Perhaps Stephen and I will get off the train in San Francisco and see where that leads us."

"Get off the train in San Francisco and see where that leads you? You say our readers won't care about what happens to a Senator swept up in a scandal they've been talking about for two years but you think they'll give a shit about what's happening three thousand miles away? I missed a step somewhere. You can't be thinking of doing this with the *Courier* in mind."

"I want to look to the future, not to the past."

Carlton scoffed. "You write like a poet, Benjamin, but you were naive about so many things when I met you and you're still naive. Take a week. Take two. Think about what it will mean for your career to burn your bridges with the *Courier*. Come to your senses and then come back to your desk."

Grainger laughed. "We had that conversation yesterday, Mercer. I wasn't any more able to talk Benjamin out of this than you are. But nobody's burning bridges. Benjamin will write what's in his heart. He'll give us a first look. If it feels right for our paper, we'll publish it and send him a few dollars. If not, he'll try to sell his story elsewhere. That arrangement seems pretty fair from our perspective."

## Chapter 49

Carlton looked at Benjamin as though he were talking to him for the first time. "Well I'll be goddamned. You're choosing to go from being one of the most notorious young reporters in the country to being a door-to-door salesman."

"I couldn't even consider this, Mercer, without the confidence you've instilled in me. Stephen and I will get by. Thanks to everything the two of you have taught me."

Carlton finally sat. He looked like a balloon losing its air. "I'll be a son of a bitch. You're really leaving."

"Let's not call it leaving, Mercer. We'll just be in different parts of the country." Benjamin was filled with sadness, respect, faith, and most of all, anticipation. He put out his hand and was grateful when Carlton finally extended his.

"One more thing, Benjamin." Grainger opened the top right drawer on his desk and took out a small white envelope. He handed it to Benjamin, who saw some cash inside.

"I remember the day Mercer bet you fifty dollars of the *Courier's* money if you could prove the Credit Mobilier stole more than five million dollars. You won the bet, Benjamin."

Grainger put out his right hand to wish Benjamin well.

"You certainly won the bet."

# AUTHOR'S NOTE

THE TESTIMONY FROM THE HEARINGS of the Poland Committee was based upon the Committee Report dated February 18, 1873 of the Select Committee to Investigate the Alleged Credit Mobilier Bribery. Thomas Nast's cartoon reacting to that report was published in *Harper's Weekly* on March 15, 1873.

An almost endless supply of information about the Johnson impeachment, including contemporaneous excepts from *Harper's Weekly,* is available on the internet. I drew much of the color of the impeachment process from those articles.

Readers interested in the bias of the press during this period and in particular in the manner in which newspapers of various political leanings reported on the Credit Mobilier scandal will enjoy reading a Working Paper written by Matthew Gentzkow, Edward Glaeser and Claudia Goldin, for the National Bureau of Economic Research, "The Rise of the Fourth Estate: How Newspapers Became Informative and Why It Mattered," Working Paper 10791, www.nber.org/papers/w10791.

While Benjamin and Susanna Wright, Mercer Carlton, T.P. Grainger, and numerous others were invented for this story, many of the characters with whom they interacted were drawn from the historical record. Their stories, of course, are fictional, created for this work.

Vinnie Ream is considered the preeminent American sculptress of the nineteenth century. She is best known for the statue of

Abraham Lincoln in the U.S. Capitol Rotunda. She was the first woman ever to win such a federal commission. Vinnie also created the bronze sculpture of Admiral David Farragut (remembered as the commander who said, *Damn the torpedoes, full speed ahead*) that stands in Farragut Square at Connecticut Avenue and 17th Street in Washington. Vinnie Ream Hoxie died in 1914 and was buried in Arlington National Cemetery under her statue of Sappho.

Edmond Ross was vilified by the Republicans for his vote against the Johnson impeachment. He never held elective office again and went into the newspaper business in Kansas. In 1885 President Grover Cleveland appointed him the Governor of the Territory of New Mexico.

Peter Dey, the chief engineer for the Union Pacific Railroad, noisily resigned his post rather than pad the contracts for the cost of construction of the line. Some historians have suggested that Dey's integrity ultimately lead to the uncovering of the Credit Mobilier scandal.

Horace Greeley was the most powerful newspaperman in the United States for over twenty years. His paper, the *New York Tribune*, had a circulation of over two hundred and fifty thousand. He lost the 1872 Presidential election to President Grant by a landslide and died before the Electoral College was convened.

Schuyler Colfax was Grant's Vice President when the Credit Mobilier scandal broke. His efforts to exonerate himself through his constantly changing stories were ridiculed, but he escaped impeachment because he received the stock before he was elected to that office. He never fully recovered from his fall from grace. He died in 1885.

After being censured by the House of Representatives for his distribution of Credit Mobilier stock, Oakes Ames wasn't nominated for reelection in 1872. He died in 1873. Ten years later, the Massachusetts legislature passed resolutions of gratitude for his work and faith in his integrity.

Pig-Iron Kelley served in the House of Representatives for nearly thirty years. He died in office in 1890.

# ACKNOWLEDGMENTS

SOME OF MY FRIENDS read bits and pieces of this story while others read complete drafts. They all made it better, so in alphabetical order, let me thank Elizabeth England, Jerry Gross, Bob Hansen, Cathy Harding, Tom Jenks, Mike Levine, Ray Schultz, Kathi and Tim Throckmorton, Margot Weinberg, Jon Weisgall, and Alan Wolf.

I completed this novel fourteen months after being diagnosed with ALS, a relentless and always fatal disease. I couldn't have done so without the support and care of my wife Nancy Alessi and my sons David, the family doctor, and Michael, a talented writer himself, who gives so much of his time and energy to my well-being.

CPSIA information can be obtained at www.ICGtesting.com
Printed in the USA
LVOW05*2017100813

347262LV00002B/5/P